THE
IMPERFECT

THE
IMPERFECT

PRASOON

Srishti
PUBLISHERS & DISTRIBUTORS

SRISHTI PUBLISHERS & DISTRIBUTORS
Registered Office: N-16, C.R. Park
New Delhi – 110 019
Corporate Office: 212A, Peacock Lane
Shahpur Jat, New Delhi – 110 049
editorial@srishtipublishers.com

First published by
Zorba Books in 2013

Revised version, 2017
First published by
Srishti Publishers & Distributors in 2017

Copyright © Prasoon, 2017

10 9 8 7 6 5 4 3 2 1

It's not mine, it's not yours
Though imperfect, but it's ours.
We gotta breathe
We gotta sleep
We gotta laugh
We gotta live.
Can you hear me?
This story belongs to us.

The Day it All Began

"**A**shu, quick… give me your economics assignment," I yelled and grabbed the closest available vacant spot.

Ashu looked up and irritatingly tossed his notebook towards me. Ashu, my friend, was an average looking guy just like me, but brilliant in maths.

As I started writing, I felt a tap on my back. A pleasant voice asked, "Rishabh, have you done the geography assignment? I need answers to two questions."

Oh baby! That was Sarah, the most gorgeous legs, I mean, girl in the class.

"Yeah, all done. You can have it," I said and passed her my notebook, stealing a glance at her ultra-awesome legs.

We all scribbled frantically. The chattering grew louder as more and more classmates poured in and joined the marathon. It was a fish market, yet a perfectly co-ordinated team effort to accomplish the unanimous goal – *complete your summer vacation homework if you value your life*.

Amidst this insane drama, a few new faces walked in, but nobody bothered to even give them a fake smile.

The frenzy was broken by the school bell. It was time for the morning assembly.

Assembly for the senior wing took place in the basketball court that also had a stage built over the parking lot. Soon the assembly ground started filling up. Queues began to spring up in ascending order from Lilliputian to Mt. Everest. Regrettably, the ladies first rule prevailed. No one envied the shortest boy who stood next to the tallest girl in the class. It was a real insult, which he aggravated by maintaining a noticeable distance.

Ashu and I were the blessed ones with an average height. This helped us to avoid any such humiliation or being hauled up by a teacher inspecting our uniforms, which normally happened at the back.

The commotion doubled as the assembly time drew closer. The crowd became raucous as friends and foes joined in the melee. Schoolbags started to fill in bits and pieces of the visible landscape as all instructions of standing in height were disregarded in all the jostling.

The assembly bell ended the shuffling. The gatekeeper slammed the school gate preaching punctuality to those stranded outside. The principal and vice-principal stepped onto the stage in their stodgy tailored suits with a few teachers approaching retirement in tow.

There was pin drop silence and I could hear birds chirping outside. The prayers were followed by a welcome note from the principal, a speech that hadn't changed since I'd entered the senior wing. Ashu whispered, "Did you see the new girl? Damn good yaar."

"Which one?" I asked anxiously.

"In our class, you moron."

"No, I didn't notice. But yes, I did see Sarah's beautiful legs," I said remembering them.

"What in the world makes you look at her so keenly?" Ashu asked baffingly.

"I just kinda like her colour."

"Really? Does she have a colour? I think she's totally bleached out," he said sarcastically.

"Huh!" I dismissed him.

Meanwhile, the principal wrapped up his lecture and smiled proudly as the students clapped at his stupendously boring speech. The school bell rang once again and we started singing the much-awaited national anthem, which concluded the assembly.

As the queues started to wobble and vanish into their respective dens, I was imagining the new girl. Ashu had really made me curious about her. My daydream was broken by Ashish and Mandeep, the Laurel and Hardy of our class. They ruined the silence in the corridor with their loud voices.

Mandeep was a bellicose Surd with a pumpkin like belly. He wore a *patka* in colour schemes quite alien to non-Surds like me and always had his collar button open to air his fat neck. On the other hand, Ashish was a scrawny fellow who seemed to have borrowed his looks from a crow. And when he spoke, it felt as if crickets were chirping. He was known for his vile wisecracks and curious habit of peeping into the adjacent urinals.

I ignored the two idiots and kept moving. They ran towards me yelling 'Neta' and punched me wildly on my back.

Irritated, I yelled back, "Kaddu and Jingur! Have some manners. Don't shout in the corridor!" Though all of us were offended by such sleazy salutations, we never expressed it. We just retaliated with worse barbs.

Once inside the class, group discussions on varied topics started. While some kept the talks limited to homework, others showed off about their summertime adventures, movies, sports, and the like.

Suddenly, the chirping in the front rows ceased as someone warned that the teacher was approaching. The frantic copying stopped and books were shoved into bags and in the desks. Miss

Betty D'Souza, the showstopper teacher walked into the class in a light blue shirt tucked into skin-tight black trousers. Her two-and-a-half inch black heels made her look fabulous. Her long hair was held away from her face with a brown clip and tiny earrings glinted from the twin piercings in each ear. Miss Betty was known to be a strict English teacher, but was equally famous among the male fraternity – be it the boys or the men in the staffroom.

"Good morning, ma'am," chanted the class, standing up almost altogether. Miss Betty smiled and waved her right hand asking us to sit down.

"So? Are you guys excited to be back with your friends?" Miss Betty asked, making minor adjustments to her chair. Nobody answered. The girls smiled and the boys drooled. So, she shifted her focus to the attendance register.

I broke the silence with "Yes miss", responding to my roll number which was regrettably the first one, something that every kid wishes not to have. As the roll call ended, a shrill voice with a weird accent shrieked, "Excuse me miss. What's my roll number?"

Miss Betty looked up from the register, "Who was that?" she asked.

All necks turned right and left trying to figure out whose voice it was. A tall, melanin-deficient slit-eyed boy stood up in the second last corner row. "Miss, it was me! I'm a new admission. I joined today," he said.

"Really? I don't have any information. Anyway, tell me your name. I'll check with the office and allot you a roll number tomorrow," Miss Betty replied expressing surprise, denial and consolation at the same time.

"Sure Miss. My name is Ben Chue," he replied confidently. Those well-versed in Hindi language slangs sniggered, extracting an abusive meaning out of Ben's name.

"Ben, can you spell your last name for me?" Miss Betty asked hesitantly. He did that and she made a note.

"Are there any more new students?" asked Miss Betty looking around the classroom once again.

"Yes miss, I'm new too," floated an angelic voice.

"What's your name, my girl?"

"Aarti Raisinghani," the girl introduced herself rather sheepishly, standing up from the second row. She tried to peep into the attendance register as Miss Betty jotted down her name.

"Okay! Now I know who Ashu was talking about," I thought to myself.

"I'm not going to take any more names after this. In case there are more shy people who need an invitation to speak, then speak up now," said Miss Betty. Nobody else did.

"Okay class, let's welcome Aarti and Ben. And, you both, come on up to the front and introduce yourselves," smiled Miss Betty. "In fact, it'll be a good idea to have a round of introductions for everyone."

A collective but silent sigh ran through the class. The introductions took off in stammers, but grew confident as the guys memorized their lines before their turn. To make things worse, Miss Betty asked us to include our last year's grades as well.

Why in the world does she want them to know the sins of our past, I wondered. *Grades are misconceptions that form people's perceptions.* That's my ideology.

It was my turn next. I stood up and looked into Aarti's walnut brown eyes, snubbing Ben. She'd had a lost expression for the last ten minutes and my gaze changed nothing. I started to speak, juggling my eyes between the fan and the wall clock.

"Good morning everybody. My name is Rishabh Aman Agrawal. I scored eighty-seven percent in class eight and stood fourth in class. My favourite subject is geography and I like playing cricket."

Miss Betty contributed to my introduction, "He's the most sincere boy of the class," she said as I let out a silent fart. I looked into Aarti's eyes (ignoring Ben again) and for the first time, our eyes locked. Aarti gave me a once over, making me feel the abashment of being ogled. But more importantly, I got noticed!

I really wanted to give Miss Betty a big hug, something that every male in the senior wing wanted to do (especially Kaddu, who had a thing for her).

It was finally the turn of the newbies. "Hi everyone! I'm Ben Chue. I come from the land of tourism, Thailand. This is my first time in India and I find it really cool. My Dad runs a restaurant chain called Thai Seven and we've recently opened a branch in India as well. I got an A grade in academics last year and my favourite sport is surfboarding," said Ben in his bizarre accent.

"We all got 'A's. What's his percentage? Ask this tour guide," hissed Ashu.

I ignored him as Kaddu, Jingur and my eyes convened to agree that we'd discovered a sponsor for our 24/7 famished souls.

"Any siblings?" Miss Betty questioned Ben.

"Yes miss. They're all in this school too. My older brother is in grade eleven, one of my sisters is in grade seven, another in grade five, two in grade four, and one little brother in nursery," Ben answered proudly, taking their names which I seriously cannot recall.

It was Aarti's turn to introduce herself. "Here comes my sugar candy," I thought to myself.

Aarti took off with élan, "Good morning class. My name is Aarti Raisinghani. I studied at Little Rose, a boarding school in Nainital for the last three years as my father was working in Kuwait. I scored eighty-two percent in the last academic year and stood sixth in my class."

"Any siblings?" Miss Betty asked once again.

"None," she replied.

"Did she say one?" Kaddu enquired.

"Yeah, one fat smelly brother called Kaddu," remarked Jingur loud enough to be heard by everyone in the vicinity.

Miss Betty interrupted, "What's so funny? Tell me the joke too." All grins evaporated immediately.

The mundane routine took over and time seemed to be standing still. Meanwhile, I took my eyes off Sarah's legs and repositioned them on Aarti. She had a wheatish complexion and her shiny black hair fell over her forehead. Small golden earrings adorned her earlobes and a miniature ponytail wagged as she spoke to her partner. A red coral glinted on her right ring finger which she toyed with every few seconds. Although Aarti's skirt was unusually shorter, her legs weren't as attractive as Sarah's. Sarah was still my favourite in that particular department.

During recess, the boys discussed the newcomers at length. While some believed that Ben's Dad may have been deported because of his offspring-making abilities, others wondered about the menu at their restaurant. Some wanted to see his sisters while still others made fun of his name.

The lover boys were, of course, only interested in discussing Aarti. Some compared her sharp features to the newly crowned Miss World while others debated about her being able to end Sarah's reign. But one thing was clear – everyone including me wanted to be friends with her!

▼

"Hi Rishabh!" trilled a sweet voice in one of the post-recess period breaks. I was at the water cooler. I turned around to find that it was the girl of the hour, Aarti.

"Hey, how is it going? Do you like the school?" I asked like an elderly person and then rebuked myself in my mind.

"Yea, it's kind of good, but I haven't seen too much of it yet," she said switching places with me at the cooler.

"What do you want to see? I can show you around," I said, grabbing the opportunity.

"Well, where's the library?" she asked.

"Looks like you're into books," I teased.

"No, not really. That's just the first thing that came to my mind."

"Oh, I see. If you want, I can take you around for a ten-fifteen-minute excursion after school."

"Can we do it tomorrow? Umm… say recess time? Pleeeease! I don't want to miss my bus," Aarti asked.

"As you wish," I said making a grim face.

Aarti suddenly changed the topic to studies. "Do you like maths?"

"Kind of. Why?" I said guessing what was about to come.

By this time a few boys had lined up behind us. One of them remarked, "Will you guys drink all the water or leave something for us as well?" Both of us grinned in embarrassment.

"Actually, I'm quite scared of maths," admitted Aarti as we walked side by side to the classroom.

"You can always take my help," I offered, pumping myself from within.

"That would be great!" she said as our shoulders brushed against each other.

"Friends?" I said looking straight into her eyes, my heart beating the way popcorns burst.

"We already are," Aarti's eyes twinkled as she raised a hand for a high-five. This was definetly a pivotal moment in my life. I raised a hand and we did an animated high-five.

As we took our seats, I was detained by an interrogation team that had been closely monitoring me. "Come here, you flirt. What was that high-five for? And what were you talking about?" barked Ashu.

"Nothing. Hi, hello. That's it," I said.

"Tell us the truth or go sit with Ben Chue and learn chowmein recipes," Kaddu said sternly, banging his fist on the desk.

"Okay, okay. She asked me to help her out with maths. Nothing more than that," I said, keeping the school excursion proposal to myself.

"And you must have agreed like an asinine baby," rasped Jingur.

Before I could reply, Ashu lamented, "As if I, the highest scorer in mathematics, was dead. Damn!"

"Look, I didn't approach her. She came and talked to me," I explained in a consolatory tone.

"I think he's right. Miss Betty is the actual culprit. She got it all set up for him," groaned Kaddu clenching his fists.

"Lucky fellow. The fish has come to the fisherman on its own!" quipped Jingur.

We decided to change the topic as Ashu had become quite grumpy. Even friends become enemies if you get what they wanted for themselves. You're treated like a traitor.

▼

"Hey Rishabh!" I heard a girl addressing me in the school bus which was otherwise full of window battlers.

"What are you doing in my bus?" I asked surprised but rather pleased.

"This is the bus I take back home," Aarti clarified.

"But you were not there in the morning?" I questioned her like a detective.

"Yea, my Dad dropped me today."

"How lucky she is," I thought remembering the languorous start of my day. "So, where do you stay? I mean, which stop will you get off at?" I asked.

"Mahanagar."

"Really? That's very close to where I live. I stay in Aliganj," I said enthusiastically.

"Wow, that's great!" Aarti said as I vacated the window seat for her. Small Bunty looked at me appalled as I'd pushed him out of there just a while ago.

Aarti and I sat next to each other and chatted all the way till her stop came.

"Bye, see you tomorrow," Aarti waved to me as she disembarked.

I spent the remainder of the day dreaming about what I would say to Aarti the next day, what I'd show her in the campus, about how to capture a seat for her in the bus, blah, blah, blah.

Infatuation at its Worst

Eighty-two. That's what my progress report showed. The past academic year hadn't been great. My only solace was that even the topper was down by two percentage points and that I was still Neta, leader of the exam scores among boys, the epithet I'd hated earlier, but now found respite in. My tuition-cum-hidden-agenda improved Aarti's maths somewhat, but not enough to boast about. Something that had progressed for sure was our friendship (and my infatuation). We were inseparable like leech, sucking each other's life, I being the dominant parasite.

A few more things had changed during this period. Miss Betty had dumped Kaddu, marrying her anonymous boyfriend, to become Ms Betty. Jingur's one-liners had got better and Ashu was already in the footsteps of the great Ramanujan. Sarah was more captivating while Ben Chue stammered Hindi like my ring-necked parrot Totu.

▼

Miss Jackson, our economics-cum-class teacher lectured us, "Children! Welcome to SSC, the most important year in a student's life. This year, I repeat, this year will decide your future. So, be sincere and dump your complacency at home."

Regular affairs resumed until Miss Tammana, our new biology teacher entered our lives. She was dressed in a light green chikan salwar-kameez and Kohlapuri chappals. Her earlobes, though pierced, were naked like mine and she wore half a dozen trinkets in both hands. She was fair and a definite threat to Ms Betty's monopoly.

Tammana ma'am wasted no time threatening our souls with the term's curriculum as her deft hands insouciantly divided the blackboard in two halves. One-half listed the chapters and reference books while the other the execution plan.

"Excuse me miss. I think you missed out the third chapter," remarked Ben. Everybody ruffled to the table of contents. There were murmurs all around as the third chapter happened to be on the human reproductive system.

"I think his Dad can teach this one better!" Kaddu said laughing at his own joke.

"No, I think he can teach the Uncontrolled Human Reproductive System better!" Jingur opened his Pandora's Box of wisecracks.

"That's intentional," Miss Tammana articulated.

"Is that out of course or do we need to study it on our own?" Ben enquired exacerbating the status quo.

"That's enough. Sit down," she said sternly. "This chapter is not in the course for the term, but will be included in the final board exams. You'll get the notes for it later," Miss Tammana dismissed the topic.

Ben had given us enough material to discuss at recess.

"Why were you laughing in Tammana ma'am's class?" Aarti asked me in the bus.

"You already know the reason, don't you?" I winked at her.

"Yeah I know what you boys think and it's not at all funny. It's just something we all should know about."

"If that's the case, then teach me the chapter and I promise to learn the diagrams on my own," I challenged Aarti, recollecting the picture of a woman's anatomy from the biology book.

"Shut up or I'll slap you!" said Aarti punching my shoulder.

▼

Things moved on smoothly until one day Kaddu's excited shrieks triggered a minor earthquake in the senior wing. "Shit man! The annual concert is coming up and the notice board says that participation is mandatory," said Kaddu gasping heavily.

That was catastrophic news for someone like me with an allergy to extra-curriculars. Faces turned gloomy in the boys' camp, but the girls became cheerful. Ms Betty called for a meeting in the recess. She announced our destinies without prior consultation. Kaddu and Ashu were shoved into something called a Rainbow Drill, probably inspired by the shades of Kaddu's patka, while Jingur was surprisingly chosen for the human pyramid acrobatics, I guess to be at the top, since he was as heavy as a feather! I was the most ill-fated one. My name starred in the dance event, that too in a ball dance! The only respite was that all the girls including Aarti and Sarah featured in this list.

"I can't do it? I don't know how to dance," I grumbled to Aarti in the bus.

"Don't worry. There will be practice sessions. It's a slow, elegant and easy going dance. High society stuff, you see. And I'm there to help you out. So, chill!" Aarti tried to console me.

I was afraid of shaking my butt in public, but the thought of getting closer to Aarti gave me strength. Sometimes in life, we do certain things, even if we dislike them, just for the greed of some materialistic gain. And I was about to do just that.

Practice sessions commenced and I messed up on the first day itself. I did a pathetic jig in front of the most desired girls of the school. It was a big blow to my reputation and a probable closure of future prospects with any of them. Aarti laughed hard but somehow convinced Ms Betty not to throw me out (which I so badly wanted) and instead, chose me as her dancing partner.

Next day before practice started

"Come on, hold my hand and take my waist," Aarti instructed me as I hesitated.

"This is not right," I said.

"What's not? We're not doing anything that the third chapter of your biology book recommends."

"No… no, I mean the dance isn't right. I won't be able to do it," I said.

"Everything is right. It's just that you're not confident and thinking about it too much," Aarti said drawing me close to her. She took my right hand and placed it on her luscious waist, then clutched my trembling left hand with her right and placed her left hand on my right shoulder.

I'd touched Aarti a thousand times, but never so intimately. Millions of bells chimed in my head as I felt her breath on my neck. A gallon of sweat, probably enough to dehydrate an elephant, dripped off my body. Aarti lifted her head to say something, bringing her lips just four inches away from mine. I turned my head sideways, dreading doing something unacceptable. Embarrassingly, the pendulum got combat-ready, making it inconceivable to control my concupiscent feelings. I deserted every other thought and recollected the worst horror movie I'd seen in my life to calm down the roaring tiger.

Over the next few days, I managed to learn some basic dance steps along with magical techniques for controlling libido. Admittedly, those were golden days, more so because I touched Aarti at places that Sarah would have unquestionably objected to.

The day of the concert soon arrived. Parents walked in with tiny tots as the gatekeeper looked on helplessly. Teachers guarded each corner of the ground like security personnel. The pandal and the stage looked much better than the assembly ground reflecting some sanity by the authorities at last. By now, my Mom was aware of who I was dancing with. She made sure that she made the time to come for the concert, not to attend the show, but to check out the girl in her son's life.

We got into our school-sponsored but self-financed brassy costumes. I wore a tuxedo with a black bowtie and matching leather shoes. To look cool, I'd smoothened my hair with a large dollop of Brylcreem and taken the refuge of half a dozen Chiclets envisioning Aarti kissing me on stage.

Aarti looked stunningly beautiful in a black and red gown with a knee-high slit. Her partially exposed left thigh grabbed my attention despite being concealed underneath black stockings. A blood-red rose resting over her clipped hair enhanced her looks to inexplicably tantalising levels. She was definitely the belle of the ball.

"You look awesome!" I remarked awestricken.

"You too," said Aarti, returning formalities.

"Can I kiss you?" the words were out before I even realised.

All eyes turned towards us.

"What? Are you mad? We're friends… looks like that biology chapter has cast a spell on you," yelled Aarti in dismay.

"I'm sorry. I didn't mean it that way. I meant… on the hand," I said, quickly changing the mood.

"Oh, okay then! You scared me," smiled Aarti and nonchalantly passed over her hand for me to leave saliva marks on. I don't know what made me do it, but it was the first time I spoke aloud what I strongly felt for her.

The soporific *Manor House of Count Blake*, a play adapted from the work of some archaic playwright was about to end. Our act was next. As we assembled backstage and the time to step onto the stage drew closer, the boys looked like they were praying and the girls were readjusting their clothes and hair.

We got onto the stage as the audience booed off the Blake party. The decibel levels were quite high. Aarti whispered something in my ear, possibly 'best of luck', but I missed it. My eyes scanned the voluble audience, looking for Mom. I finally spotted her wedged into a seat some eight-nine rows from the front. She was gazing at Aarti as I held her hand. I'd have left the clutch at once had I not been on stage! Sometimes you're so flummoxed in life, you can't even smirk, even if you're with your most desired possession.

Music started to play and we slowly started moving our feet and buns in an anticlockwise motion. The cameraman captured this live as his minion manoeuvred his lights on us. The parents started clapping insanely, enjoying the intimate act of their non-adults. We all bowed at the end of our tango and slipped away. I soon forgot what Mom would think about her not so virtuous son.

▼

Soon, the dates for the most important exams of our life, as prophesied earlier, were announced. Inactive teachers suddenly came to life, bombarding us with notes, extra-classes, mock tests, predictive questions and other such bloodcurdling stuff. With each passing day, attendance reduced as students started to burn the midnight oil. Even the not-so-needed farewell party had only a ten percent attendance! It was a grave situation. But all this failed to bother me as I had far more important things in life to think about — Aarti, Aarti and Aarti.

"I'm worried about the exams. I can handle all the other subjects, but maths… god help me," Aarti confessed in the bus on our last day at school.

"Don't worry. I'll help."

"I know, but you won't write my paper."

"True. But I can always help you prepare better," I said confidently, as if I was setting up the paper.

"Can we study together? At my place?" Aarti asked.

Wow! That would be awesome. But how to pole vault the unconquerable hurdle – Mom? I thought desperately.

"Mom won't allow me to get out of the house. We need to find another way. Let me think of something," I replied.

Aarti's face fell. I continued, "By the way, we'll soon be getting a telephone connection, within a day or two. A sarkari one, so no restriction on the number of calls."

"What's the number? If not study together, we can at least discuss things over the phone," Aarti's face lit up immediately.

"I think it is 32-28-32, but I'm not sure. That's what I noticed Dad scribbling on the paper yesterday."

"Is that really your number or somebody's vital statistics? What's your Dad up to?" Aarti giggled, reflecting a sudden change in mood. What *was* that? Looks like the hormones are getting to her as well.

We talked over the hotline over the next few days, more about other things and less about studies. Whenever my sister picked up the phone, she'd tease me endlessly before handing me the receiver. Mom would usually disconnect after cooking up some excuses while Dad did the simplest – he added answering the phone to his 'Not to Attend' list (just like the doorbell). I figured out a straightforward solution for myself – spring at every 'tring'.

I called Aarti only when Mom was out, which didn't happen often. But each time I called, some servant picked up and put me through a detailed enquiry and then put me on hold. Almost always,

I'd hear the pressure cooker whistling. It took almost ten minutes for Aarti to reach the phone. Sometimes after waiting for even longer, I got responses like 'she is sleeping' or 'not at home'. One in five times, the servant even forgot that I was holding on. So, I stopped calling.

One day Aarti invited me to her place. I slipped out after fabricating some convincing lies and cycled to her residence at Mahanagar. Twenty minutes later, I stood, sweaty and exhausted, at the Raisinghani residence. There were three buttons next to the gate, but with no signs about which was for what. I decided to use my better judgment and opened the latch of the rust-brown wrought iron gate. Suddenly, a bushy white canine with a comma-like tail barked its way out in response to the metal's creaking sound. My stimuli took over and I rammed the half-open barrier on its face.

Someone peeped from the balcony to check out the trespasser. It was Aarti. She gestured to me to wait and reappeared at the porch within seconds. She quickly picked up her dog. Aarti was wearing knee-length blue shorts and a white cable-knit sweater.

"Hi Rishu, how are you? I'm sorry about Jackie. Did he scare you?" Aarti asked.

I carefully parked my bicycle next to a row of flower pots and pulled out the books from the carrier. Honestly speaking, Jackie's incessant barking had made me quite uncomfortable.

"I'm fine. Am not scared of dogs unless they're Dobermans or Alsatians," I said keeping a safe distance from the still agitated fellow. Maybe it had smelt my intentions.

"Better to keep away from him. Spitzes bite too!" Aarti cautioned as we entered the house. "Please take off your shoes. Mom is a bit fastidious about cleanliness."

I quickly took them off and followed her into a large drawing room with a giant chandelier. There were huge paintings, two tapestries, a rosewood centre table, a three-piece sofa set and a lovely

Persian carpet. The lavish set-up was something I'd seen only in Sooraj Barjatya movies. Looks like her Dad has minted a lot of money in the Gulf, I thought feeling the softness of the carpet with my feet.

As I settled on the sofa, Aarti called out, "Rajjo, paani."

A dusky girl, possibly ten and barefoot, hurried into the room balancing a crystal glass precariously on a white tray. She must be the one picking up the phone, I thought to myself, as she offered me the water.

Being a steel tumbler guy I drank cautiously from the crystal glass. Aarti's eyes were on me as she settled into a seat right in front of me, one leg over the other, right elbow on her knee and palm on the chin, shaking one of her slippers vigorously. That was the first time I saw her feet without socks and shoes. I looked at the silver nail paint on her toenails and somehow managed to restrain my eyes from wandering higher upwards.

As I returned the glass, Aarti shooed away the girl with a wave of her hand. I thought there might be something to eat too, but she didn't offer anything.

"So? How are the exam preparations?" Aarti asked to begin the conversation, even though she knew the exact status, thanks to our daily calls.

"It's okay. How about yours?" I returned the formality.

"I'm a little concerned about maths, otherwise it's cool," she said rising from the sofa. "Come, let's go to my room."

"Would that be okay with everyone?" I asked sincerely.

"Nobody's home! That's why I asked you to come," Aarti said smiling mysteriously. I wondered what she was up to as dirty thoughts started to capture my mind.

As we climbed the twenty steps next to the dining area, my heart started pounding faster and faster. I heard the pressure cooker whistle loudly – a noise that was the trademark of the Raisinghani household. Aarti leapt onto her bed as we entered her room. It was big, bigger than our drawing room, and very well lit. Two big posters from *DDLJ* and *Dil To Pagal Hai* adorned a wall. The cupboard was half-open and I could see her pullovers neatly piled one on top of the other. A wooden rack full of books and audio cassettes was squeezed next to the study table while a tape recorder was plugged in over the same. A classy table lamp and a fully satiated pen holder rested on her study table along with a few open books.

"Make yourself comfortable," Aarti urged as I dragged a stool from the corner. "Come, sit over here," she said gently tapping the bed. It's a weird feeling when a girl asks you to come to bed, even if it's just to park your posterior.

As ordered, I sat on the bed, tightly gripping my books and my mind. "Okay, let's start studying. I don't have much time," I said to release some tension, definitely my own.

"What's the hurry? Let's do it after a while," said Aarti putting her hand on my books.

What should I do now? Close the door and give my best at everything else except studies or spifflicate Jackie and run away or give Aarti a tight slap for making me feel awful.

"Please Aarti. We can always chat, but not today. Try and understand. It's exam time," I begged.

"Okay fine. I want help in trigo. It seems so easy but is extremely difficult to apply. Hardly a handful of formulae, but they're enough to make you mad," Aarti said stretching her hand to pick up the books from the table. Just then, her sweater gently curled up to reveal the most beautiful navel I'd seen in my life. All my formulae got enervated as maths got thoroughly mixed up with biology.

Over the next one hour, Aarti tried to get her doubts clarified. But only a handful of her queries were answered as I was in a filthy state of mind. I left the Raisinghani residence a short while later after Aarti bid me a zippy farewell, Jackie a lot more passionately.

▼

It was the final board exam, that too maths, the most feared one. "I'm getting butterflies in my tummy," Aarti said apprehensively.

"Don't worry. Be confident," I comforted her. Those who are in deep shit shouldn't do that. My other board exams hadn't gone well so far.

"Look, my hands are so cold," Aarti said shoving her hands into mine. Latent heat got exchanged and the poor fellows went numb. I could barely feel my fingers!

The five minutes before the three-hour exercise were really gripping this time around. The question paper pattern had changed, to everybody's consternation. But everything that happens in life isn't negative. There were more options for choice-based questions, making it easier to score. Each trigo question had a non-trigo alternative and its effect was quite evident on Aarti's face.

I too became more confident after scanning the paper and consulting my neighbour. But my hands seemed to have failed to recognize me. Contagion from Aarti had palsied them. I held the pen like a toddler, writing illegibly at tortoise pace.

When things start to go wrong, they keep going wrong. Ashu worsened the situation calling out for a supplementary booklet after just an hour. More booklets were handed out thereafter, interrupting the hour-long pin-drop silence. I think bastards like Ashu should be thrown out of the examination hall for making others feel miserable. I definitely wasn't going to require an additional booklet. Instead, I could have happily donated a few pages if needed!

Knowing almost all the answers became a curse. My godly discretionary powers made me choose the complex and lengthy problems. The end result didn't need any predictions. I screwed up a lollipop paper.

Screwed by a Mile

"**G**et up Rishu, get up. Get up you lazy boy… Rishuuu… your results are out!"

I sprang out of bed. "What? Are you serious?" I asked suspecting the news to be a prank.

"Ah, I was just joking," Mom smiled.

"You scared me!" I exclaimed and pulled back the sheet. Instantly, a ferocious tornado struck, disrespectfully blowing away the piece of cloth.

"Aarti called two minutes back. She said the results were out. You'd better get up and find out. It's eleven and you're still sleeping," Mom grumbled.

"Didn't she tell you my grades?" I asked stupidly.

"Wow! Look at you. First you sleep till eleven and then expect someone else to go and look at your result. Shame on you, Rishu."

"Okay fine. I'll go after lunch," I said as I lay down again.

"Enough of your nonsense. Leave now or you won't get lunch," Mom said firmly, picking up a slipper.

"Okay, okay. I'm leaving. At least give me time to freshen up."

"I want you out of the house in the next thirty minutes. And don't forget to take your admit card along. Aarti said the result has only the roll numbers... no names," said Mom slamming the slipper on to the floor.

I wasted no time as Mom returned to the kitchen after re-reminding me about my admit card. It was ten past twelve when I entered school.

A sea of students thronged the ground floor of the senior wing. The results were enclosed in a glass box which, by now had far more fingerprints than there probably were in the CBI records. I contributed mine too as I searched for my roll number in the list. I finally found it.

English – 69, Hindi – 71, Maths – 74, Science – 86, Social Studies – 73

My heart skipped a beat. Was it really mine? Rechecking changed nothing. One fellow was using a wooden ruler to reconfirm that he was reading his own results and not anyone else's. Maybe the result dismayed him as well. Using his technique went in vain as none of the digits changed their mind. Percentage calculation was now a mere formality.

I had scored 74.6%. Not even honours.

The most important result of my life was screwed by a mile. My shoulders drooped and my head hung low as I pulled out of the crowd. The thought of the reactions at home haunted me more than anything else. Lunch for the day seemed a distant possibility and a few slaps here and there couldn't be ruled out either.

Amid a steadily escalating sense of premonition, I noticed my friends sitting on the stairs at the end of the corridor. They looked pretty content and I wasn't in a sound state of mind to listen to their success stories or share my dismal bust.

As I started trudging back to the main gate, I heard Kaddu hiss ultrasonically, "Neta!"

The buzzing at the notice board halted for a second but was restored almost immediately. I ignored the disgraceful salutation and kept walking. I suddenly felt a human bulldozer ramming into me from behind. "Can't you hear? I've been calling out to you for the last two minutes," Kaddu fumed.

"Hey man. How are you? I'm sorry. I didn't hear you through the noise," I said, rubbing my back. His hand had felt like a hammer.

"How did you do? Come let's talk… see, everyone's waiting for you," Kaddu said pointing towards the stairs. Aarti must have informed them about her phone call.

"Yaar, can we please talk later? I've some really urgent work at home," I said.

"Don't act smart. Nothing will happen in five minutes," chided Kaddu and pulled me towards the gang.

"Netaji. How are you? How was your result? We've been waiting for you since half an hour. Where were you? Sleeping?" I was bombarded with questions.

"I'm fine. My results are okay too," I replied looking down. "And yours?"

"We all failed miserably and plan to commit suicide in another ten minutes. Now tell us yours so that you can also join in," said Jingur. There was an explosion of laughter.

"Come on! Speak up man," urged Ashu adding to my mortification.

"I've failed you all. I've dishonoured my teachers, my parents and my friends… I… I'm… I…," I broke down.

Everybody went silent. No questions, no wisecracks and no guffawing. Aarti, who had looked spirited till now, stood up and came down the stairs to put her arm around my shoulder to comfort me.

"What happened? Is everything alright?" Aarti asked in a heavy voice. I took out my hall ticket and passed it to Aarti who passed it further on to Ashu. He studied it for a bit before broadcasting my *fait accompli*.

"What's his overall percentage?" Kaddu asked striking the final nail in my coffin.

"Two marks short of honours," said Ashu.

All of them mourned my non-performance with a two-minute silence. Aarti kept her hand around me, gently rubbing my arm. Kaddu tried to lighten up the situation with a famous dialogue from the movie *Baazigar*.

My friends were sensible enough not to disclose their results, until I asked for them (but only after finding solace in Aarti's ten-minute half embrace). Each one had passed with overall honours. Ashu had scored a perfect hundred in maths. Surprisingly, Aarti too had managed eighty-three. It was only Kaddu who had a mark less than mine. As per Ashu's statistical computation, my rank was somewhere around seventy-five in our batch of a hundred and seventy-one – a real disgrace by my standards.

"I'm not your Neta anymore," I lamented looking at Kaddu, almost bursting into tears again. Aarti re-embraced me, this time even more cosily.

"One instance ain't going to change my perception. You're still my Neta and will always be," asserted Kaddu, making the atmosphere congenial again.

Public memory is amnesic. Post the mawkish drama at home and defamation at school, everybody, including me, forgot the debacle.

There were hundreds of applications for the maths stream. Dad got me to apply for it too, not only in my school but also several others.

The notice board announced our fate once again as the first list was put up. My name was second from the bottom – probably a fluke as the cut-off for PCM was eighty percent and I had a perfect eighty.

An extremely serendipitous finding was Aarti entering the maths section too! Ashu was a default selection. His name was also second on the list, but from the top.

Sarah moved into bio to dissect some frogs while Kaddu and Jingur opted for commerce, and so did Ben.

▼

That summer vacation we got a cable connection. It was a pleasant change from the dull DD channels. The days of steering the antenna over the rooftop was now a thing of the past. The telephone lost its importance as the TV remote became the most desired possession. I developed a taste for English movies too, especially those that came past midnight. The first movie I saw five times was the blockbuster epic *Titanic*.

Days later, Aarti brought up the movie topic in the school bus, "Have you seen *Titanic*?" Before I could reply she gave me her own opinion, "Awesome movie. A must watch. Leonardo just made me fall for him. He's so handsome."

"O my dear Senorita! What will Shahrukh do now?" I teased.

"I still like my sweetu," she said remembering her childhood love.

"Oho! Two men at the same time. Wild fantasies huh?" I winked and grinned.

"Shut up. Have you watched *Titanic* or not?"

"No, I haven't. Why is everybody so mad over it these days? What's so great about it?" I said loudly as her 'shut up' had echoed way too far, making people turn to look at us.

"You should watch it to understand why. The story is so touching, the actors so adorable and the music so romantic," Aarti praised the movie.

"But I've heard that it's only for adults," I said coming to the point I was interested in.

"You always think crap. Watch it in the theatre. All such stuff is edited out," Aarti said looking at me in disgust.

"How do you know which scenes have been pruned? I'm sure you've watched the original one. One where the heroine drops her..."

"Okay, that's enough. I don't know why I talk to a filthy mind like you," said Aarti exasperated.

"I'm sorry. Promise not to do that again," I pleaded.

"Get lost," Aarti huffed and shifted her focus outside the window.

▼

Raksha Bandhan, the festival that strengthens the bond between a brother and a sister, arrived. I was lucky to have Roshini didi as my sibling. She must have been the first sister who didn't demand high-ticket gifts over a rakhi. Instead, she gifted me a Batman t-shirt which I immediately fell in love with.

I showed off my rakhi like a gold bracelet. Aarti became pensive as she admired it, "I don't have a brother. Not even a cousin. I've always tied a rakhi to Laddu Gopalji."

I looked at her, terrified that she'd tie me a rakhi. Girls are quite unpredictable. They give you hints and then out of the blue, make you their brother!

Just then, Aarti took out three rakhis from her school bag. I almost got a cardiac arrest. No god, no... please. Anything but not rakhi.

"I've brought these for Ashu, Mandeep and Ashish," she explained.

I was relieved to hear the names. My three friends were soon to get a lovely sister while I was to get three bloody brothers-in-law!

Once in the school, Aarti caught Kaddu unawares on the stairs. He grimaced at first but then grinned as Aarti planted a kiss on his hirsute cheek. Ashu saw this sisterly love and vanished for assembly. During recess, Kaddu pulled him out of the loo and dragged him through the stairs to the gallery. Aarti tied her rakhi to Ashu as Kaddu held him by the scruff of his neck. Ashu was almost teary-eyed as he was heartbroken. I always knew that the bastard had feelings for Aarti.

I tell you, a tormented lover always tries to screw the prospects of other lovers. A sad, no sad $^{(infinity)}$ Ashu yelped, "What about Neta? Aren't you tying a rakhi to him?"

"Rishu already has a sister, much better than me," Aarti replied immediately.

"No problem. He can have one more," Ashu grunted.

"No, I don't want to be his sister. He's a friend."

"We too are your friends. Then why this brother-sister thing?"

I was red-faced and ready for violence by now. "What's the problem man?" I snarled.

Kaddu spoke for the first time, "Leave it Ashu. Neta won't be able to touch our sister. If he does, we can break his bones."

Aarti elbowed me in the stomach. It did hurt, but not as much as it could have.

Jingur was another bastard with dirty feelings for his sister. He had given school a miss that day. Ashu reminded Aarti about tying a rakhi to Jingur the next day, but she said Jingur didn't deserve to be her brother. I was dejected because the trick had worked for him.

Gift of Y2K

"What do you plan to do after twelfth?" Aarti asked me and Ashu at recess. We had just entered another watershed year of our life, HSC.

"Teach maths to primary classes," Ashu replied sarcastically.

"That sounds pretty exciting. I'll send over Rajjo, our gardener's daughter. She's a very bright student. Please give her a discount," Aarti jibed.

I interrupted before Ashu could speak. "Astronomy."

"What? You took up maths to be able to read people's hands and prepare horoscopes?" asked Ashu incredulously.

"You idiot, that's astrology!" Aarti shot once again.

Ashu was miffed and stood up. I'd have kept quiet had it been Jingur and Kaddu. Their bickering is always fun to watch. But this one needed to be doused. I put my hand over Aarti's mouth. When that didn't work, I folded my hands and bowed before the bloodthirsty vampires. They exchanged dirty looks, but fell silent. I tell you, ego is like cyanide. Instantly kills dialogue. Always needs to be kept satisfied.

Thankfully, I'd managed to convert an impending war into just a cold war.

I began from where we left. "Astronomy is all about stars, planets, solar systems, galaxies, etc. I want to become an astronomer."

"So basically, you want to look for aliens?" Ashu enquired, revealing what he understood about the profession from sci-fi movies. Aarti stopped herself from smiling somehow.

"That's not exactly what it is. It's much more than that."

"Whatever it is… are you sitting for IIT or not?" asked Ashu looking concerned.

"Actually, I don't want to, but Dad thinks astronomy is all rubbish. He says I was born to become an engineer," I said pensively.

"I think Uncle is right. We took up maths to study engineering. I'm not settling for anything less than IIT Kanpur, no matter how many years I need to invest," Ashu talked like an insurgent strongly supporting his leader, which over here, was my Dad.

"You should first explore a bit. What are the available courses, in which colleges, what are the employment options and likewise. Have you done that?" Aarti asked, brushing aside Ashu.

"No, I haven't."

"Why not? Who'll do it for you? First explore and then decide. Your future depends on the decisions you take now," Aarti preached.

"The truth is I'm confused. Don't know what to do in life," I confessed.

"Then you should go with Uncle's decision," said Aarti. Ashu supported her opinion nodding vigorously without saying anything. Ego is truly a dialogue killer.

"Parents always want the best for their children. My Dad says I'll do well in computers, so I'll take it up of my own volition," Aarti continued.

"Of my what? Valuation?" I asked surprised.

Aarti laughed at my interpretation. "Nothing Mr Galileo. I'll go by my Dad's decision."

▼

As was bound to happen, Dad hurled me down the path to IIT. I was admitted to DST, a coaching institute that extravagantly advertised its successes at JEE. They charged heavily as well – seven thousand per subject and twenty for the entire package. Dad happily donated sixty percent of his monthly salary for this. Parents really do make sacrifices.

Aarti too joined the same coaching institute, more importantly, the same batch. Ashu applied the time and distance formula and chose a correspondence course instead as he didn't want to waste ninety minutes on travel – five days a week, twenty days a month, and approximately a hundred and fifty days of the academic year. That's actually a lot of time, but who cared!

It was the first day of coaching class. I quickly gobbled up my lunch, took Dad's scooter and muscled my way through the busy lanes of Lucknow. These days Dad basked in the glory of a chauffeur-driven official vehicle, a bottle green Maruti Gypsy. And yes, I'd finally been able to learn driving during the summer break. But I didn't have a license yet, though I always had fifty bucks handy to meet exigencies such as being caught by the cops on the road.

The coaching class was in a total ruckus. It was a big hall that resembled an auditorium by the style of furniture it contained. The semi-circular front row seats were already taken by the twenty or so girls. The boys, who were in majority, took the seats behind them. Though it was deadly noisy, but thankfully, the class hadn't started, though I was a good ten minutes late.

Aarti was already there, conversing with a really hot girl, correction, mermaid. As she waved at me, I felt three dozen eyeballs turn to look at me. I waved back and looked around for a seat. I found one in the window slab next to the desert cooler. A tall dark fellow in faded grey denims and a red t-shirt walked right up to me and requested me to shift.

"Sorry boss. No space," I said trying to convince him to look elsewhere.

"Please shift. I think both of us can fit in easily," he said and pushed his bum in, almost sitting on my lap. I had no choice. "Hi. I'm Raman Ahuja," said my neighbour proffering his hand.

"Rishabh Agrawal," I said shaking hands with him.

"I too just came in. Thank god the class hasn't started yet. Any idea when it will start?" I asked.

"Not before three-thirty. Tripathi never comes on time," said Raman viciously.

"Three-thirty? I thought this was the best coaching institute in Lucknow," I said amazed.

"It is. That's why nobody values our time. They have six such batches – each full of two hundred and fifty morons like us. Why would they bother about time when their business is flourishing like a brothel?"

Raman's scathing remarks raised a very valid point. For a moment, I thought Ashu was quite wise to study on his own. But then, my eyes wandered towards Aarti and all such thoughts vanished into thin air.

"Agrawal sir, what are you thinking? Planning to join these bastards after engineering?" Raman asked.

"No, no! I was just checking if we'd be able to see the board from here," I clarified.

"Who the hell can see or listen from here?" Raman stood up, dusted his jeans and sat down again.

In the next half-an-hour, Raman and I exchanged a wide variety of thoughts. We started with coaching, gradually moved on to cricket, then to movies, and then to bikes. Finally, when all topics were depleted, we shifted our focus to girls.

Raman was right. At 3:35 p.m., a bald man with stylish goggles entered the class, swinging a keychain around his finger. He went up to the podium, attached a wireless mic onto his collar, did some 'Hello, hello, mic testing' and announced pompously, "Hello students. I am Manish Tripathi. Ex-IITian. 1985 batch. I'll help you to crack the physics paper."

"Do you know why he's an ex-IITian?" whispered Raman.

"Why?"

"He had a one-night stand with a professor's daughter and was kicked out! And now he teaches others how to get into IIT... son of a bitch is using us to take revenge," said Raman savagely. Both of us chuckled and re-joined Tripathi's hogwash.

"Today, we'll start with babes," Tripathi declared smiling at the babes in the first row. "Who'll tell me what a babe is? There's a five-hundred-rupee cash prize to the one who defines it correctly," tempted Tripathi. There was silence. Not one person raised a hand to answer. Tripathi turned around and wrote WAVES on the whiteboard in capitals. Almost everybody raised their hands now, suppressing their smiles. I wasn't the only one who had misunderstood him.

In the next eighty minutes, we became familiar with a wide variety of 'babes'. Some were transverse, longitudinal, surface or electromagnetic, but all were 'babes'.

At exactly 5 p.m., Tripathi's chronograph watch beeped. He looked at it, looked at us and then looked at it again. "That's all for today. We'll continue on Wednesday."

"Is that it? I thought it was a two-hour class," I said in surprise.

"You should be thankful that Tripathi came and gave you his time. He's nothing less than a film star," Raman replied.

"Why should I be thankful? I've paid him fees," I snarled.

"Everybody has paid fees. You need him. He doesn't need you."

That line from Raman made it clear that getting into IIT was our concern, not Mr Tripathi's or any of his colleagues at DST. If we clear the exam, the coaching institute would take credit, but if we didn't, it'd be our fault.

"What did you think of the class?" Aarti asked.

"The teachers are knowledgeable, but don't respect time," I gave my opinion.

"Ya, that's true, but they're really fandu. What clear concepts," gushed Aarti.

"How have you come?" I asked changing the topic.

"*Tempo*. And you?"

"Scooter," I responded with a grin.

"Really? Now do I need to tell you that I'm riding pillion?"

▼

Aarti was now a regular with me on the scooter for the coaching classes. Of course, nobody from our families knew about it. The coaching class boys had also got accustomed with our fictitious liaison. Overall, it was all going well, except for the most important thing – the IIT preparation (at least in my case).

After days of smooth talk, Aarti introduced me to the bewitching mermaid she was talking to on the first day of our coaching. The nymphet's name was Priyanka Sharma and she too came from Aliganj. Exchanging phone numbers with her was the most euphoric moment of my life.

One auspicious day I got the golden opportunity of dropping both the girls home on my scooter. Priyanka sat sandwiched between me and Aarti. What a wonderful experience! Two girls behind me, bumpy roads and super sharp brakes!

I was so excited that I strongly considered making Priyanka a regular pillion. To be true, her touch, feel, smell and everything else was delicious. But I didn't have the guts to ask Aarti to start using the tempo, so I just resigned myself to give Priyanka a lift whenever Aarti was absent. That included two golgappa sessions as well. I hoped Aarti never found out about all this.

▼

The DST troika (Das, Singh, Tripathi) and demons at school kept releasing oodles of gyan until the day for the IIT JEE arrived. To my consternation, that year the JEE pattern changed! It was now split into two stages, screening and mains. Screening was an elimination round and was purely objective in nature (aspirants were required to answer by blackening bubbles on pink OMR sheets).

My examination centre was the same as Aarti's, possibly because we filled and posted our application forms together. Ashu had a different centre, much to my satisfaction.

It was the 2nd of January, the first Sunday of the Y2K year. Extreme cold wave conditions swept North India; the best time to be in a cosy bed with some hot magazines to stare at (of course, with a lot of action under the quilt). But IIT had other plans for many of us.

It was 8:15 a.m. and I was standing with Dad at an unknown place surrounded by numerous strangers. It looked like the weekend rush for a movie. Some guys were madly revising their notes while others shivered in the foggy conditions. Some even had the sacred red teeka on their foreheads!

Minutes later, Aarti arrived with her Dad and spotted me in the crowd. "Hi Rishu! Howdy! All set to crack the JEE?" she yelled, not noticing Dad standing four-five steps to my left.

I went dead for a second but then responded judiciously with an elementary "Hi" and a "Namaste Uncle." Her Dad nodded looking at me with suspicion. He was as tall as a coconut tree, with a nice-looking moustache resting under his nose. I understood now how Aarti was so good looking even when she wasn't fair in a colour-obsessed country like ours.

"Who's he?" Uncle asked Aarti.

"He's Rishabh, Dad. My best friend, classmate, bus-mate and also DST-mate," Aarti replied.

"Baby, you forgot soul-mate," I said in my mind.

"Is he the one who messed up his board results?" Raisinghani Senior shot a poison-laced arrow. I smiled tawdrily and said, "Yes, unfortunately."

Aarti changed the topic quickly. "You've come on your scooter in this cold? You should have brought the Gypsy." Uncle looked at her confused but then left us alone to explore the crowd. I turned my eyes to Dad. He looked surprised.

"Actually, Dad anticipated a parking problem. That's why the scooter," I tried to tell Aarti that I wasn't alone.

"Oh, come on! Don't always think like a baniya," said Aarti, referring to the niggardliness of my community. Don't know how Dad must have felt hearing such unsavoury remarks from the Raisinghani duo.

"It's so cold. I can't feel my nose. Even my hands have frozen," Aarti lamented, still not realising the situation. Then suddenly she took off her gloves and caught my wrist and started to rub her hands in mine.

I yanked my hands away from her and shoved them into my jacket pockets. "Take your hands out," Aarti ordered playfully and tried pulling them out.

"Meet Dad," I curtly ended the struggle before something irrevocable happened. Aarti realised her blunder and then quickly tried to cover up, "Hello Uncle. Wish you a Happy New Year. Rishu, you're so stupid. Why didn't you say that Uncle was also here?"

Only if you and your Dad had kept your indelicate mouths shut, I thought. Dad smiled and nodded, scanning Aarti through his glasses.

"How's Aunty feeling now?" Aarti asked Dad.

Now where did that come from? I slapped my forehead mentally. Aarti was good at handling situations, but super blockheaded as well. Her question made it clear that she knew the day-to-day affairs of our household. Dad looked at her surprised. "She's fine," he replied.

By this time, Uncle was back. I introduced him to my father as they shook hands and exchanged a few pleasantries. This Lord-Rama-meets-King-Bharata drama was aborted abruptly as the gatekeeper called out something about a change in the seating plan.

"Please check mine too," Aarti ordered, handing over her hall ticket to me. I joined the posse but was hardly able to move a step over the next few minutes. So, I came back saying that I'd check once the rush lessened.

"What? You're good for nothing," said Aarti, rudely snatching the hall tickets from my hand.

She returned within a minute.

"I've to go to GF-3 and you've to go to FF-5," she announced returning my hall ticket.

"What's FF-5?"

"First floor, room five," she replied and mumbled, "Full-blown fool" (which all of us heard quite clearly).

Aarti's Dad smirked while mine feigned ignorance. After about five minutes, we left our fathers in each other's company as they literally frogmarched us to confront the JEE conundrums for the next three hours.

The wait wasn't long. The results of the not-so-pleasurable bubble game were out by the end of the month. As expected, the year 2000 began with affliction. Two of my friends happily left the remaining three zeros for me. They advanced to the next level, leaving me to prepare solo for other not-so-prestigious competitive exams. Even the DST brothers preferred differentiation over integration. Batches were reorganized. Prospective IIT brains were separated from the rest of the crowd. They were given all the attention while the others were totally neglected. Thankfully, Priyanka was there as a centripetal force, keeping my interests alive.

Time for Ciao

Should I? Shouldn't I? I think I should. What if she rejects me? Worse, slaps me?

I started to contemplate on this just a week after the IITs declared their coveted list. The reason was simple. It was time for our farewell party at school – triggering a countdown to part with friends, foes, competitors, demons, crushes and lovers.

The last week at school was the most memorable one. There was an unmistakeable exuberance in the air as the teachers gave us the liberty to do as we wanted all day. Classrooms were flooded with slam books. The slam book tradition started by the girls gradually infiltrated to the boys and suddenly there were slam books everywhere. You must be wondering what a slam book is. Let me define it for you. A slam book is a postcard-sized diary which has a ridiculous set of questions to be answered by the person privileged to be asked to do so!

Since this was the last chance to impress the girls, the boys applied their innovation to glut these frivolous databases. I was privileged to be asked by Sarah to fill in and sign her slam book. She gave it to me at recess and got busy with her friends. The cover of the pink and white diary had a lot of flowers around it, and at the centre, a rotund bear licking honey from a jar. My mind started racing as I imagined myself to be the bear and Sarah the honey!

It's always fun to read others' entries in someone's slam book (especially for contact details of other desirable girls). As I flipped through Sarah's slam book, Jingur's entry caught my eye.

What the hell? How could he be so vulgar and blatant? I thought as I went through his lecherous entry. I was sure that Sarah hadn't seen what filth Jingur had written about her and some of the other girls from the school. That bastard had also mentioned my two-year-old sob story and Aarti's mommy-type consoling. I wish him immortal celibacy.

I filled the slam book like a normal person, copying nothing from either Jingur or anybody else. Over the next two days, I filled in two dozen slam books, including Aarti's.

▼

It was Sunday night, the night before the farewell. For the entire week, I wondered when and how I should propose to Aarti, but just couldn't muster enough courage. I decided to put forward my proposition at the farewell. Now the question was what to say, when to say and how to begin? It had to be something rocking and not shocking.

"Aarti, I want to tell you something... it's much more important than IIT, Shahrukh and everything else that matters to you in life. We've been friends for almost five years now and hopefully understand each other very well. Once we pass out from here, we'll go to different colleges and get busy with our lives. We'll make new friends, but not as loving as childhood buddies. If I say I want to be your best friend forever, will that be possible? If I say I want to live life's ups and downs with you, will that be possible? If I say I want to be beside you till my last breath, will that be possible? If I say I love you, would you say no?"

I'd practised that soppy speech to perfection. I decided to team it up with some red flowers and a valentine card since the farewell party was on Valentine's Day.

I spent almost two hours deciding what to wear for the party. Finally, I closed in on my one and only single-breasted suit, big snouted leather shoes and one of Dad's ties. As the day was super special, I shaved for the first time ever, gifting myself a minor cut over the chin. Dad's Old Spice worked wonders on it, though it did hurt initially. I liked its fragrance so much that I added a few extra drops to my neck and behind my ears too.

Mom was pleasantly surprised, "You're looking human!" she praised me, "but... wait... why so much perfume?" She smiled, knowingly sniffing the aftershave.

"Today's our farewell party. It's an important day. Everyone will be dressed like this," I replied avoiding eye contact.

"An important day will be the one when you get selected somewhere," said Mom sarcastically. I made a face and walked out of the house.

I went straight to Archies Gallery at Kapoorthala. A lot of florist kiosks had mushroomed around the shop overnight. Looking at my attire, the shopkeeper guided me straight to the love section that had a lot of heart-shaped balloons suspended from the ceiling.

After much research, I decided on a card showing two kids holding hands and kissing each other. I paid thirty bucks and left to pick up the flowers. I balanced myself on my scooter seat to inundate the card with some love quotes before driving towards the school.

I entered the school and who should I bump into, but Kaddu. He looked me up and down and said, "Wow Neta! You're looking so young!"

"I *am* young Kaddu. Younger than you," I replied miffed.

"Who told you to shave? What's going on? Tell me you bastard. Are you going to propose to Aarti?" Kaddu winked.

"How do you know I'm going to propose?" I was surprised.

"Are you... really? I didn't know... just said it like that," he responded immediately.

"Yes! Today I'll propose. But to Betty. She turns me on every time I see her," I changed the name just to piss him off.

Kaddu roared, "You bastard. Speak of her with respect. Or else I'll kill you."

I broke into laughter as Jingur leaped in from behind with a wisecrack, "Oh my, just look at that. Netaji is a suited-booted sahib today. All shaved too. I wonder what's happening... some girls are going to die today!"

"And a woman as well," I replied winking at Kaddu.

"I desperately need some fresh bones," Kaddu growled, folding up his shirtsleeves.

"Leave it bro. He's just teasing you. Let's check out the girls," Jingur quickly diverted his attention from me.

"Let's wait for Ashu," Kaddu responded, looking unfazed now.

"He's not coming. He has some mock test for the IIT mains," I informed them.

"What man? IIT can only give him a degree, not true friends," Jingur said crestfallen. Agreed. IIT cannot guarantee true friends but definitely a bright future and a successful life. And probably, a sexy wife too!

The class eleven girls welcomed us into the party hall by sprinkling rose water over us. We were ushered in by a beautiful girl with a magnetic mole on her upper lip. Five minutes later, Sarah entered the hall in a red chiffon sari with matching earrings. She'd used red lipstick and wore pencil heels.

"Wow! She looks hotter than Pamela," Jingur whispered staring at her longingly.

"What's happened to you? Looks like you have a crush on her," I asked innocently.

"Yes man. I do have a crush on her. But yaar, she's not been talking to me since the time I filled in her slam book," Jingur admitted.

"I read what you wrote, bastard! You've written all filth in that. Not even spared your friends."

"What has he written about me?" Kaddu asked.

"That you see an elder sister in Betty," Jingur responded.

Such retarded bickering continued until Aarti entered the hall. She wore a dark blue sari with perfectly matching accessories and very subtle make-up. She had a totally new hair-do which made her look even better than she usually did. I just stared at her as she took her seat five rows ahead of us.

The farewell show commenced with a speech by Ms Betty. Kaddu listened transfixed as the rest of us yawned. The juniors had prepared a skit and a few dance performances to entertain us. Afterwards, Ms Betty got off the stage and went to the students asking questions over the mic. People curled up in their seats to try and hide themselves from her. Strangely, her fourth victim was Kaddu.

"Mandeep, right?"

"Yes ma'am," Kaddu stood up immediately. "Tell us Mandeep. Who will you miss the most after school? Which friend will you miss?" Ms Betty pressed Kaddu's shoulder to make him sit.

"No friends, ma'am," Kaddu replied, "I'll miss you. You're my favourite teacher. You're what I love most in the school," said Kaddu seriously.

The crowd fell silent. Jingur and I bent down to pretend tying our shoelaces. "Thank you Mandeep. Wish you all the very best for the future, love you too," said Ms Betty smiling. Kaddu turned scarlet as he heard those words. Aarti started to clap and everyone joined in gradually. Fatso had finally spoken his heart out.

Ms Betty brought the eventful party to a close by passing around the class photograph taken a few days earlier. The photo showed the principal seated right in the middle without him being physically present for the photoshoot. Quite distasteful from a person of his stature.

One of the juniors took over the mic from Ms Betty and directed everyone to the snacks counter. People made a beeline as if it was relief material being distributed at a refugee camp.

"Hi Rishu," Aarti greeted me.

"Hey Aarti. How are you? Haircut?" I asked.

"Yep. Is it nice?"

"Yes, it is. You look beautiful."

"Thanks. You look good too. Oy! Wait a second. Where's the fuzz gone?" Aarti asked as she caressed my cheeks.

"I've just shaved. That's it," I clarified.

"You're looking pretty handsome. Always stay like this."

"You're embarrassing me," I said stroking the hair at the back of my head.

"No, I mean it. You're looking really nice," Aarti said touching my cheek again.

I grinned and said, "Your sari looks pretty nice too."

"This? It's a pathetic thing. It kept coming off till finally Mom draped it for me."

I kept silent thinking why I wasn't there when this sari coming-off episode was happening.

"Hey listen. I want to tell you something important," I came to the point immediately.

"Uh-huh, I'm listening."

"Not here. Alone."

"Why? Is it a secret?" asked Aarti wide-eyed.

"Yes, a big secret," I put a finger on my lips to make her feel the weight of the matter.

"Okay… if you say so. But do tell me before we leave. I can never sleep with unsolved stuff in my head."

I confirmed with a nod as Aarti got busy with the snacks. I devoured a pastry and some chips to reinforce my courage for the post-party proposition. Jingur and Kaddu joined us a little later.

Soon after, we started our photo session, in all possible combinations. Sarah also joined us. She avoided eye contact with Jingur even as he kept staring at her. Half-an-hour later, people started to stream out as it was beginning to get dark. By six, almost everybody had left, sparing ten-twelve of us. Kaddu and Jingur also moved out ten minutes later. I stayed back with Aarti as she waited for her Dad to arrive.

Is this the right time to propose? I asked myself. Yes, of course, it is. Speak up you moron, someone rebuked me from inside. My heart was beating unnaturally fast. "Aarti, I want to tell you something."

"Oh yes, the secret thing. Please go ahead. I'm all ears," she said putting two fingers behind her right earlobe.

"It's much more important than IIT, Shahrukh and everything else that matters to you in life," I continued.

"Then it must be really really important," Aarti winked and drew closer to me. I felt like kissing her instead of begging for love as physical contact can sometimes convey much more than words.

But that needed guts, which, unfortunately, I was born without. So, I preferred to beg.

"We've been friends for almost five years now and hopefully understand each other very well. Once we pass out from here, we'll go to different colleges and get busy with our lives. We'll make new friends, but not as loving as childhood buddies. If I say I want to be your best friend forever, will that be possible? If I..."

Aarti hugged me tightly before I could say out the most critical lines of my proposal.

"Oh Rishu! I'll always be your best friend. I promise nobody else will ever take that place," Aarti promised crossing her heart and kissed me on the cheek. Guys left on the premises watched us embrace and kiss anxiously. They must have been thinking that the girl was set and now the boy would enjoy the pleasures of life.

"I... I..." I tried to come out of that shocking intimacy but couldn't find the right words.

"Don't say anything or I'll cry," Aarti said and hugged me again, this time even more intimately. For the first time since the unforgettable ball dance, I felt her body against mine. The guys checking us out moaned, wanting more of this amorous play.

Aarti suddenly let go of me. "What's that you're hiding?" she asked digging her hand into the inside pocket of my coat.

"Nothing," I said grabbing her hand from over my coat.

"Remove your hand. Let me see what it is," she said and took out the roses which had almost wilted by now.

"Red roses. For whom?" Aarti asked rolling her eyes. I didn't reply.

She asked again, "Come on Rishu. Don't be shy. You can share it with me. I won't tell anyone. But please, don't say that you brought them for me."

"Yes, I brought them for you," I spoke the truth.

"Idiot! Friends are given yellow roses. Red ones are for valentines."

"Then be my valentine," I said meekly.

"Hmm... let me think," Aarti said tapping her cheek with her index finger. After five seconds of fake acting she said, "Okay, I'll be your valentine. But tell me the truth. For whom did you bring these? Priyanka?"

"What nonsense! You and your imagination."

"I know everything about you, Rishu. Even the way you think. So, don't play games with me. I know you've been secretly dating her since our batches changed. Phone calls, golgappas and..." Aarti started to laugh.

"Are you spying on me? How do you know all this?" I asked shaking her shoulder.

"Bond... James Bond!" Aarti said and pretended to blow off smoke from the roses, as if they were a pistol.

Her Dad arrived just then. She carefully put the flowers in her purse and said bye to me as I accompanied her to the car. Uncle offered me a lift but I had my scooter, so I politely declined his offer. Once Aarti left, the boys who had been watching us, walked up and congratulated me as if I'd been declared the next Prime Minister.

I can't explain the trauma I went through that night. I kept twisting and turning, often weeping (Jingur was right in his slam book entry), before falling asleep with the valentine card under my bed.

Fiasco King

History is taught so that we don't repeat the mistakes committed by the greats of the past. I wasn't great, nor were my mess-ups big enough to find their way into history books.

Even though Aarti didn't invite me for combined studies this time, I was mentally with her day in and day out. My books were open for almost twelve hours a day, but only to deceive the people at home. I dreamt about topping the board exams, if not the IIT, to win back my reputation. The only thing missing in this noble idea was focus on my books.

Exams came and went. I improvised better than the last time, but it was way short of materializing into what I'd dreamt about. As can be expected, I screwed up my board exams once again!

It was May when the results for IIT mains were declared amidst much touting by the media. I called Aarti. She picked up the phone herself for the first time in almost two-and-a-half years.

"Hello Aarti. Rishabh here," I said, as if she wouldn't recognize my voice.

"Hi Rishu," Aarti replied coldly.

"IIT results are out. Did you make it?" I came directly to the point of interest.

There was a long silence before a melancholic "No."

"I'm sorry. You'll definitely get through next time," I consoled her.

"I'm not wasting another year. It's very painful to fail even after giving your all."

She continued woefully, "Ashu's cleared the mains, by the way."

"What?" I screamed in surprise.

"Yes, he got AIR 594," Aarti informed me in a super sad low-spirited tone about the super success of her foster brother.

"Really? Let me call him. Talk to you later," I hung up without asking about anything else. I called Ashu's place. His Dad picked up the phone and kicked off the conversation asking about my rank. He didn't sound disappointed at my elimination in the prelims. He went on to extol the virtues of self-study and a strict time table. When I finally got the chance to ask for Ashu to wish him, I was told that he'd gone to the temple to offer his thanks, probably with some big money offerings. I sincerely felt like going to the graveyard.

The HSC results followed soon after. I scored a mediocre seventy-six percent. Yes, it was an honours this time. Aarti scored eighty-four while Ashu missed ninety by a whisker. Kaddu was also at seventy-six while Jingur got seventy-nine.

Over the next few days, more results poured in, spreading the wound of failure like septicaemia. I kept touching new lows while Ashu thrived. I was stunned to find his name in a seemingly endless list in DST's Olympian advertisement. Those bastards had paid his Dad a handsome amount for this. For them, education was a business and they could prosper only by showing off exceptional results. It was all for attracting unsuspecting students like me. There were no ethics in it at all. Amid this drama, Aarti too got mediocre ranks in other competitive exams, her best being at the state engineering test. I failed to score a rank even in that. After all, I was the world's new fiasco king.

▼

It was counselling time. While everyone was occupied with exploring their options, I was busy getting rebuked at home and joining other coaching institutes for a dead duck seat at IIT next year. Ashu, the achiever who had hit bull's eye, got Mechanical at IIT Kanpur, his dream institute, a name that had started giving me nightmares. Aarti too joined engineering, opting for Computer Science at PILOTS, a local private engineering college. Even Priyanka, the mermaid from DST had got a decent college through CET Karnataka. Jingur went on to pursue B.Com. from some not-so-reputed college in Delhi while Kaddu's burning desire to avenge the Kargil war was soon to bear fruit. I don't know how he did it with his weight, but he got into the NDA.

"College starts next week but I can already feel the butterflies in my stomach," Aarti admitted her jitteriness sipping a Coke at our regular haunt near Archies.

"Don't worry. Everything would be alright," I said.

"These days, ragging has become very physical. Just yesterday I saw on TV that two freshers committed suicide due to ragging. I'm getting really scared."

"You're thinking way too much. I know ragging happens, but only with hostellers."

The bubble of positivity was short-lived as Aarti restarted the ragging subject a while later. I gave up and listened patiently, stifling my yawns. I offered her a lift back home and she hopped on to my scooter as always. Everything was okay till two rowdy fellows on a bike whistled at her and stepped on the accelerator at full throttle.

"Follow them Rishu. Follow them. I'll break their bloody noses," Aarti screamed.

"I can't. They're on a bike. This is a scooter," I cried.

"Then buy a bike," Aarti ordered as if she was asking me to buy a lollypop.

"Just ignore them. You'll come across many such rascals at college. What will you do then?"

"I'll chase them till the end of the world and beat them black and blue."

"How? Will you run after them?" I mimicked a running athlete with my fingers.

Aarti was silent for a while before asking me seriously, "I want to learn how to drive. Will you teach me?"

"You and drive? What a joke!"

"Will you, or won't you? Answer me."

"Okay, okay, I will. But what will you drive? A scooter?"

"I'll ask Dad to buy me a Scooty. You just teach me."

Aarti was a hard nut to crack. I surrendered to her demands and agreed to free tutorials. What a comedown — from a maths teacher to a driving instructor.

Aarti was a quick learner but a witch as well. She drained out my skills. Earlier it was maths and now it was driving. I can't explain how it was sitting so close to her, with my legs around hers, hands clasping her soft hands and her sweet-smelling hair tickling my nose. Those intimate driving lessons nearly made me insane.

▼

It was my birthday, almost nine months after I approved Aarti's driving capabilities. Getting her a driving license was her Dad's headache. We hadn't met ever since the driving lessons got over, but just chatted a couple of times on the phone. And yes, the bubbles on the OMR sheet had busted me yet again. I just wasn't made for the IITs, or maybe it was vice versa. After all, it was the age of objectivity, where subjectivity held no meaning.

Aarti gave me a surprise call at five in the evening. By default, Mom picked it up. I was busy making love to M.L. Khanna, the Bible of Mathematics. What a noble way to celebrate a birthday!

"Rishu, it's for you… Aarti's calling to wish you," Mom yelled from the drawing room.

I stopped my rote memorizing, shoved my pen into the parabola chapter and ran to hear the voice I'd been longing for.

"Happy birthday to you… May god bless you…," Aarti sang her own version of the birthday song to me. I blushed and drew shapes on the sofa. "Thank you Aarti. Thank you very much."

"What thank you? Party man! I want a party."

"Party for what?"

"Oh, come on Rishu! You're coming to Archies at six. I'll wait over there," Aarti commanded and hung up before I could complete my crooked parabola over the sofa. Mom was in the kitchen, pretending not to listen in to the conversation. As I passed her, she commented, "Looks like you need to see someone."

I grinned and dropped my head. "It's my birthday Mom. And she's the only friend who's called me. You know that," I said looking down.

Mom mulled over something and then took out two hundred bucks and handed it to me, "Here, take this and go have some fun."

I shaved twice and reached Archies exactly at six. I parked my scooter and lounged over it to wait for Aarti.

She arrived ten minutes later on a pink Scooty with a slightly dented mudguard. She wore body hugging denims with a matching top and had a cute satchel slung on her shoulder. The earrings had given way to the more demure tops and she wore stilettos instead of her usual sandals. Her ponytail was back and so was her petite elliptical watch. In short, she looked extremely sexy.

Smokers in the vicinity turned to stare, taking long drags on their cigarettes, as Aarti parked and gave me a tight hug and wished me happy birthday.

"What the hell are you doing? Move away. People are looking at us!" I protested.

"Let them watch and envy your luck," Aarti replied, her eyes twinkling as she loosened her embrace.

"My luck?"

"Yes, your luck. Otherwise why would a beautiful girl come and hug you in public?" Aarti said with her nose up in the air, her hands still encircling my neck.

"You're saying I'm ugly. Get lost, no party," I said removing her hands from my neck.

"I'm simply saying that I'm beautiful!"

Aarti was right. She was much more gorgeous than ever before.

"So? Are we going to stay here or go elsewhere?" she asked.

"You tell me. Where do you want to go? I have only two hundred bucks."

"Tsk, a true baniya! Can't spend even on your own birthday."

"Have you come to call me names or celebrate my birthday?" I said pretending to look hurt.

"Let's go to CCD."

"And what's that?"

"Celebrate Cheaply Dude!" Aarti pinched my freshly depilated cheeks and chuckled.

"Tell na!"

"Cafe Coffee Day, up there on the first floor. It opened last month. I've been there once with Mom. It's an awesome place to loosen up. A perfect hangout," she explained.

I looked up and saw a cheerful-looking place with a friendly ambience. I was hoping it wouldn't be too expensive. We got a table near the glass wall where we could get occasional glimpses of the traffic on the street. Aarti wrested the menu card from my hands and ordered things I'd never heard of before – a doughnut and a muffin along with two regular cappuccinos (I still don't know how to pronounce it). I quickly glanced at the prices, mentally calculating the expected bill. I was terrified that the bill would cross two hundred. Thankfully, it didn't.

"I have a surprise for you," Aarti opened her satchel and took out a tiny box along with an envelope. She placed both the items in front of me at the centre of the table.

"What's in it? Perfume?" I asked rotating the box.

"Open it and you'll know."

I tore the wrapping paper and opened the box. There was a small Ganesh idol inside.

"It's to give you mental strength. Keep it on your study table and you'll definitely get into a good college this year," Aarti said solemnly as I frowned mentally. But then, I realised that the gift showed her concern for me and I kissed the idol to show my appreciation.

"Idiot! Touch the feet. Don't kiss it. You're insulting Ganeshji," she rebuked me.

"I'm sorry," I apologized and touched the idol's feet to my head.

"Check out the card," Aarti pushed the envelope towards me.

I opened the envelope and took out the card. The cover had beer bottles on it with a message inside it, "For my dearest of dearest friends who missed it just by a day. But that doesn't matter because he is what he was supposed to be. Dated 2nd April 2001."

"You mean to say I'm a fool?" I grunted pointing my finger first at Aarti and then at myself.

"Did I say that?"

"What else does this mean?" My finger pointed to the card.

"It means a first-class person like you doesn't deserve to be in the second category," she interpreted her message laughing.

"I know you're making this up. You actually meant I was supposed to be born on April Fools' Day."

"Assumptions my dear, assumptions…"

We bickered over the insulting birthday wishes until our order arrived. The cute white hearts floating on the coffee changed our mood. We switched to our regular 'how have you been' kind of stuff.

"Hey, what's that?" I questioned pointing to a mark on Aarti's temple.

"Stitch marks. I had an accident last year."

"How? What happened?"

"I started using my Scooty to go to college. One day it was drizzling and my Scooty skidded when I braked to avoid a pothole. Got three stitches. Ever since, Dad doesn't let me take the Scooty to college. I take the bus again."

I leaned forward to check the scar with my fingers.

"What the hell are you doing? Move away. People are looking at us!" she protested.

"Let them watch and envy your luck," I said it exactly the way she had done at Archies.

"You scoundrel!" she slapped my hand.

Suddenly, there was a shattering sound. A dude and his date, seated diagonally opposite to our table, had spilt their coffee.

"*Phuck!*" the fellow shrieked at the top of his lungs.

Aarti laughed uncontrollably hearing his pronunciation.

"You understood what he meant?" I asked surprised.

"I understand how it's done as well!" she replied smugly as she stirred the foam in her cup.

"Really? Come Closer Darling, and show me how," I said touching her scar and gradually moving my fingers towards her sensual lips.

"Do you want to get slapped on your birthday?" Aarti spurned my advances, hitting me hard on my knuckles with her spoon. I instantly retracted my hand and started to nurse the injury.

"You know what? You just need a chance to start on a filthy topic! That's why I've given you the idol of Ganeshji. I wish he cleanses your mind and helps you concentrate on more important things in life," Aarti said looking serious. That's what I'm doing baby, I thought.

The bill came to a hundred and eighty-nine bucks. A closer analysis revealed that I'd forgotten to include service tax in my calculations. I paid the bill and was forced to tip the waiter as Aarti fluttered her eyelids over her hypnotic brown eyes. Returning home with a one rupee coin was mortifying, so I gifted it to an old beggar woman who wished us a happily married life with more than a dozen kids. Aarti tried to explain the actual relationship to her as I thanked her (in my mind) for the blessings.

A Strange Pick

Ironically, all the competitive exams seemed to have turned their backs on me. Only the state engineering test held out a flimsy hope, but nothing more than a non-reputed private engineering college. Dropping a year had turned out to be a total waste of time and money. Pursuing a B.Sc. in Astronomy from Lucknow University would have been a far better choice.

It was a hot and humid Saturday evening when Dad called me to his room. "How is PILOTS as a college?" he asked.

"Umm, I have no idea, Dad. But I can ask," I replied looking down at his slippers.

"Ask whom?"

"Aarti."

"Who's Aarti?" Dad took off his glasses.

"The girl we met at the IIT entrance test last year. Remember?" I said looking straight at Dad.

"Oh yes! I do remember meeting her... is she studying there?" he asked excitedly.

"Yes, she took admission last year," I replied.

"Paid seat?"

"No, free," I answered and repositioned my eyes onto his slippers.

"Give me her number. I'll talk to her father."

"You can directly talk to her. Why bother her father?" I suggested.

"Just give the number and go to your room," Dad said sternly. I passed on the number and went to my room. Five minutes later I heard Dad saying hello to someone. I snuck out of my room and took a chair at the dining table. I was quite worried about the conversation.

Dad introduced himself and started to talk straightaway. Surprisingly, Aarti had answered the phone. I tried to listen in to the infrasonic conversation with a throbbing heart. All I could make out was PILOTS being mentioned at least seven-eight times. Two minutes later, Dad hung up repeating, "Okay, tomorrow at six." He put the receiver down and stared at me for a while before speaking, "Raisinghaniji is out of town. So, I've called your friend tomorrow at six."

"Where?"

"Here. You've to meet her at Kapoorthala and bring her here. She doesn't know the house," he said.

That night was the longest night of my life. Aarti was coming to meet her future in-laws for an extremely sticky reason – to submit a college's advisory report so that the man she would marry could get admission there.

The next day at around 5:45 p.m., I met Aarti at Kapoorthala and guided her to our place, obviously on separate vehicles. She was sensible enough to wear a salwar-kameez instead of the bootylicious outfit she wore on my birthday. Pandey Aunty, our neighbourhood nosey parker watched us from her balcony as we parked our vehicles side by side. I avoided all eye contact with her lest she asked me some embarrassing questions in front of Aarti. Mom opened the door and let us in. I introduced the battleship to the nuclear submarine. "Mom, this is Aarti. Aarti, my Mom."

They exchanged formalities as Totu, my parrot, started to chant 'Aarti Aarti Aarti'. Aarti couldn't control her smile and exclaimed, "Wow, it talks!" Totu repeated her words. She was mighty impressed and went near the cage for a closer look. Totu showed her its best dance moves, twirling in its cage, calling out her name more than I did in a day.

"Sit beta. And don't touch the parrot. It might bite. Has a very sharp beak," cautioned Mom. Aarti immediately retracted her hand as she was about to touch Totu's rose-ring. She bid farewell to it and found herself a place on the sofa. I stood in the corner. Dad entered the drawing room cleaning his glasses with his kurta. Aarti stood up and greeted him, "Namaste Uncle."

"Namaste beta. Why don't you sit down?" said Dad.

Their discussion on the PILOTS' faculty, branches, facilities, results, placements, etc., started and I listened intently. The focus shifted on me as Dad told Aarti, "Your friend has performed poorly this year too. I don't know if he can get anything at PILOTS. What do you think?"

"Uncle, he should go for computers. The future lies there. Paid seats don't get filled easily because the fee is almost thrice that of the free seats," she told him. Dad took off his glasses and glared at me. Three free seat bright students would graduate in the amount of money his undeserving son would consume alone! As the discussion on finance bankrupted my mind, I picked up the newspaper and buried my face in it. Mom arrived just then with tea and snacks and so did Roshini didi.

Didi had got married a few months ago, and had come to spend some time with us before she and Jijaji migrated to UK. Jijaji was an engineer from IIT Delhi and Dad was very proud of this. At least his son-in-law was an IITian, if not his own good-for-nothing son.

Mom gradually took over the discussion that was supposed to be limited only to PILOTS. She deliberately insulted me as much as she could. Her most hurtful remark was, "I was going to use him as domestic help had he not got a rank this year too. He just eats and sleeps. Doesn't understand the value of money. Asking him to study is like casting pearls before swine."

On hearing this, Dad left the room while Aarti chose to intervene, "Forget it Aunty. That's in the past now. I'm sure he'll make you proud as an engineer."

Mom smirked at the stupid suggestion and then suddenly changed gears. She got under Aarti's skin asking her personal details. Aarti looked displeasingly at me when Mom asked her if she had a boyfriend. But then she patiently said 'no' which made me gloat as if she had said she loved me. I think Aarti was relieved to finally leave our house after twenty minutes of intense interrogation. I apologized on the staircase for such scrutiny.

"All parents are like this. We should just be patient with them. I'm sure you'd have done the same for me too," replied Aarti.

"Yes, of course."

"Then why are you feeling sorry?"

I thanked Aarti once again before saying bye. All through this, Pandey Aunty was trying to see what we were saying or doing. I ignored her as much as I could to avoid wicked enquiries.

Our drawing room became a discussion forum as the night grew darker. Out of curiosity I eavesdropped on the conversation hiding behind the door. Dad was pretty impressed by Aarti's general awareness while Didi was enchanted by her pleasing manners. Expectedly, Mom was gushing about her beauty and unfathomable friendship with me. She was quite defiantly vocal when the topic of admission to PILOTS popped up.

Regrettably, the counselling got delayed as Allahabad High Court had put a stay on it. Someone had petitioned a PIL asking to withdraw the undeclared introduction of Women's Reservation in college admissions and the matter was subjudice. As per the rules, we already had a fifty percent quota to emancipate the minorities. Had more seats been reserved, most of the general category boys would have probably left for Chambal.

Amidst all this mudslinging between the state government and the petitioner, the woman at home showed me hell on earth. Mom taunted me so much about my academic fiasco and the upcoming three-fold expenses that I felt like rotting in a dungeon rather than living in my own house. I was free, yet bound. All that suffering made me understand Totu's pain. It had everything a bird could ask for in its minuscule life, except the freedom to fly in the sky.

Watching the pigeons take flight on Independence Day, I decided to release Totu. Mom resisted but Dad supported the good cause. As soon as I went to the terrace, Totu looked up at the skies as if searching for its family. I became emotional and opened the cage without delaying it any further. Totu ambled out in style and took two rounds of the terrace, much like Dad used to do post-dinner. Strangely, minutes later, Totu walked back into its cage. I got frustrated and caught the bird by its wings. It shrieked my name in discomfort but I didn't relent and lobbed it up in the air like a tennis ball. Having been held captive for more than eight years, Totu had forgotten how to fly! It came crashing down as if it had been shot. But then a little wing stretching, aided with the mating calls from the nearby eucalyptus trees, worked wonders. And Totu flew up, up and away...

I smashed the cage and returned to my room with a teary heart. I'm sorry Totu to have used you as an object of entertainment these many years. I hope you lead a liberated life till your last breath.

▼

Counselling finally happened, a month post the tragic 9/11, when the court gave its verdict surprisingly in favour of the plaintiff. But that clemency was applicable only for the current academic year.

As recommended by the people I loved, I enrolled for a paid seat at PILOTS, that too for Computer Science, overall an unbelievably strange pick. Everybody referred to the college as PILOTS rather than Professor Imarti Lal's Oracle of Technology & Science (a name totally contradictory to its acronym).

▼

"Congratulations Rishu. I'm so excited. We'll be together again," said Aarti gulping down her Coke at our Kapoorthala haunt near Archies.

"Yeah, but as junior and senior," I said sadly.

"Of course, you bloody junior. Start practising from now. All the senior girls are your sisters!" she said and started to giggle.

"What nonsense!"

"That's the code of conduct, my dear. Senior girls are sisters, super senior girls are mothers and super super senior girls are grandmas," she added gleefully.

Aarti revealed that ragging was a thing of the past and nothing more than introductions was permitted these days. But as far as the senior girls were concerned, the senior boys were extremely possessive about them. Any sort of philandering could be injurious to health. I was relieved to hear about the no-ragging rule, but wasn't very happy to know about the security services run by the senior boys to protect their adorable sisters.

▼

Dad got me a snazzy CBZ to commute to PILOTS. It was a mean machine that zoomed to seventy-eighty within seconds. More importantly, it was far better than driving an uncle-type scooter to college.

It was my first day at PILOTS. I entered the gates close to 9:30 a.m. A group of rowdy looking guys was hanging around the parking stand. One unsuspecting fellow asked for directions to first year classes and was caught immediately. As the crowd got busy with him, I parked my bike and sneaked out.

The seniors hovered around like wasps on each floor inside the building. Since the first-year classes were on the topmost floor, there was no escaping them. I looked for a way to reach the top safely and was lucky to discover a mechanical door staff lift concealed behind the stairs. Seeing no elderly people around, I boarded it without a second thought and jabbed the third-floor button. As the lift rose upwards, I pumped my fists in jubilation. After all I'd outsmarted a colony of thirsty wasps!

I trotted into the lecture theatre fearing getting caught in the corridor. To my surprise, it was just like the DST classroom. Most of the people seemed to be in black and white. The boys had crew cuts or mohawks while the girls had oil dripping from their plaited hair. I sensed that Aarti had lied to me. Ragging was still prevalent and tough days awaited me with a fat garland.

Being a regular backbencher, I made my way to the last row. A tall waifish fellow with a hairstyle like a bird's nest came and sat next to me. He looked at me, smiled and said, "Hi, I'm Karan."

"I'm Rishabh."

"Day scholar?"

"Yes. You?"

"Same."

"2001 passout?"

"No... 2000."

"Oho! You too made the same mistake. See! This is what we got," Karan said raising his palms in air.

I nodded in agreement. "Anyway, what was your rank?" Karan asked the question I was dreading.

"Does that really matter?" I responded making a face.

"Actually, no. But just tell me whether it's a house number, aces in a deck, pandavas, postcode or unvalued?"

"What?"

"Tsk. I mean three, four, five or six-digit rank? Or no rank? Simple management quota," Karan explained his weird terminology about the ranking system.

I didn't reply as I was reluctant to disclose my rank.

Karan tried again, "Everyone here is either a four or a five. What's yours? And for the record, I'm number five."

I was relieved. "Same here buddy."

Karan sneered back and said, "I was lying. I'm number four! But anyway, we're still brothers. I'm also a paid seat." I cursed my foolishness. Even if I'd said three, Karan wouldn't have checked with the admissions office.

Just then, there was a hush as a forty-plus lady entered the class. She wore a light-yellow sari with matching bangles and gold earrings. Her hair was tied neatly into a bun with a pinch of vermilion in the parting. She was moderately fair and her hair had grey streaks, but she was quite a beauty even at this age. I'm sure she'd been a firecracker in her younger days.

"Hello everyone! I'm Mili Furniturewala. I'll take Professional Communication," she introduced herself to us cheerfully.

"What's Professional Communication?" I whispered to Karan as we recaptured our seats.

"English. Boss, this is an engineering college. There's a professional way to communicate everything. Like... like she's a..." and then he came up with a filthy acronym.

Our next class was taken by a bearded fellow in a mustard coloured safari suit. His name was Fakruddeen Abdul Kitabi. He was a senior lecturer from the Mechanical Engineering department. Karan took no time nicknaming him as well.

It was lunch break — the time to understand who we'd have to endure for the next four years. But alas! There entered a junta of despotic rulers banging the door and slapping the duster on the teacher's desk.

"Get up, you morons! No lunch today," one of our tormentors hollered.

Grabbing a girl's lunchbox, a fat senior took guard at the entrance. All of us stood up, our eyes partially downcast. The monsters strolled through the class trying to target their first guinea pig. A short fellow from the third row got caught.

"Chintu, come on up to the board! And the rest, eyes on the third button," someone ordered. Everybody complied subserviently as Chintu (only god knew his real name) stepped onto the podium.

"Tell your friends the code of conduct," the same voice commanded.

Chintu started speaking looking at his third button while we all listened looking at our own third buttons.

"Boys need to wear white full-sleeved shirts and black trousers, no jeans and no belt. Black leather shoes with white laces are a must. The third button of the shirt needs to be red and the collar button must be buttoned. Your hair must be no longer than one centimetre. No pullovers/coats/jackets allowed. You're not to visit the canteen or the library before the fresher's party. Smoking and cellphones are also strictly banned till the end of the year. Day scholars cannot visit friends in the hostel and are supposed to push their vehicles to and from the parking stand once inside the campus. None of you should even try to look at or talk to a senior girl until asked to.

They must be respected like your sister, mother and grandma. Most importantly, make sure that as soon as you see a senior, wish him or her by bowing down ninety degrees, applicable even in the loo."

Chintu continued like a parrot, "Girls need to follow the same set of rules too. Only the dress code is a bit different – you'll wear black and white salwar-kameez and your hair needs to be oiled and braided with red and white ribbons. Hairbands or any other type of hair accessories won't be tolerated. Those who have short hair will wear a white scarf with your name sewn on it. Nail paint, rings, earrings, bracelets, anklets, hair colour, tattoos, etc., aren't allowed. And if anyone of you is caught wearing heels or flip-flops to the classes, then such footwear would immediately be confiscated." Chintu fell silent after that rather harrowing list of protocols.

"Chintu beta! Are you sure you didn't miss anything?" asked one of the seniors patronisingly as he petted Chintu's head as we normally do to a dog.

Chintu jerked as he recollected what he'd left out, "Girls must treat all the senior boys like your husbands and entertain them whenever they ask for."

"Bravo, bravo..." a huge round of applause filled the class. We also clapped seeing the front rows clap. Chintu returned to his seat and was allowed to sit for his exceptional oration.

After two minutes of short intro rounds, Karan and I were caught. Our attires were totally non-compliant! We were called up to the front. I was told to impersonate a lizard by crawling over the side wall, which I did immediately, while Karan was asked to introduce himself followed by a series of double meaning questions.

I heard a girl asking him, "What's between your legs?"

"Ma'am... Ma'am..." Karan stuttered.

"Is ma'am between your legs?" guffawed one of the seniors, sending the others into peals of raucous laughter.

"No laughing, freshers. Only seniors can laugh. Everybody, eyes on your third button." The class turned into a morgue again.

"Ma'am, it's my hammer," Karan declared bluntly.

Somebody slapped him. "Is this how your Dad speaks to your aunt? Don't you have knees between your legs?"

"Yes sir. I do."

"Say sorry to your sister."

Karan apologized at once. One of the senior girls came on up to the board and wrote in bold letters, FUC. "How would you pronounce it?" she asked Karan.

I swivelled around to read what it was as Karan kept silent. I know he was thinking of a possibly clean answer which the seniors were expecting. But what was it? "Quick or you'll have to kiss your lizard friend," someone threatened.

I turned towards the wall and prayed for Karan to say it quickly. Pat came the reply, "Fuck," followed by two slaps this time.

"Haven't you read set theory? Isn't this F Union C?" the senior girl reprimanded Karan.

"Sorry ma'am, my set theory is pretty weak," Karan apologized yet again.

"But your sex theory is pretty strong!" remarked one of the senior boys as people started to guffaw again. The duster was slammed hard on the front desk and everyone turned into scarecrows again. The senior girl gave Karan a last chance to answer correctly, asking if he'd done intercourse. Karan confidently denied having such a terrific opportunity on which she proclaimed, "All your seniors have done it. Even I've done it. How did you get admission in engineering without doing intercourse?"

Karan gave the most idiotic reply one can think of, "Ma'am, give me one chance. I promise I'll do it tonight."

The seniors laughed boisterously as the senior girl threw a piece of chalk at Karan in exasperation. She shouted back petulantly, "What kind of a chance are you talking about?"

"Ma'am, I just need a little co-operation," said Karan.

"Like what?"

"Certain contacts from where I can hire such services. In case you know any, please pass them on."

That was it. Five slaps from the senior girl this time for indirectly calling her a pimp. She went ahead and wrote on the board 'INTER-COURSE'. That's HSC.

The senior who'd commented on Karan's strong sex theory fumed, "This guy is trying to act smart. Let's ask him some direct questions."

"Hey you! Tell me the name of an adult film," he asked.

"Sir, no idea," said Karan, although I seriously doubted him after learning that dirty acronym in the Professional Communication class.

"We'll spare you if you answer correctly, Mr Sex-Starved Soul," crowed a voice from the back. The salutation suited Karan.

"Sir, *My Father Your Mom*," Karan replied with an exceedingly disrespectful choice of name.

There was wild laughter. Even the seniors were thumping the desks in enjoyment. Sanity returned as the wounded senior slapped Karan almost ten times, hurling mother and sister cuss words.

"Madam, looks like you enjoyed the joke a lot. Come on, *out!*" another senior girl screamed clouding the atmosphere with gloominess again. It felt like a known voice but I couldn't dare to look back. Karan was dismissed to the back of the class after yet another round of slaps. He was told to become a murga and crow like a cock once in every thirty seconds.

I was asked to come out from my lizard avatar and report at the board. The lawbreaker was made to stand face-to-face with me, with no eye contact at all. I noticed a pretty pair of hands. They were markedly small and had a mild henna effect going up to the nails.

"Hold hands," the same known voice ordered.

I froze but the girl obeyed promptly. What's this bitch going to ask next? I thought.

"Propose to each other like Romeo-Juliet."

My partner's hands started to tremble.

"We don't have the entire day for this. Propose quickly," said another voice.

"You're beautiful," I said.

"Is that how you propose? Somebody else would sleep with your girlfriend right under your nose if you're so shy," the known voice scolded. That was cheeky enough to awaken my feelings of affection. I blurted out publicly what I always wanted to, "I love you." Aarti was still mouthed mentally.

I received a standing ovation from the persecutors and the victims for that act of bravery. Karan too appreciated my efforts by crowing out loudly.

"Your turn, lady."

A teardrop fell on my hand. My partner was crying! Her hands were trembling. But I was helpless.

"Speak," the bitch shrieked. I strongly felt it was Aarti screaming. Probability had always betrayed me, so I didn't look up. I didn't want to give anyone a chance to deposit slaps on my face.

"I... I love you... too," my date falteringly proposed and dropped two more tears on my hand. There was a loud round of applause. She was spared and instructed to go wash her face, but return in precisely three minutes, else she'd have the distinguished company of Mr Sex-Starved Soul right inside the washroom.

I thought I'd be told to get lost as well. But no, ignominy had just started to gain momentum. A senior pulled out five guys from the class and asked me to rate them on their sex appeal. This was suicidal. An answer would definitely kill all my prospects with any of the girls. As I took my time to rate the boys, I felt a rough hand land on my left shoulder. It was about time that I too got some slaps.

But just then, the sentry at the entrance yowled about a lecturer been sighted near the loo. The seniors dispersed as quickly as cockroaches do at night when you suddenly turn on the light. Everyone heaved a sigh of relief. I too found my way back to my seat.

Karan welcomed me, "Great man. You proposed to a hot chick on the first day."

"I was forced to. I don't even know who she is," I responded trying to search for her in the front rows.

"So what? Maybe next time they ask you to make love to her!"

I chuckled and enquired, "Did you notice who that senior was?"

"Yes man. She was damn sexy. I'd love to have her."

"You're sick dude. You've been talking sex since morning."

"What's sick about it? We all are products of unprotected sex and are born to have free sex," asserted Karan. I chose not to debate any further.

Classes got over at four. People packed up quickly to leave as fast as they could. Karan and I took refuge in the loo until the floor was deserted. When it seemed quiet enough, we made our exit.

"Fuck! Back off, back off," Karan screamed as Chintu crawled out of a senior class on all fours. Thinking that there were still a few seniors loitering about, both of us made a quick retreat. Now we were left with no other option but to board the staff lift. We were lucky. We reached the ground floor safely, but the danger was still not averted. Getting out safely from the parking was the final frontier.

We were unlucky this time. The senior with the crow-like voice (who Karan had insulted with the adult movie name) recognized us as we cackled over a joke on our way to the parking stand. We were abused and frogmarched into the hostel for some 'cultural events' by the four seniors. Once in the hostel common room, all four grabbed chairs as Karan and I stood near the door, awaiting their commands. The crow senior sneered at us before bluntly instructing us to strip. I know the bastard was taking revenge on Karan who had dared to propose a union between their parents. But why me? I didn't do him any harm. I froze, but Karan obeyed his command gleefully. He removed his clothes without the slightest of hesitation and started entertaining the molesters. As the seniors got engrossed with Karan's performance, I tried to break loose. But I tripped on the staircase. Everybody deserted Karan's Oscar winning act and came after me 'effing' loudly. We played a little parkour before I was cornered. The bastards swooped down on me like a pack of hungry wolves. They thrashed me like a dog until a security guard appeared from the heavens to rescue me. Had he not intervened, I'd have been beaten to pulp.

As I stepped out of the hostel premises, one of the four boys cussed menacingly from a window of the common room, "I'll catch you tomorrow, asshole. My name is Imran. Remember that name!"

I hobbled to the parking lot with an aching stomach and a bleeding nose. Aarti bumped into me near the library, a prohibited place as per the code of conduct.

"Hey! What happened?" she asked checking out my nose.

"Remove your hand. That hurts," I kind of cried.

"Who did that?"

"Some senior boys. They dragged me to the hostel and…"

"I know the story. Can you recognize the boys?"

"Definitely. I can never forget their bloody faces."

"I'm pretty sure Imran was behind it all. He's a goddamn bully," said Aarti angrily.

"Yes, one of them was Imran. He said he'll catch me tomorrow again."

"He can't do that. Come on, come with me!" Aarti said clutching my wrist.

"Where?"

"To the hostel."

"Are you mad? That's the boys' hostel!"

"I don't care."

Aarti didn't listen and forced me to accompany her back to the wretched place. The gatekeeper stopped us, "Girls not allowed," he said sternly.

"Reserve that statement for your daughter and call Imran Ali right now," Aarti screamed at the gateman, maybe for being loyal to his duty when it came to girls entering the hostel, but not in the case of freshers being kidnapped into.

The gatekeeper was taken aback and stared transiently before announcing over the mic, "There's a girl to see Imran Ali. She's waiting at the main gate."

Imran came down immediately. He noticed me standing next to Aarti. "You bastard. How dare you? Aarti, did he say anything to you?" Imran howled.

"You tell me first. What did you do to him?" asked Aarti menacingly.

"That's none of your business. Why are you so bothered about a fresher?"

"He's my friend. You and your friends dare not touch him. I'm warning you," Aarti jabbed her forefinger on Imran's nose as she issued that word of caution.

"We will not only touch him, we will kick his ass. What will you do?" Imran said grabbing my collar, his biceps struggling to burst out of his t-shirt. Imran was much taller than me and quite rugged. I can't imagine myself in such top physique at least in this life.

By this time, Imran's friends and some other boys from the hostel had gathered around the gate. Karan was also there, zipping in his hammer back to where it belonged.

"Leave him!" Aarti squawked and tried plucking Imran's hands off my collar.

When he didn't loosen his grip, Aarti did the unimaginable. She kneed Imran below the belt!

Despite being a bodybuilder, Imran released me in a flash and collapsed on the ground clenching his groin. He wailed with pain, mentioning his mother again and again.

"Listen carefully you fucking bastards. If I find any of you ragging my friend, I'll crush you all like this. That's a promise," Aarti threatened and kicked Imran at the forbidden place. Imran cried again for his mother, this time with a lot more passion.

There was pin drop silence at the hostel gate. Nobody moved an inch. Even the gatekeeper covered his privates with his hands suspecting a kick.

"I'm coming with you till the fresher's party," Aarti conveyed the verdict as we walked towards the parking. She also kept cleaning my nose with her handkerchief.

"Coming where?" I asked.

"To college. You're not safe anymore. They'll definitely try and hurt you again."

"I'm more concerned for you. You shouldn't have taken panga with them," I said apprehensively.

"Don't worry. Nothing will happen. That Imran is a flirt who's been after me for the past year. He was with me today when we made you propose to that girl!"

"So, it was you! Very bad. That girl will never talk with me."

I cursed Imran mentally for wooing my girl and wished him eternal impotency. Aarti should have planted a few more kicks to make my wish come true.

"She'll definitely talk with you. I can give this to you in writing. Today's interaction has demolished the shyness between you guys. No matter how bad ragging is, it's pretty good for personality development. It helps people connect with each other, but only till the time it's verbal," Aarti said.

"And by the way, you're a pathetic proposer," she added.

"You're a pathetic friend. First you lied to me about ragging, and then instead of saving my ass, you screwed me yourself," I grumbled.

"Hey! Watch your words!"

"Why should I? I heard how you spoke only a few minutes ago!"

"I rarely use language like that. It was just a one-time thing, understand?"

"Oho! So, you use that extraordinary vocab of yours only on special occasions."

"Look... I didn't know all this before joining PILOTS. Over here, everybody uses such lingo. And so, I picked it up. But one thing's for sure – abusing is a great stress buster!"

"Yup, damn fucking right," I added for extra measure.

"This is the last warning. Don't use such language with me or else you'll soon get what Imran got," warned Aarti.

I instantly went into mute mode.

"Wow, a bike! When did you buy this?" Aarti broke the silence as I put the key in the ignition.

"Last week. Now you can chase all the rowdies you want to and break their bloody noses."

"Yeah, but not just their noses anymore," Aarti giggled. I shut up immediately again.

▼

The next day I reached Gol Market, the place Aarti took the city bus from. It'd been a while since she'd quit the college bus. You know why? Because the annual charges were raised by a mere eight hundred bucks. Huh! And such people call me a baniya. Bloody hypocrites!

Aarti arrived two minutes later, exactly at nine. She was wearing a black cardigan over tan trousers, an ensemble that made her look very classy. She looked me up and down and burst out laughing.

"Yeah! I know... it's weird," I said in my defence.

"When the hell did you get this?" she asked feeling my cactus hair with her palm.

"Last evening at Stylo Men's Parlour."

"Really nice and stylish. You look top class."

"Oh please Aarti, don't embarrass me. I know it looks idiotic."

"My friend, you don't need to look it, you already are one."

I groaned, "Do you want a lift or not?"

"No, you may leave. I'll go on my own. But then... umm, who's going to save you in college Mr Stylo?" Aarti said tapping a finger on her chin, looking up at the sky.

"Okay, I'm sorry! Please sit and let's go," I said tapping the pillion seat of my bike. Only an idiot can apologize for being called an idiot!

Aarti hopped on immediately.

▼

The Imran bashing news had spread like wildfire. Seniors from all corners came to see who I was, ragged me, but didn't hurt me. All of them just wanted to know if Aarti was my girlfriend. I vowed on my life that she wasn't, which in reality was true. Luckily this made some of them so happy that I was given a permanent hiatus from the 'no canteen' rule.

Karan asked, "Agrawal, tell me something, how did you manage to befriend that sexy senior?"

"Hey, mind your language. She's a childhood friend," I admonished him.

"Oh, come on! What's the problem with that? She's a sexy chick. I'm sure you've nailed her by now!" he winked.

"Bastard, shut your dirty mouth."

"Why are you so offended boss? If not till now, you'll get to do it one day. Don't let her escape. She's hot man. Bi…." I didn't let him finish.

"Screw yourself sisterfucker," I said slamming the book on the table.

Karan apologized immediately, "Sorry man. I didn't mean that. I promise not to say anything about her again. But please, don't tell me you're not in love with her."

"That's none of your business."

"I got my answer dude," Karan smiled and drew a tiny heart on his notebook, piercing it with a monster arrow.

▼

It was practical class for workshop practice a few days later. Even though we were not mechanical students, we had to study all branches in the first year to get a feel of every aspect of engineering.

The lab technician, a fellow in his mid-thirties, watched us as we looked around and fingered the machinery before finally settling down. He looked more like a mechanic rather than someone who could actually teach us the concepts. He divided the batch in groups of three, alphabetically. I got two girls in my group – Ria and Ruhana. Ria looked like a distant cousin of a buffalo while Ruhana was her antithesis.

"Hello everyone! My name is Arun Kumar and I'm your lab instructor. Today you'll learn about a metal work process called filing. Listen to my instructions carefully and keep your hands off the tools that don't need your attention," said the instructor. "There are three metal pieces on each workbench. All you need to do is to file them to the required dimensions," he added and turned to the board to write the specifications.

Moments later, we all huddled around him as he demonstrated what filing was. It looked so damn easy when he did it. We were given filers, rulers, markers and all other requisites (along with a repeated warning about touching other tools or machines).

Ria clamped a metal piece between the jaws of a fitter's vise and started to file. Within minutes, she was wheezing. "I'm tired," she said and plonked her butt on one of the wooden stools.

I took a turn and joined her after two minutes. Ruhana too gave up after a while. This round robin marathon went on for ten-fifteen minutes until Karan walked over to us wearing a strange smile.

"Come here Agrawal. I have something important for you."

"What?" I asked.

He gestured that I should follow him. "Yes, what is it?" I said moving close to him.

"First you tell me. What the fuck were you trying to do?" Karan asked.

"Filing. What else?" I said, guessing he thought I was trying to impress Ruhana (obviously, not Ria).

"What will you get from this fucking filing? We're computer guys. We don't do such menial jobs. Dump the filing and come with me. I want to show you something interesting."

I was curious about what he wanted to show me, so I went with him until he threw his filer on an unoccupied workbench and propped his bum against it. Karan gestured gleefully, "Just look at Sapna." I turned my eyes towards Sapna. She was panting, perspiring, visibly tired but still filing with utmost devotion. Her neckline was moderately deep and her stance at the workbench revealed a considerable portion of her big wobbly chest.

"Fuck!" I said with my mouth agape.

"You like it?"

"Of course," I nodded dementedly, staring hard at the most common male fetish. Sapna, the enchantress, had made my dream come true.

Suddenly, we heard a loud voice, "You two. Are you done with the assignment?" It was Kumar sir.

"Sir, tired. Just taking some air," Karan replied wiping non-existent sweat from his forehead.

"Get back to work or I'll give you both a big zero in the internals," he threatened.

We cursed Kumar under our breath and returned to our workbenches. Ruhana was busy pulverizing an innocent metal piece, her cardigan tied around her waist. My eyes peeped inside her top. But I only got access to the strap of her black bra.

While I attempted to slide my eyes deeper, Ruhana noticed what I was doing and stood straight all of a sudden. "What you're doing is not right," she said sternly, looking into my eyes, sweat dribbling down her flawless neck.

Oh fuck! She caught me! I anticipated a flurry of slaps or maybe the application of the artillery that Kumar had warned us against. Worse still, if Ria offered a helping hand, I'd be dead!

"What's the use of having you in our group? Instead of taking the lead, you're roaming around," grumbled Ruhana wiping her lovely face and neck with a mini hand towel.

"Yeah! She's right," Ria joined the protest thrusting the filer in her shock-absorber palm; thankfully not over my head. I sighed in relief and thanked god for saving my butt.

Over the next half an hour, I toiled like an ass while the girls gossiped about the latest movies and the most charming men in the industry. Of course, Shahrukh was their unanimous choice!

Once we, correction, 'I' was done with the filing, Ria took my, correction, 'our' samples to Kumar for approval. As Ria left, Ruhana asked, "Do you remember me?"

"Sorry?" I asked wiping my face, neck and arms which were all soaked in sweat by now.

"I'm the one you proposed to. Remember?" she said smiling.

I apologized immediately, "Sorry." Isn't it amazing how the same word can have different connotations in the way we say them?

"Don't be sorry. That was just a part of ragging. Totally unintentional," Ruhana made a joke of my first ever proposal.

"Thanks for understanding," I said sheepishly. Ruhana smiled back in return.

Ruhana belonged to Sultanpur. Her father was in the police, something that terrorized most of the boys. Nobody dared to flirt with her. We became good friends in a few days' time, mainly because of our grouping in various practical classes (best being the pin-dovetail aka male-female joint in carpentry).

Ria tried clinging on too but I snubbed her advances. Unfortunately, Karan had an all boys group, so he was always trying to sabotage my blossoming friendship with Ruhana.

The fresher's party was called off because the seniors were busy campaigning for the university to reduce the pass marks from fifty to thirty. We, the freshers were screwed for free. Not even a samosa party for us. Our only respite was that the code of conduct was now rescinded. That meant that the junior-senior hegemony had been dropped and was now passed on as a legacy to us to torment the next batch.

▼

The semester exams arrived in January. Thankfully, Aarti wasn't there to paralyse my hands this time around. Instead, she gifted me all her previous year notes and question papers with some tips on how to expand the answers as well.

It was my first non-competitive exam after HSC. I was very nervous looking at the results of my seniors and begged god to send in some help. And it arrived. My partners for the practicals were doctorates in the cheating domain! I was amazed to find the reams of miniature photocopies in their possession, thanks to Bhatia Xerox, a bulk photocopying den outside the campus.

The good thing with girls is they can hide chits in places the men in the flying squads would never dare to check. And women are hardly a part of such nonsensical teams.

For the first time in my life, yes, for the first time – I cheated openly as my new friends (especially Ruhana) did everything possible to help me with the required answers.

The results were out in a flash, that too online. Karan informed Mom over phone while I was asleep on a lazy February Sunday. I didn't have a computer at home and hardly knew how to use it. Yes, I'd opted for Computer Science, but it has nothing to do with my current computer literacy.

Going to a cyber café wasn't a great option lest the guys there died laughing learning that a prospective computer engineer needed their assistance to check his progress report. So, I called Karan. He was celebrating as if he'd topped the university. After all, he'd successfully avoided a *suppli*, the supplementary paper, along with securing a net percentage of sixty-nine, which happened to be his favourite number. As far as my result was concerned, Karan apologised for not being able to check it because his dial-up connection was extremely slow and kept getting disconnected. I requested him to keep trying and hung up. Next, I called Aarti. It was my good luck that she, and not Rajjo, picked up the call.

"Hello Aarti. Rishu here. My results are out. Can you help me find out how I did?" I said in one breath.

"Really! That means mine will also be out in a day or two," Aarti started worrying.

I repeated my question, "Aarti, can you please check my marks?"

"Of course, I can. Tell me your roll number. I'll check and call back. Be ready for a party in the evening," Aarti said excitedly.

I gave her my roll number and waited patiently next to the phone. Aarti called twenty minutes later. I'd got a seventy percent, the benchmark for being an average student at PILOTS. The internals and miniature photocopies had a huge role in making that percentage. Thankfully, the university had acceded to the demands of failures; sorry, respected seniors. External passing marks were unbelievably reduced to thirty. Otherwise I would have had a suppli in five out of six subjects, a real disgrace.

"I'll e-mail your result to you. Tell me your id," Aarti asked.

"I'm sorry I don't have one."

"Really? You don't keep an id. You should have made one by now."

"Can you make one for me?"

"Sure, I'll create it for you."

"But it's free na."

"Yes, my baniya boy. It's absolutely free!" and she started to laugh uncontrollably.

Mom, who'd mastered the art of eavesdropping, asked me to get a printout of the result instead.

"Do you have a printer?" I asked Aarti.

"Yes. Why? What happened?"

"I think a printout would do for the time being. I need one from you."

"No way! I'm not wasting the precious ink of my printer on your wretched result. Do you know how much an inkjet cartridge costs?"

"Okay, fine. I'll get it from somewhere else," I said and disconnected the phone.

It rang back almost instantly. Mom picked it up. It was Aarti. Mom listened silently and nodded a great deal, which wasn't how she typically was, and then hung up. She turned her gaze on me and said, "Aarti is calling you to collect the printout. And also saying that you throw tantrums like girls do!"

"I don't want a printout," I said in frustration.

"Arrey, go na. Cyber café will unnecessarily charge ten-fifteen bucks," Mom cajoled me demonstrating the traits of a typical baniya.

"Do you know where she lives?"

"Yes, but I'm not going," I said crossing my arms on my chest.

"Don't be adamant. Pick up the keys and leave. But don't stay longer… and… wait a second. How do you know her place?" the spirit of Sherlock Holmes suddenly entered Mom's body.

"I dropped her home once when she missed her bus," I lied.

Just to avert cyber café mortification and further questioning from Mom, I set out for Aarti's place. It was almost four years since I made my lone visit to the Raisinghani residence. Jackie greeted me this time too with the same passion in his bark.

A fat lady with fat lawn scissors opened the gate. "Yes?" she asked.

"Namasteji. My name is Rishabh. Aarti's friend. Is she at home?" I said keeping an eye on Jackie as well as the deadly gardening tool.

"Are you Rishu?" the lady asked raising her brows.

"Yeah, I'm Rishu. How do you know me?" I asked surprised.

"Betaji, I'm Aarti's Mom. She always talks about you but somehow, we just never got a chance to meet. Come. Come inside," Aunty said shielding me from Jackie.

"Actually Aunty, I've never come to your place before. That's why we've never met," I lied.

Aunty welcomed me to her abode but not before forcing me to get rid of my shoes. The interiors of the mansion were just as opulent as I saw them last; the only difference was in the colour of the distemper which had turned lavender from turquoise. Aunty gestured to me to sit as she called out, "Rajjo, paani." I think Aarti learnt those lines from her mother.

Rajjo, now taller than earlier but still barefoot, appeared with a glass of water, pressure cooker symphony buzzing in the background. She stared at me with puzzled expressions and then enounced, "Bhaiyaji, aap?"

Aunty looked at me with raised eyebrows once again, minus the happiness she evinced earlier. I started to look inside my glass as if something had fallen in it. Aunty shouted, "Nonu, O Nonu. Rishu has come."

I got flummoxed as to who Nonu was. As Aunty hollered again Aarti came running down the steps. She was wearing a white top with a winking Donald Duck and a pair of stonewashed blue denims that seemed to have shrunk. A black thread encircled her left ankle and she'd dark red nail-polish on her toenails.

"Hi Rishu. Come, come up," she shouted from the staircase gesturing to me. I didn't want to. My last experience upstairs was nothing less than a nightmare, I thought.

I shivered as the pressure cooker shrieked again. Unable to figure out an amiable response I shifted my focus towards Aunty. Her eyes were suggesting a big 'no' to Aarti.

"Oho! Get up yaar," Aarti urged coming forward and pulled me up from the sofa. Aunty immediately sent Rajjo after us to keep an eye on us.

I entered Aarti's room moments later. It was completely transformed. The music system was gone and so were the cassettes.

A vast collection of CDs sparkled from a wooden trolley with a hulky deck relaxing idly on its top. The posters though, were still there, Shahrukh only, but this time from *Mohabbatein* and *K3G*. Aarti's bed had a Jaipuri quilt along with two pillows stacked one over the other. An off-white monitor rested on a computer-cum-study table with fat books and stationery items eating up the rest of the space. The most important thing, the printer, was forcibly adjusted on a tiny side stool lying next to the table.

"Who's Nonu?" I asked as Aarti left my hand.

"Who do you think it is?" Aarti grinned shyly.

"Okay, tell me Nonu, what's this that you're wearing? Are they your childhood jeans?" I asked pointing to her shin-length jeans.

"No, you stupid! It's called a capri. And don't you dare call me Nonu again."

"And what's that thread for?"

"To ward off vulture-eyes like yours. Now don't ask what Donald Duck's doing over here," she replied irritably, pointing to her chest.

I grinned as Rajjo cackled from her hideout. Aarti reprimanded her quite rudely and told her to leave the room.

I pulled up a chair as Aarti opened my subpar result which she'd saved in some html format. "Phew! Thank god. I passed in all the subjects," I said leaning back on the chair.

"But it's a pretty poor scorecard. Had you been in my batch, you were fuc... gone," Aarti corrected herself just in time.

"Who cares? It's a seventy percent. The overall percentage matters," I said resting my palms behind my head.

"I got eighty percent in the first semester."

"Good. But I'm not you. I'm doing engineering because I've been asked to. And computers because you suggested it to Dad."

"Awww, my little baby. How obedient!"

"Shut up and give me the printout. I have to go," I said.

"What's the hurry? Stay for a while," Aarti urged as she gave the print command.

"What will we do? Look at these stupid posters?" I asked, looking around.

"Nothing that has SRK is stupid."

"SRK?"

"Shahrukh, you dumbo. Anyway, leave it. Let me show you something really amazing," said Aarti.

"Yes! Finally," I exclaimed thinking something what boys normally think about. Their scope of thinking reduces drastically in presence of girls.

Quite unfortunately, Aarti showed me something else. The monitor read, "Enter a number from two to nine."

"Rishu, enter a number," Aarti asked me to jab in a digit, her voice fervid.

I entered eight. Instantly an inverted green triangle with eight rows showed up on the screen.

"How did you do that?" I asked, my jaw dropping eight inches.

"Magic!"

"Tell na!"

"C."

"What should I see?" I asked looking carefully at the screen.

"No stupid, that's C language. It's in your next semester," Aarti said pulling out a book called *Let Us C*.

I flipped through it, but understood nothing. "How will I ever do it?" I said with a creased forehead.

"It's easy man. But for coding, you must have a computer."

"How much will it cost?" I asked.

"It depends on what configuration you choose. I'd strictly recommend P4, 7200 rpm 40 GB HDD, 256 MB DDR RAM and a decent graphics card. The choice of peripherals would entirely depend on your budget."

"I didn't understand a word of what you said. Please help me out with computers," I clasped Aarti's hands begging her.

"Leave me you idiot. Rajjo might see and build up a story for Mom," Aarti retracted her hands from mine.

Within ten seconds, Rajjo barged in with tea and papad. Aarti gave me a dirty look before passing over a stool to Rajjo.

As Rajjo left, Aarti kicked my chair two feet away from hers. "Sit over there. Have your tea and leave. You almost got me killed today."

"I'm really very sorry. But please... please help me with computers. I need your tutorials, notes, question papers, books and everything else that could help me clear engineering," I begged her.

"All you need is self-confidence and a bit of determination to do well," Aarti lectured me while devouring a crunchy papad.

"Don't preach. Tell me clearly. Are you helping your so-called best friend or not? Or was that promise made at the farewell just a publicity stunt?" I asked.

"I don't make false promises. Had I not been your friend, I wouldn't have kicked that bloody Imran in his...," Aarti fell silent.

"I'm sure that bastard would never be able to use his 'dash-dash' to make kids."

"Shut up! This is my house. You'll leave with your idiotic printout, but I have to stay. I have to face Mom and her silly questions," Aarti rebuked me. So, I wasn't the only one who feared the woman the world calls Mom. People like Aarti too had apprehensions.

Finally, after much of bootlicking, Aarti agreed to lend her study related belongings along with personal tutorials whenever she had the time. My only job was to get a computer financed by Dad, and of course, approved by Mom.

Twenty Unforgettable Months

As advised by Aarti, I managed to convince Dad to get me a computer. Mom acceded too, but with a no-printer clause. After all, Aarti was there for those once-in-a-while pricey inkjet printouts.

After a ten-minute long lecture on how many sacrifices were being made to make me an engineer, Dad gave me forty thousand bucks in hard cash. Aarti agreed to help me choose the best configuration after I promised her a coffee at CCD. So, we went to Naza, the computer and electronics market at Hazratganj. Its lanes were secluded, shops pretty congested and shopkeepers extremely foxy. After a bit of window shopping and a few failed negotiations, we finally struck a decent deal at C-Zone.

Aarti hired a tempo and got the components loaded. Although I insisted that she come with me on my bike instead of the tempo, she decided to sit in the tempo while I followed.

Mom and Pandey Aunty appeared in their respective balconies on hearing the tempo.

"Bhabhiji, computer!" Pandey Aunty exclaimed.

Mom nodded smiling widely. We took out the boxes with the driver's help and dragged them into the house. I quickly hopped up the stairs and shut the door before Pandey Aunty started quizzing me on the details.

"Where's the parrot Aunty?" Aarti asked.

"Dead," I said.

"No, he set him free," Mom clarified.

"As I don't see him every day, he's as good as dead to me," I said.

Aarti looked at me shocked. "That means when you go out to work, we'll be dead for you," said Mom.

"Applicable to pets only," I said making a face.

Mom tried to say something, but I ignored her and got busy transferring the cartons to my room. I was in a bad mood because of the insult I had to bear from her earlier in the day. She'd whined that forty thousand was more than Dad's monthly salary and I was now turning out to be sort of a black hole for the family.

Aarti changed the topic and started telling Mom how she'd bargained at C-Zone. I interrupted her, "It's all done. Can we connect now?"

For the first time ever, Aarti entered my room. She did a quick scan and sat on the bed. Mom came and sat next to her. I unpacked the cartons and cleared the study table. Aarti asked me to place the components on the table. She then went down on her knees to attach the peripherals. Suddenly, the phone rang and Mom got up to answer it. Aarti continued with the wires while I got bowled over by a beguiling view. Aarti's tee had curled up, revealing part of her panties from the top of her jeans.

Suddenly, Aarti turned to pick up a wire and noticed me staring at her back.

"What the hell are you looking at?" she said getting up, pulling her jeans up and pushing her tee down. I wish it had been the opposite.

"Nothing. Just trying to understand how you're attaching everything together," I stammered.

"Don't lie to me. I know wha..."

Suddenly, Mom entered the room with two glasses of orange squash. I seized the opportunity, "What was that red thing Aarti? Can you show it to me again?"

Aarti looked at me irritated, "Sure, but you've got to bend down for that!"

"Aunty, look at him, he wants to learn all this standing five feet away!" she said pointing to the wires.

Mom gestured me to squat and vanished into the kitchen as the pressure cooker started whistling.

"Do you still want to see that red thing?" Aarti said pulling my ear hard.

"Ouch! That hurts. What the hell are you doing?"

"Just checking if it comes out or not...!"

"It's my ear, not some silly wire."

Moments later, the computer was all hooked up. Aarti inaugurated it by playing some MP3 songs – unfortunately of SRK movies. She made some changes in the system settings and installed a pirated version of Microsoft Office which C-Zone had gifted us. "Hey, never realised your initials are RA – exactly the opposite of mine!" Aarti remarked as she customized the MS Word application. I didn't reply as Mom was still around, but thought about the theory of magnetism where opposites attract. Maybe one day Aarti will be as attracted to me as I am to her.

"Thank you, beta. Thank you very much for your help and time. Please teach him how to use it as well," Mom thanked Aarti with a smile.

"Aunty, you're embarrassing me. It was nothing. Of course, I'll help him. But please ask him to study hard. His first sem result wasn't good at all," Aarti replied, guzzling her squash.

That was it. Mom whined over my result for the next ten minutes. I offered Aarti a ride back home which Mom said was only fair considering the amount of time she had spent setting up the computer for me.

We stopped by at Kapoorthala for a cup of coffee. Aarti got me to buy a not-so-required Windows XP Professional beginners guide from Universal Bookstores as well.

▼

A week later, it was Ruhana's birthday. After the Engineering Graphics class, we went to the canteen. Karan joined us uninvited as we marched along with our drafters and sheet holders the way Contra soldiers carry assault rifles.

"What would you like to have?" Ruhana asked as we settled next to the desert cooler.

"Rishabh? Are you listening?" Ruhana said shaking my shoulder.

"Yeah, I'm listening," I responded quickly.

"Call him Rishu. People who love him call him that," Karan interrupted.

I gave him a cold stare. "He's just joking. I'll have chhola-bhatura," I said.

"Rishu is a nice name. I'll call you Rishu. What will you have, Karan?" Ruhana asked.

"Call him KS. It suits him," I interrupted this time.

Karan returned a dirty look as both of us understood that KS not only meant Karan Saxena but also *Kamasutra*, the ancient text giving rules for sensual pleasure. This name fitted Karan's personality more than anything else.

"Karan?" Ruhana snapped her fingers twice.

"Umm... I'll also take a chhola-bhatura and also a drink, if you don't mind... Sprite or something," Karan replied with a silly smile. Ruhana nodded and decided on a chhola-bhatura for herself as well.

"Fuck you, Agrawal. I'll spoil the party if you don't apologize right now," Karan abused as soon as Ruhana went out of audible range.

"Oooh! Look at me, KS. I'm shivering," I made fun of Karan's name and then went on after his surname.

"Bastard. If you don't say sorry, I'll say bad things about that hot friend of yours," Karan threatened.

I apologized immediately. "I'm sorry dude, but please don't say anything about her."

"I promise," Karan said touching his throat.

"Thanks," I said relieved.

"But you can't stop me from thinking dirty and...," Karan started to laugh.

"You sister..."

Ruhana returned just then with two bhatura laden plates, making me swallow my sweet words for KS. She asked Karan to collect his order from the counter. I too got up to get water. Moments later, all three of us were looking down our plates. Karan was the first one to deflate his bhatura and start a conversation.

The food was delicious but spicy. Within minutes, we all began to sweat like pigs with our tongues hanging out. I got up and adjusted the panes of the cooler to change the wind direction. And shucks! Something irrevocable happened. The crispy leftovers from the bhatura flew off my plate and got stuck on Ruhana's chest. All three of us sprang from our seats almost instantaneously.

"I'm so sorry Ruhana," I said trying to remove the stuff from her neck, and inadvertently, chest.

"Don't touch. I'll do it on my own," Ruhana said and got up to go to the water cooler.

"Boss. What the hell were you trying to do? Have a complimentary sweet dish with this fucking bhatura?" asked Karan smiling slyly.

"You're brainsick dude. I was just trying to help her."

"Me? Me brainsick? It was you who was trying to grab her fun bags."

"Shut up. She's coming."

"I'm really sorry Ruhana. Totally unintentional," I apologized.

"Leave it. Let's finish this. It's already cold," Ruhana said tearing the bhatura on her plate.

Later both Karan and Ruhana decided on fruit cake for dessert while I savoured a cream roll.

As we were walking out of the canteen, Aarti walked in with Imran, my tormentor. I gestured to her to ask what she was doing with the broken balls guy, but she snubbed me. Karan gave me a knowing smile, poking the middle finger of his right hand into his curled left hand. It was an invitation for a fight, but I ignored him.

"What were you doing with that bloody Imran?" I asked Aarti later at the parking lot.

"None of your business. Did I ask what you were doing with that girl?" she shot back.

"It was her birthday. She gave us a treat."

"Only to you?"

"No, Karan was there too."

"I didn't see anyone else."

"That's not my problem and also not the answer to my question."

"Look, there are certain things which I cannot share with you," Aarti said seriously.

"Like what? Like you like that asshole?"

"Mind your language! He's just a friend."

"Friend? My foot! He's a lecher who wants to…" I fell silent.

"Who wants to what? You just worry about yourself. I'm old enough to understand what's right and what's wrong. Today onwards, I won't ask you any questions about any of your friends and you need not ask me any about mine," she said angrily.

"But…"

"That's it," she said slamming my visor shut.

Thousands of questions plagued me. How had that Imran managed to strike a friendship with Aarti? Were they seeing each other? Has she slept with him like Karan pointed out? Was Aarti only using me as a driver to pick and drop her from college to home?

▼

Feeling quite frustrated and helpless at the thought of Aarti seeing Imran, I finally borrowed the prohibited CDs from Karan to cheer myself up. I'd managed to learn how to use the computer and had in fact, become quite adept. Once I managed to copy the volatile content to my disk drive, I spent most of the time inside the loo than in my room. It was a real stress-buster!

One Sunday, Aarti dropped by without notice. Although Dad didn't really like girls coming to our house, I think he believed Aarti to be a cultured girl and a bright student who could help his son in computers. Mom didn't mind as well as Dad had given her instructions to allow Aarti in as an exceptional case. Aarti conversed a bit with Dad before my computer literacy topic popped up. Mom asked her to test my knowledge. So, we booted up the machine and Aarti started her assessment with some elementary questions. Mom listened for a while but lost interest pretty soon. She silently snuck back into the kitchen.

"Hey, I've created a mail id for you. Give me some paper. I'll write it down for you," Aarti said.

"Put it down in a notepad file and save under D:\Personal Docs," I replied casually.

"Oho! You've become quite tech-savvy!" Aarti commented as she typed in something on the notepad.

I leaned forward to read my first mail id, riagra@hotmail.co.in. Password – baniyathegreat.

"What the hell? What kind of a username is this?"

"What happened? Don't you like it?" Aarti said showing concern.

"Like? I hate it. It sounds like Viagra," I explained my reason for unhappiness.

Aarti started laughing. "Viagra for a not-so-hot male. Really nice one! I didn't even notice that," she said hiding her smile behind a hand.

"Didn't you get any other name?"

"I tried rishabh.agrawal, agrawal.rishabh, rishabhagrawal and many other combinations, but they were all taken. The system gave a few suggestions and I selected this one. Now if the Hotmail guys have become naughty, what can I do about it?"

"What about the password? That isn't funny either," I said pointing at the screen.

Aarti giggled. "Honestly, this one I kept intentionally! You can always change it. But your username will always remain viag... sorry sorry riagra!"

I ground my teeth and closed the notepad. Aarti had forgotten to write her own mail id (aartiraisinghani18@rediffmail.com), so she checked the 'Recent Items' list. She clicked on SRK.DAT before I could say anything. Suddenly, two naked blondes appeared on the screen doing unbelievable things with a lucky dude. Thankfully, the speaker was on mute.

"Oh shit! What the fuck is this? I thought it was some Shahrukh movie!" Aarti hit Alt+F4 to close the application and stood up.

"I'm sorry," I apologized. Actually, that was *Six Russian Kittens*.

"Sorry? My dear, this is porn. I'm going to tell Aunty. You're in deep shit," Aarti started to move out of the room.

I blocked her way, pleading inordinately, "Sorry, sorry Aarti. I'm really sorry. I won't watch it again. Please, please. I'm begging you not to tell Mom." I grasped her hands.

"You're sick. And... oh my god! Let go of me. Now I need to wash my hands," she said pushing me back.

"What happened?"

"You must be watching porn and then... yuck! The keyboard must definitely be yucky," Aarti made a face.

"I don't do it here!" it was out before I realised.

"Bastard!" Aarti yelled at me and ran into the loo. I followed her crying like a baby.

Mom barged into the loo hearing our voices. "What happened?" she asked solicitously.

None of us spoke. "I'm asking you both. What happened?" Mom repeated her question.

"And Rishu. What exactly are you doing over here?" Mom enquired seeing me stand at the door.

"Aunty, the computer gave me a shock. And it's pretty dirty as well," Aarti spoke the truth in a sort of muffled mode.

"What? Are you okay?" Mom asked with a worried expression.

"Yeah, I'm okay now," Aarti said looking at me disdainfully.

Mom went inside the room and touched the monitor. Nothing happened, so she gingerly touched the mouse and then the keyboard.

"It looks fine. No shock-vock. Still, I'll ask Uncle to get it checked by the electrician. Might be some earthing problem," Mom surmised.

She left the room to get us some snacks. Aarti kept shaking her head for almost two minutes after Mom left. "I'm not going to touch your computer anymore. And not going to help you with your studies either," she declared.

"Please, don't do that to me. I promise I'll never watch that thing again."

"Then delete it. Now. Right in front of me." Aarti was asking for something extremely painful.

I had no choice but to destroy my precious treasure. Aarti was amazed to see the number of folders under which I'd buried the files, in hidden mode. She finally touched my computer, but only after wearing her driving gloves.

▼

The next semester exams came and went. Expectedly, my result remained the same. Quite luckily, I cleared the 'C' paper managing exactly thirty percent, that too because of Ruhana. By now our friendship had touched a new level – she being a bit smitten. But I didn't give it much importance as it was Aarti who was on my mind. I moved into second year with surprisingly no supplis while Aarti moved into third year with expected honours in all subjects.

▼

The scorching heat of 2002 made us realise the comforts of the college bus. Life on the bike was hell. When finally monsoon hit our city, clouds obscured the sun and there was huge excitement. Students bunked classes to enjoy the weather in the lawns, canteen verandah and other places. I went to the canteen with Ruhana as Karan was busy with something in the lab, probably downloading some hot stuff. The bastard had made friends with the lab assistant and they often exchanged CDs.

Ruhana suddenly remembered that she had to complete some tutorials and left for her hostel. I decided to join Karan in the lab and started walking towards the main building. Just then, I noticed Aarti sitting on the library stairs with the pig I hated. They were smiling and talking. It was obvious that there was something on between the two. Aarti saw me and gestured. "Rishu, Rishu, here, over here," she called out.

I ignored her. She ran up to me and said, "Hey. I need your help."

"Yes, what is it?" I asked curtly.

"Why are you being so rude?"

"Just tell me what you want?"

"I want your bike for half an hour," Aarti requested rolling her brown eyes.

"Why? What for?"

"I have to go somewhere."

"With him?" I asked pointing to Imran.

"Yes, with him. We have some urgent work."

"What kind of work? I'll take you," I offered.

"No, it can be done only with him."

"In that case, I cannot give my bike," I said.

"Oh, come on Rishu! It's urgent. I promise we'll be back in half an hour."

"No. I'm not going to be part of some illegal stuff," I said loudly.

"Shut up! If you don't want to give it, don't! But keep your fucking mouth shut," Aarti yelled back at me.

"Don't cross the limit. Talk politely," I warned her.

"You talk politely too."

"Aarti, please listen to me. That Imran isn't a good guy, trust me. Whenever I do something, wrong, you always correct me. Remember those adult movies? I always listen to you. So, if I'm saying something, please listen to me. I'm your friend, not your enemy," I changed to a softer mode to convince my future wife not to sleep with a lecher. Though the movies were back on my computer.

Aarti was silent for some time. "Do you have any more classes to attend?" she asked.

"No, why?"

"Let's go back home," she said.

I nodded and patted her back. She remained expressionless for a while and then suddenly gave me a tight hug. I saw Imran jump up and down like a monkey on the stairs. Aarti waved goodbye to him as I escorted her out of the college as fast as I could.

"Where were you going with Imran?" I asked on the way.

"Forget it. I listened to you," said Aarti.

Minutes later, a car almost rammed into us at one of the intersections. I screamed through my helmet, "You bastard, can't you see?"

"No, I was looking at your super-hot sister! How much for one night?" the driver leered.

"You son of a bitch!" I stopped the bike at the corner.

"Let him be Rishu. Don't be impulsive. These are all gonads," Aarti tried to interrupt me.

"How can I leave him?" I said taking off my helmet.

"I'm asking you to leave him. Please. Let's go," Aarti requested and caught my wrist.

The bastard was waiting eagerly in his car. He spat out of the window with another round of abuses. I became red and released myself from Aarti's grip. She blocked my way and hugged me tight. The car driver showed me the middle finger and zipped off. Aarti had made me weak. I killed the warrior inside me and got back on the bike.

"Looks like you love me a lot," Aarti commented. I didn't answer.

"Hello? I'm talking to you."

"What do you want to know?" I asked.

"I see that you're getting too possessive about me. First Imran, now this."

"You and your assumptions!"

"Whatever it is, I really liked the way you came forward to protect me," Aarti said putting her hands around my waist and planted a kiss on my helmet.

"Should I take it off? It'd taste better," I said turning to her. Aarti slapped my helmet playfully.

▼

Two days later, I fell ill. The fever was extremely high and the dysentery even more intense. Everyone at home suspected malaria, but the tests revealed typhoid.

Aarti initially paid me two flying visits and then called up several times, maybe because it became hard to travel sans her driver. Karan also rang up, but didn't pay a visit fearing a lecture on grades. I slept and slept like a koala.

After almost ten days, I was finally back on my feet. I was preparing for college the next day when Mom came in and asked, "Who's Ruhana?"

"She is my batch-mate. How do you know her?" I said shocked.

"She called up a few days back. She was saying you got sick because you ate a cream roll in the canteen. Is that true?"

"Yes, I ate one, but it could be something else that caused the infection. How can she be so sure?"

"I'm not talking about the cream roll."

"Mom! Ruhana and I are just friends. The way me and Aarti are."

"Why is it that you don't have male friends? Why only girls?" Mom asked.

"Oho! I have male friends as well. Mandeep, Ashish, Ashutosh…"

"I'm asking about college, not school."

"Karan," I said.

"Apart from him?"

I was silent. "Listen. Don't make friends with Muslim girls," she said. Mom was a conservative lady who believed in making friends within the same community. But then, why didn't she have a problem with Kaddu, I thought to myself.

"Why? What's wrong with Muslim girls?" I asked.

"Such friendships are unacceptable. Actually, friendship with girls is unacceptable. Girls and boys cannot just be friends."

"Really?" I asked raising an eyebrow.

"We're already bearing one of your girlfriends. I don't want more. Pandey Aunty keeps asking me about Aarti. Even suggested that we get you married!" Mom grumbled.

I felt like giving Pandey Aunty a big hug. She had understood the need of the hour.

"Tsk. How can Aunty think like that? Aarti is just a friend. You know that, right?" I said something that had no truth at all.

"Only time will tell whether she's a friend or something else. But let me be very clear. I'll never accept her as my daughter-in-law. She's not from our caste," Mom waved her index finger and issued a diktat.

I dropped the argument. There was no point in carrying it on.

I went to college by bus the next day. Mom forbade me from using my bike for at least a fortnight till I regained my strength. The city buses were very crowded and the people horrible. I experienced that first-hand. Real lechers. Whenever the driver braked, they pretended to be thrown off their feet to be able to touch and feel up the women passengers. I made Aarti sit near the window to keep her safe.

It had been about fifteen minutes since we got on the bus. "There's a surprise for you!" said Aarti excitedly.

"Really?" I asked.

She opened her bag and took out a little brown purse. From one of its pockets, she pulled out a tiny cellphone. "See, I got a phone! That too with a coloured screen!" said Aarti, sporting a broad smile. Almost everybody in the bus turned to catch a glimpse of the instrument. I pressed a few buttons and turned it around to look at it properly, "It looks great. What's the number?"

"Its 9415… I'll tell you later."

"Why? What happened?"

"People are listening. I don't want pesky calls."

I understood her concern and started to study the device. I opened the inbox. It had a few messages, the top two by someone called Immu. One was a silly Santa-Banta joke while the other had a senti shayari.

"What the hell are you doing? Those are my personal messages. Give my phone back," Aarti snatched the phone as soon as she noticed me go through her messages.

"Who's Immu?"

"None of your business."

"A cousin?"

"Nopes, a friend."

"Imarti Lal?" I said and laughed.

"Bingo!"

"Tsk. Tell na, who is it?"

"Imran."

"That sister…"

Aarti warned me to stop by wagging her forefinger in front of my face. I was depressed. Aarti wasn't ready to hear anything against her Immu. Fuck! What the hell am I saying? Imran, the sis…

▼

Over the next couple of months, life moved on as usual. But a few things did change. Like my results nosedived from seventy to sixty-six, Ruhana started giving unexpected calls at home, much to Mom's displeasure, Karan's craving for women became irrepressible, and Aarti's relationship blossomed with Imran the… I think you got the name.

▼

During the summer break, Aarti got busy with her internship at some local IT company. I was kind of free, so I enjoyed my time sleeping, consuming the material supplied by Mr KS and daydreaming of employing Bill Gates once I successfully created the inverted green triangle program (after almost eleven attempts and some cheating from Aarti's code).

▼

It was soon time for campus placements. Aarti was very tensed as only eighty percent of her senior batch had got placed. Since she wasn't interested in preparing for either of GATE, GRE, MAT or CAT, this was a do or die situation for her.

Accenture was the first company to visit. They had outsourced the written test to some external agency. Unfortunately, Lal allowed students from other engineering colleges to participate as well. All of a sudden, the PILOTS campus turned into a Kumbh

Mela. I accompanied Aarti to the workshop building, neglecting my own classes. I waited for her under the blazing sun for almost three hours. She came out looking confused.

"What happened? How was the test?" I asked.

"I don't know. It was a very confusing paper. And there was a lot of cheating too," she replied.

"Cheating! In recruitments?" I was surprised.

"Yeah! That was bound to happen. Just look at the number of people. I don't know why the fuck Lal allowed students from other colleges to sit for our placement tests," Aarti said sourly.

"Don't get nervous. Only the best ones will clear," I comforted her.

"I don't care. I just want to clear the cut-off!"

"I'm sure you'll get through. Calm down. When will the results be out?"

"At five."

"What? It's only two. What will we do till then?"

"Let's go back home. Imran will call me when the list comes out. And anyway, the interviews will happen only tomorrow," said Aarti.

"I think we should wait. Why trust Imran?" I suggested abusing Imran in my mind.

"People don't lie about such things. Even if he does, the placement cell will inform me in any case. PILOTS is thriving just because of its placements," said Aarti nonchalantly.

She had a valid point so we moved out after gobbling two lumpy samosas in the canteen.

"Hello. May I speak with Rishabh?" there was a dog barking agitatedly in the background drowning out the voice.

"Yes, speaking. Who's it?" I asked. Getting personal calls from females is always a strange feeling.

"It's me, idiot! Don't you recognize my voice? I've cleared the written. My interview is scheduled for tomorrow morning," Aarti informed me excitedly.

"Really? That's great news. Party!" I shouted over the phone. Thankfully, Mom was with Pandey Aunty in the balcony.

"I still have to get through the interview. And that's what really matters. This time Accenture is sending its own guys. So, it's gonna be real tough. I'll need to study all night. Come home at half past eight sharp. The interviews will start around ten. Understood?" Aarti ordered me.

"Yeah, understood."

It was 4:40 p.m. I was soaked in sweat and smelt awful. Thankfully, Ruhana's company helped me survive those seven-and-a-half hours. Suddenly, I saw Aarti coming out with Imran, holding hands. As soon as she saw me, she left his hand. She ran up to me and said, "Guess what happened?"

"You got kicked out," I teased.

"Idiot! I got selected," she said thumping my shoulder.

"Awesome! I knew you'd make it," I said offering a handshake.

"Is this how you congratulate your best friend?" Aarti said slapping my hand.

"Then? Should I give a party?"

"That I'll give. You just give me a hug," Aarti said and hugged me like a teddy bear.

The crowd became less noisy and Imran stared at us. It was the first time that I too put my arms around Aarti and hugged her back. "Leave me you scoundrel. You'll break my back. And chhee! You smell awful," Aarti pushed me and made a pukey face.

"It's musk baby. It's musk," I said smelling my armpits.

Aarti grimaced at my filthy act. She quickly jumped to the facts and figures. Only thirty-four students were given offers from the hundred and forty-three interviewed, with just eleven belonging to PILOTS. "Imran also got through. Isn't that great?" Aarti said enthusiastically.

"Great? That's the saddest news of my life!" I said making a face.

"Don't say that. He's not that bad. Come with me. Imran wants to say sorry," Aarti started pulling me towards Imran.

"No, thank you. And do let me know if you're interested in going back home. Or will the city bus be your choice today?" I said freeing my hand from her hold.

"Okay, okay. Don't get angry. I don't want to spoil anybody's mood today."

Aarti waved to Imran as we left the college premises. From there we went to the Hanuman Mandir down the hill near the Monkey Bridge. While Aarti offered her prayers, I stared at the midriffs of the crouching female devotees. Totally indecorous behaviour!

Once Aarti was done with her prayers, I forced her to give me a treat at CCD. She ordered without considering my choice, as was expected. In the meantime, I flipped through the documents in her folder. Her resume was perfectly drafted and looked great with percentages over seventy-five starting from SSC till the sixth semester of engineering.

Suddenly, I heard someone call out, "Neta!" Aarti and I turned to see who it was. It was Jingur two tables away! He'd put on a little weight, lost a bit of melanin and sported a funky hairstyle. His jeans were torn at the knees and a wad of wristbands clearly suggested that he lived in Delhi.

"Jingur!" both Aarti and I exclaimed in excitement. People sitting around started inspecting the floor anticipating real jingurs. A few of them even folded up their legs!

Jingur walked up to us, dragged a chair and sat down sporting his trademark donkey grin.

He looked into Aarti's eyes and said, "*Vadi Sai*, you look far hotter than those LSR chicks." Aarti was taken aback but didn't show it.

"Hey Ashish! How are you buddy? Where have you been all this time?" she asked.

"I'm rocking! Just completed my graduation from Delhi," Jingur replied.

"So? What next? Job?" I asked.

"Definitely, but only after I complete by MBA."

"Are you preparing for it or you've already taken admission?" I grilled him.

"Joined."

"Where?" Aarti asked curiously.

"IIM Lucknow."

"What?" Both me and Aarti screeched in surprise. I never thought Jingur would go that far.

"Yeah! What's the big deal?" Jingur said casually.

"Congrats man," I said offering a handshake, mentally cursing myself for coming to CCD.

"Neta, you haven't changed at all. Same looks and everything else," Jingur said shaking hands with me.

I grinned. Then he dropped the bomb, "So, how is it going between the lovebirds? I always knew there was something cooking between the two of you."

"No, you stupid. Nothing like that. We're only friends," Aarti said dabbing the table.

"Really? Quite unbelievable. Anyway, what are you guys doing here? Any special occasion?"

"Your *Vadi Sai* is giving me a party," I spoke hiding my sadness at the 'only friends' statement that Aarti had just made.

"Party for what? Has her boyfriend proposed or is she getting married?" Jingur asked, making me feel like putting a live jingur inside his shorts.

"Hold on, hold on. I just got my first job," Aarti clarified.

"That's great man… sorry… lady. Can I also join you? Oh, what a silly question. Of course, yes. I'm joining you guys," and Jingur whistled to the waiter. Aarti looked at me irritated as Jingur ordered a long list of eatables.

Over the next one hour, we exchanged details of the past three years. Jingur enlightened us with Kaddu's heroic acts at the academy along with Ashu's intellectual growth at IIT. At one point, I thought about my own achievements and ambitions. I couldn't think of anything. I couldn't even boast of a budding love life.

▼

I saw a transformation in Aarti after that day. She became egotistic and a little immodest. After all, she had a job. She took the initiative to tutor me on alternate weekends as I was having a hard time with OOPS, DBMS and DAA. Don't get frightened. These are all computer subjects with frightening concepts.

On one such Saturday, Mom wasn't home. She and Pandey Aunty had gone grocery shopping. Mom had listed out a few tasks for me before she left – move the milk vessel to the refrigerator once it gets cold, bring in the clothes from the terrace, and help myself to Maggi for lunch.

Such opportunities were scarce for me so I wasted no time in getting naughty and playing some hardcore stuff. I was deeply engrossed watching the lovely women when I heard a scooter. Shit! It was Aarti. I bid adieu to the ladies, cleaned up the recent items, deleted history from the media player, hid the treasure, changed my wallpaper from Shakira to Shahrukh and turned off the computer. The bell rang. I opened the door as if I'd been woken from deep sleep.

"Hi Rishu. What took you so long to open the door?" Aarti questioned me.

"Feeling lazy. I woke up with your bell," I lied stretching my arms.

"Wake up dude. Time for some C++ puzzles," Aarti said patting my cheeks.

"Yea," I said latching the door.

"Isn't anybody home?" Aarti asked. "Mom's gone shopping. She'll be back in an hour or so," I said imitating a yawn.

"I think I'd come later on. What if she comes and finds me over here?" Aarti said showing concern.

"What?"

"What will she think?"

"What?" I asked again.

"You understand what I'm saying. Don't act foolish," Aarti said staring straight at me.

"What if she sees you leaving? Then what will she think? 'Aarti came during my absence. Did something-something with my boy and left before I came'," I said, my eyebrows dancing.

"Shut up! I'll kill you," Aarti screeched and tried to catch hold of my collar.

I dodged behind the sofa and ran to my room. Aarti came running behind me and stubbed her toes on the bed. She lost her balance and fell on me. I too lost my balance and fell on the bed, with Aarti in my arms. We were in a double-decker set-up, lying face-to-face over a thirsty bed, nobody at home for at least an hour and lots of stuff on the computer hard drive.

I looked into Aarti's confident yet shy brown eyes. Our lips were two inches apart, her warm breath talking to my nostrils and hair all over my face. She tried to get up and unintentionally placed her knee on my groin. "Ahh...!" I screamed.

"I'm sorry. I'm really really sorry Rishu. I didn't mean to hurt you," Aarti apologized. "Lie down, lie down straight. Don't move. You'll be alright in two minutes," she said stroking my face.

"You should try for the Guinness World Records. Extremely talented in crushing men," I cried.

"Now you're overreacting. I said I'm sorry. Had that been intentional, you'd have lost consciousness by now," Aarti said lying next to me. Her hand was on my chest. My hands were still comforting the poor thing.

We remained in that position for another two minutes looking at the fan swirling above us. "Give me your hand," said Aarti.

I passed my groin-infected hand to her. She made a pillow out of it and rested her head on my shoulder. I freed my groin and drew my fingers through her hair.

"Rishu, you're the only person I trust as much as my parents. I don't know what I'll do without you once I start working," Aarti said emotionally. I turned my neck to look at her. A tear rolled down from the edge of her eye.

I got emotional too even though I had other desires bubbling up inside my system. "I'm glad to know that you trust me so much. If you ever feel lonely at any time in your life, remember that there's one person on this planet who'll always have his doors open for you. Anytime." I promised mawkishly, my eyes back on the ceiling fan.

There was no reaction from Aarti so I twisted my neck once again to look at her. And fuck! It happened right then. Aarti kissed me. Hard on the lips. Fair enough to be put into the category of a smooch. As that first expression of love happened, Aarti got up in a flash cursing, "You bastard, I was pecking you on the cheek."

She spat into the air as if she had swallowed a housefly and then scrubbed her lips with her lovely little hanky. I was dead – enraptured by her two-second taste of love. I came back to life only after Aarti hit me repeatedly with her tiny little handkerchief, calling me an opportunist, which I undoubtedly was.

"I didn't kiss you. You kissed me. But overall it was great. Can we do it again?" I replied swirling my tongue around my lips.

Aarti was furious, "This time I'll hit you intentionally," she warned pointing a finger at my groin.

"Just kidding. Forget it! A mistake from both of us," I handled the situation.

Aarti got off the bed and went to the bathroom to remove my germs from her lips, while I savoured each bit of the moment. The phone alarm made me remember the jobs assigned by Mom. I ran to the kitchen to put the milk vessel into the fridge. Finding me missing from the room, Aarti came to the kitchen. "What are you doing?" she asked.

"Mom assigned me certain tasks. Just completing them," I replied.

"Can I be of any help?" she asked.

"Why not? Just take off the clothes."

"What?"

I had said it intentionally. "I mean, bring the clothes from the terrace," I quickly translated.

"Don't use those double meaning sentences with me," reprimanded Aarti.

I grinned as Aarti scrambled to the terrace. Meanwhile, I got engrossed in cooking Maggi noodles for both of us. After five minutes Aarti returned to the kitchen. "They're done. But I haven't folded them. Do I need to?" she asked.

"Leave them. Mom will do it. Is there anything left or have you brought everything inside?" I asked.

"Your pants are still wet. So, I didn't take them off," Aarti replied.

This time I reprimanded her, "Don't use those double meaning sentences with me."

Aarti sensed what she had just said and imitated jabbing me with the kitchen knife. The Maggi was ready. We ate from the same plate, but with different forks. C++ was kept aside as Aarti switched on the computer and played some SRK songs. But she didn't forget to wear her driving gloves!

TARFU

It was time for another farewell party. But this one was different. First, Aarti was the lone ranger; I was out of the reckoning. Second, it was finally time to say goodbye to our daily bickering. And third and most important, I was determined to propose to her despite having doubts on her relationship status. My mind was made up. It was rock solid this time. I planned to execute it just before the farewell party.

Inter alia, Aarti had received her joining letter from Accenture. She had to report at Bangalore, the IT hub of India. My only solace was that Imran got his posting in Navi Mumbai.

9th April 2004 – the day of the farewell party, a week after my birthday and a month before my semester exams. It was 4 o'clock. I reached Aarti's place to pick her up. She was waiting for me and seemed to be brooding.

"What's the matter?" I asked.

"Aa… I, umm, there's something I need to tell you… but l'll tell you on the way, let's go now," Aarti said adjusting the pleats of her sari.

"Is this what you wore at our school farewell?" I asked pointing to her dark blue sari.

"Really? I don't remember. How does it matter? You're the only one who was there. So, besides you, no one else will know," she said unselfconsciously. Aarti was very different from other girls in that respect.

"Are you ready to leave?" I asked.

"Yes of course. I can't wait."

"Why?"

"On the way, on the way... chalo," Aarti said tugging me to the main gate.

Once we crossed the Nishatganj flyover, she put her arms around my stomach and exclaimed, "Rishu. I'm in love!"

I slammed on the brakes instantly. The car behind us managed to manoeuvre just in time and the driver stuck his neck out of the window and abused me earnestly.

"What's wrong with you Rishu? You almost got us both killed," Aarti screamed at me.

"I'm sorry," I apologized and swerved the bike towards the pavement to stop.

"You're in love?" I asked taking off my helmet.

"Totally and fully," Aarti said crossing her fingers.

"Then say it," I was getting butterflies in my stomach with the excitement.

"Really? Should I say it right now?"

"Yes, say it. Why wait?"

"I... I... I'm getting nervous," Aarti blushed.

"Oh, come on! What's the big deal?"

"Yeah. You're right. But... I can't say it while we face each other."

I turned around immediately. It was a giddy feeling waiting for her to declare her love to me in the next few moments.

"I have to tell you something. Something I can't keep in my system any longer. It's more than two years since I... I mean... I... I love you. I love you Immu. I love you."

I swivelled around immediately. Aarti was talking on the phone and not to me! Fuck! Aarti was in love with Imran. All my dreams were shattered right there in one go.

Please don't be in love with someone else. I can accept rejection, but not this. I begged Aarti in my mind as I walked away from the bike. While I lamented on my fucked-up one-sided love story, Aarti embraced me from behind. "I said it Rishu, I said it. Thank you for giving me the strength to say it. You know what... Imran loves me too!" she said excitedly.

I couldn't take it. I released myself from her grip and put on my helmet.

"What happened? Aren't you happy for me?"

"No, of course not! Not when it's Imran. I hate him more than your Jackie," I said irritated.

"Watch your language. Imran is now my hubby," Aarti warned.

"Hubby? He's just using you for his dirty ambitions."

"Huh. You're simply jealous of him. Actually, he got what you wanted for yourself."

"Myself? Really?"

"Don't pretend to be innocent. I know what you feel for me. I understood it the day you didn't give me your bike and then fought with that car driver."

"Really? What makes you think so? Have I ever said anything to you?"

"You never had the guts to. You're nothing but a bloody loser."

"Guts? Loser? Ha! What do you think of yourself? Some Miss India? I wouldn't touch you even if you came for free." It was a cheap thing to say to a girl and a terrible thing to take in.

"Shut up you bastard. I'm not some cheap slut who'll sleep with sex addicts like you."

"Me... a sex addict? Get lost, you bitch! Go and warm that bastard's sheets," I said rudely, pushing her back.

"How dare you... fuck you, son of a bitch!" And she raised her hand to slap me. But I had my helmet on.

I twisted Aarti's arm and pushed her once again. "Fuck off, bloody whore!" I abused her in anger.

We looked at each other with fiery eyes before Aarti spat on my helmet and flagged down an auto. I kicked my bike in frustration and sat down on the pavement. It was over, I had a feeling.

▼

After that day, Aarti stopped talking to me. She didn't respond to my calls or e-mails either. I even got roughed up by Imran on two separate occasions. I started to get into a depression. Each night I sat on my computer thinking about Aarti. Mom thought I was studying, but no, I was just talking to myself – thinking about where I went wrong. Exams came in a flash and so did the results. For the first time ever, I got two supplis. My percentage sank further – from a below par sixty-six to a flimsy fifty-nine. That was the nadir of my academic record. Summer training was also a mere formality. I paid five grand to a training institute in return for a certificate and a fake project report. My life was *totally and royally fucked up* (TARFU).

I tried to meet Aarti and went over to her house eight to ten times only to be told by Rajjo every single time, "Nonu didi has gone with Sahib-Memsahib to Bangalore. I don't know when they'll be back." She refused to divulge their contact number saying she didn't know it because they called her and she never had to.

The final year classes commenced. When Karan and Ruhana saw me, they were shocked. I'd lost four kilos and looked haggard. I told them that I was having some problems at home. Thankfully, they didn't ask any more questions.

▼

I wasn't the same person that I used to be. And it didn't go down well with Ruhana. She really did believe that I had a genuine problem at home and so she kept assuring me that things will be okay soon. Then one day Ruhana suggested a trip to Kukrail, a reserve forest cum alligator rehabilitation park. I think I needed more rehabilitation than those big-snouted stinking reptiles. I had no interest in going, but went along as Ruhana was insistent. It was her first time on my bike. Actually, it was the first time I had someone other than Aarti riding pillion with me.

We entered the forest after a fifty-minute ride. The temperature suddenly dropped by around three to four degrees. Ruhana clasped my tummy as I accelerated on the solitary track inside the forest. Once inside, we bought the tickets and took a stroll around. Each of the enclosures had a pond of murky water with alligators of all shapes and sizes lying around, absolutely still.

"Let's go into the forest," said Ruhana pulling my hand.

"No, it's dangerous. There are lots of monkeys and there could be some goons lurking around as well," I said worried.

"Nothing will happen. Come na," Ruhana urged and tugged me towards a secluded lane. We kept walking for almost ten minutes without saying a word. Suddenly, we noticed a dilapidated bench. I plonked myself on it and said, "Let's take a five-minute break and then get out of here. I'll drop you at the hostel and then go back home."

"Rishu, I want to tell you something. But I don't know how to start," Ruhana said looking at the ground.

"Something personal?"

"Yes, kind of," she said kicking a pebble on the ground.

"Okay, I'm listening… what is it?"

"Leave it. I'll tell you some other time," Ruhana said looking sideways.

I placed my hand on her shoulder. "You can trust me. I won't share it with anyone," I said.

"No, it's not about that. It's…"

"Okay just think you're alone. I'm closing my eyes. You can tell me now." And I closed my eyes.

There was silence for a minute. Then suddenly I felt a breath on my face. I opened my eyes and, oh my god! Ruhana kissed me on the lips. It was *almost* a wet kiss. I jerked my head back and shrieked, "What the hell are you doing?"

"Let me do it Rishu. Let me love you." Ruhana sat herself astride my lap, her bosom almost on my face. Before I could say or do anything, she grabbed my face and planted another kiss on my mouth, this time even more intense. I couldn't believe it was Ruhana!

"Ruhana, please stop this insanity. This isn't right. Let's not complicate things and regret later," I said pushing her back.

"I'm never going to complain. Just love me for today, if not for your entire life," she begged me and then without warning, planted yet another kiss on my lips.

The wolf inside me urged to go with the flow, but there was still some morality left in me. I pushed back Ruhana so fiercely that she lost her balance and fell on the ground. And then in the heat of the moment, I gave her two tight slaps.

"What the fuck do you think you're doing?" I barked.

Ruhana started to sob loudly. I was worried about someone coming by… they'd think that I was trying to rape her. Who knows if all this took a religious turn? Her Dad was in the police and I've heard horrific stories about third degree torture. I started to sweat profusely.

"Look Ruhana, I didn't mean to hurt you. I'm sorry. Please forgive me," I said wiping her tears. I took her hand and made her sit next to me on the bench. I could see the impression of my fingers on her skin. I hated myself for it.

Ruhana was inconsolable, so I pulled her close. I held her tightly. "Calm down Ruhana, calm down. It's okay."

Ruhana kept sobbing for a while and then pushed herself back.

"Look up Ruhana. Look at me!" I said. I lifted her chin to make an eye contact. "I'm sorry Ruhana. I'm really sorry for hurting you," I apologized.

Ruhana snivelled and spoke with a trembling voice, "No, it's not your fault. I just couldn't control my emotions."

"Who said I don't love you? I love you. But as a friend. Try and understand. Our culture, our families, and our upbringing… everything is different. The society that we live in is quite conservative. It won't approve of our relationship; not even our parents. Please understand that. You're a beautiful girl and I'm pretty sure you'll get a good boy someday. Someone who's not a loser like me," I said.

"No, you're not a loser. You're a hero. Had it been some other boy, he'd have ruined my life," Ruhana drew forward and hugged me hard.

I kissed her on the forehead. She started to cry again, this time in remorse. It took a long time to make her sober again.

I dropped Ruhana to her hostel, promising to keep the secret locked deep within the walls of my heart. It was another sleepless night for me. This time I thought more about Ruhana and less about Aarti. I was sad. Sad for making Ruhana feel awful. But also satisfied to have taken the right decision.

Found at Last

It was time for campus placements. While everyone was busy preparing for the interviews, I spent my time playing cricket on my computer. Those with pending supplis weren't allowed to sit for the placements and since I'd just bagged two, I wasn't eligible. When Mom found out about it, she added to my woes by constantly berating me. To appease Mom, I gave up playing on my computer, and to avoid her, I spent most of my time out of the house – either at Karan's place or with Ruhana on campus. By this time, Ruhana had got over the Kukrail incident.

Karan and Ruhana sat for interviews while I took on the role of providing psychological support, just like the previous year, even though I needed the support more than anybody else. Though Karan was a sex maniac, it didn't come in the way of his securing a job at a small IT firm based in Pune. He celebrated his success by donating his entire CD collection, which the lab assistant and I accepted gleefully.

Ruhana had yet to get a placement. We were nearing the end of the season with only one more company left to visit. "I don't think I'll make it anywhere. I can clearly see my future. Either I'll have to struggle at some walk-in, or worse, join a call centre," Ruhana lamented in the canteen.

"Don't give up. You'll definitely get through somewhere," I consoled her.

"How do you know that? Do you've a 'setting'?" Karan asked.

"No setting-vetting. I just sense it," I replied.

"Really? Then Rishu baba, tell us what other things you sense too! What about her?" Karan said pointing to a girl in a super tight top.

"I sense that you'll be slapped soon," I retorted.

"If she doesn't, I'll slap you for sure. Don't act smart just because you've got through," Ruhana added scornfully.

"Acting smart? Me? What a joke! My dear, just go and study. Don't waste time with us. Otherwise you'll lose this chance too," Karan said to Ruhana quite rudely.

"Thanks for your not-so-required advice," Ruhana said disdainfully.

"Karan, yaar please. Ruhana needs motivation, not discouragement like this," I quickly said.

"You? You'll motivate her? First clear your supplis dude!" He laughed derisively.

I felt I'd been hit by a train. Sometimes the truth is so painful that even a slight mention of it drowns you in an ocean of dejection. I just looked down and didn't say anything. And then, I heard a loud smack. Ruhana had slapped Karan!

Before I could react, he'd caught Ruhana by her hair.

"Karan, Karan… what are you doing? Leave her…," I intervened.

"Leave her? How dare she? Bitch. I'll screw her. Girls like her look good in brothels and not in engineering colleges," he shouted, abusing not just Ruhana but the entire female fraternity.

This was unacceptable. I couldn't control myself and did something that I'd probably have done only for Aarti. I picked up my helmet and smashed it on Karan's head. He fell to the floor, bleeding profusely. A crowd had gathered around us, but nobody intervened.

"You bastard! If you dare say another word to her, I'll kill you. Had your sister been alive, she'd have become the most sought after street girl by now," I said whatever came to my mind.

Karan stood up holding his head. He hobbled towards me and kicked me in the shins. In a matter of seconds, his elbow was curled around my neck. We grappled for a bit till I kneed him in the privates. He fell to the floor once again. I repeatedly kicked him in the abdomen before Ruhana caught my hand. "Leave him Rishu. Leave him!"

For a moment, I felt as if it was Aarti speaking to me. She used to call me Rishu just the same way. I looked into Ruhana's eyes. They were brimming with tears. I held her hand and pulled her out of the canteen. I literally dragged her to the parking stand. I forced her to sit pillion and zipped out of the gate.

"Where are we going?" Ruhana asked clipping back her hair.

"I don't know. Just want to get out of this filthy place," I screamed back.

After meandering on the roads for almost twenty minutes, I took the road to Kukrail.

"Are we going to Kukrail?" Ruhana asked as I turned my bike towards the woods.

"It's the only place free from chaos," I said driving at a dangerous ninety.

Some thirty odd minutes later, we were sitting at the bench we were on roughly a month back.

"What happened to you today? I never saw you so angry. You looked like you'd kill Karan," Ruhana asked. She was visibly quite shaken up.

"Don't take that bastard's name."

"Calm down, Rishu, calm down!" She shifted closer to me and started to rub my shoulder.

I don't know what made me do it, but in that instant, I grabbed her face and forcibly planted a kiss on her lips. Ruhana tried to push me back, but I was too strong for her. I kissed her for a while before sliding my hand inside her top.

"Stop it Rishu. Stop!" Ruhana said grabbing my hand.

"This is what you wanted. Right? Let's do it today," I said trying to take off her top. Ruhana resisted hard, but I pulled off her top roughly.

"No Rishu, no… what are you doing? Please leave me. I was wrong that day and you showed me the right path. You're a good person," Ruhana cried for mercy, covering herself with her hands.

I was unmoved. I went on to unbutton her jeans, barking like a mad dog, "Good person? Bullshit. I'm a loser. A double suppli guy. A guy with no job. A guy with no guts. A guy with no Aarti."

Time froze as I took that name. It was my longing for Aarti that had made me so pathetic, so broken, and so vulnerable.

I let go of Ruhana and fell to my knees with my head hanging low. And then I broke down.

Ruhana quickly wore back her top and leaned over to embrace and caress me with her gentle hands.

"Get up Rishu. Get up. Tell me what happened between you and Aarti," she said.

I cried like a two-year-old as I narrated the tragedy of my life to Ruhana. How I fell in love with Aarti, how I could never declare it to her, how I felt when she told me that she was in love with someone else, and how I'd hurt her feelings thereafter.

Ruhana listened to me patiently. She kept rubbing my shoulder and back all the while. "Rishu, Aarti is gone. She loves Imran. That's the reality. Just let go of her. You've your whole life ahead of you. Aarti isn't the end of the road," she said softly.

"I can't forget her. I'll die if she isn't mine," I snivelled.

"What are you saying? Don't do anything foolish."

When I didn't respond, Ruhana continued, "Promise me that you'll fight it out. It was you who guided me that day. And you were so right. If ever in your heart you've felt something for me, then please do this for me." Ruhana drew my face to her and kissed me on the cheek. "Rishu, not all of us are lucky to have the person we love. I know how hard it is to stop loving the person who means everything to us. But we need to learn to live with it and gradually move on," she continued.

My eyes filled up again. Ruhana's love for me was immaculate. I hugged her close and apologized for my actions. "Ruhana, I'm really really sorry for my behaviour. I shouldn't have done that. And I'm so sorry for not being able to understand your true love and concern for me. Please forgive me. I'm extremely sorry."

Ruhana patted me on the back and rested her head on my shoulder. A tear rolled down her face. I kissed her on the forehead and led her out of the area that was rumoured to have witnessed two half-rapes in the last one month.

▼

I lost another friend as Karan stopped talking to me. He had to get three stitches on his temple. I seemed to be destined to lose friends who got stitches directly or indirectly because of me!

▼

Ruhana was quite tensed, as it was the final day for placements. I wished her best of luck and prayed for her success. I just wanted to see her happy. After waiting for almost four hours, Ruhana emerged smiling radiantly like a bride. I ran up to her. She hugged me in public for the first time ever. "I got it Rishu. I got the job!" she exclaimed.

I felt as if I'd got the job. "Proud of you Ruhana… so proud of you. I always knew you'd get through," I said.

We went to the canteen for a small party of sorts and then snuggled at a secluded spot behind the library. I don't know whether it was friendship or support or plain need for each other, but we'd shared warm hugs around a dozen times after my Kukrail sobbing episode.

▼

Ruhana took it as her duty to get me through engineering by taking time out to study with me. She also took an additional risk of supplying me with chits during the exams.

The results came and I was back in the seventies after five long semesters! I gifted a t-shirt to Ruhana to show my gratefulness to her and also as a replacement for ruining one of hers. For the final year project, Ruhana chose me as her partner. She did all the work. I just had to type, format and get the printouts done. The last semester exams also arrived pretty fast. I had the additional burden of clearing two supplis this time around.

Soon, the exams were over and the circular to vacate the hostels was pinned up. Ruhana was sad as we had only a few more days together. So, to cheer her up, I decided to take her out for a picnic. And Kukrail was the name that came to my mind without a second thought.

This time around, we took an actual interest in exploring the place. I must say, alligators, the green savages are so deadly by their appearance that they make one go real weak in the knees. Ruhana clutched my arm whenever we went close to an enclosure, even for those that had just metre long young ones. We went on to see the museum that depicted the vast history of this beast.

We also had lunch in one of the few delis that were the sole source of survival inside the park. Afterwards, we went out for an aimless stroll across the various wretched tracks.

Forty minutes later, we were on our favourite bench. We chatted for a while, hand in hand, and then out of nowhere, things got messy. We kissed softly, then intensely, and at last wildly. It was clear that we badly wanted each other.

"Wait, wait, wait! I don't have any protection. We need to be careful," I said as Ruhana tried to unbutton my jeans.

"Oh man, I can't wait."

"No, we shouldn't be reckless."

"Oh, come on Rishu! Nothing really should come between a couple except love. That is what morning-after pills are for." And then without wasting any more time, Ruhana simply pulled up her top and unhooked her bra.

Fuck! It was live! Something I'd seen a lot in digital format but never in reality. Ruhana was quite ripe, an S-curve that needed no augmentation. She also had a tiny mole over the right one, quite enough to turn an animal breeding centre into a human copulation ground. As it turned extremely difficult for me to keep my eyes away from her milk white casabas, I decided to go after them.

We did it twice in the next one hour. Ruhana wanted more, but I had no more reserves left. So, we restricted ourselves to kisses only. "I'll remember this day all my life," she said.

"Me too," I said ruffling her hair.

Ruhana told me that her father would soon be starting to look for a groom for her now that she had got a job. That didn't hurt, more so because we both knew that there was no future for us, although we'd just had sex, that too twice. Actually, we were too timid to confront our families and face the atrocities of society.

"Your husband will be a really unlucky fortunate man," I said with a smile.

"Meaning?" Ruhana asked playing with the lump of hair over my chest.

"He'll be fortunate to have you as his wife, but unlucky not to be the first one to have you!" I said running my fingers over Ruhana's smooth behind.

"You!" Ruhana knuckled me on the forehead. I yelped in pain.

"Sorry, sorry. I didn't mean to hurt you," she apologized and kissed my forehead.

"This is nothing compared to the pain of not seeing you. God only knows what will happen to me," I said holding her hand.

"You'll do okay. Just keep in touch. And by the way, this was your first and last time doing it with me. The rest is all for my hubby!" Ruhana giggled.

"As you wish, your majesty. It was a pleasure to serve you," I said winking at her.

Both of us laughed and kissed again. I was ready for one more session by now. Ruhana wasn't interested as she had to be back before dark. I convinced her that this would be the last one as my water table was almost depleted. Our final union was so close to primitive man – on the ground, among the trees and watched by god knows how many species on earth.

We got dressed and kissed one last time before leaving the place that had everlasting memories for us.

▼

Ruhana left after a week or so. Thankfully, the morning-after pill worked well. I went to the station to see her off. As the train started to move, my eyes filled up. I gave her one last kiss on her lovely little hands, the first and the last thing I saw of her.

▼

Ruhana and I had exchanged e-mail ids to stay in touch (For the record, I'd stopped using the 'riagra' account). I had removed everything that reminded me of Aarti as she wasn't a part of my life anymore. She had not tried to contact me in the past one year and I hadn't bothered to either.

In the meantime, I tried to get myself a job at some local companies, but none of them even shortlisted my resume. It was only my final semester result that could have brought me some relief. When it was finally out after a month, it turned out to be the most satisfying scorecard of my life. I had cleared all the subjects, including both the supplis! And surprise of surprises, for the first time in four years – I got honours! And it was all because of Ruhana.

I wrote an e-mail to thank her once again for all the support she had given me although I'd done that a zillion times in the past month already! Ruhana replied within minutes, showering me with compliments that I wonder if I actually deserved. She too had got honours. She then informed me about her joining work at Hyderabad in October.

Mom and Dad heaved a sigh of relief as I had finally fulfilled their dream of becoming an engineer.

Dad reached out to his influential friends and after a little over two weeks, got me my first job in a small company at Gurgaon, that too without appearing for a written test or an interview! There was only a telephonic HR round. I mailed my documents to the HR department and my offer letter arrived on e-mail as well as by registered post. I had kept Ruhana abreast of these developments and she was very happy about my job. I was about to enter yet another watershed year of my life and it was to commence on the 5th of September 2005.

NCR

Arora Uncle was one of Dad's colleagues, whose son Atul worked and lived in Gurgaon. Atul came to receive us at the station. We reached his place almost around midnight. His super sexy ultra-modern wife opened the door in an enticing nightie. She touched Dad's feet and showed us the guest room. We were already full, so we just had tea and then hit the bed after a few minutes of talking to Atul and his wife. Next day, after having a refreshing bath and a graceful breakfast, we left in search of an accommodation for me. By one we'd scoured half of Gurgaon, but without any luck. Exhausted, we took a break at a tea stall in one of the colonies. The tea vendor spoke in some South Indian lingo to the people crowded around us. Atul ordered three teas. "It's very difficult to find decent accommodation these days," he said.

"Looking for a room sir?" said a voice in fluent English. All three of us turned. It was the tea stall owner named Ramesh. "What is your requirement sir? Single room, one BHK, two BHK or PG?" he enquired.

"Single room or PG. Both will work," Dad replied.

"Budget?"

"Three to four thousand."

"Who'll be staying? How many people?" Ramesh asked pointing his finger at each one of us one by one.

"One person... he's my son... we're looking for accommodation for him," Dad responded, pushing me forward.

Ramesh took out his Nokia 1100 and made back to back calls juggling between Hindi, Haryanvi and the alien South Indian language. By the time our tea arrived, there were three heavily bearded men on bikes ready to show us places! They were all brokers. Ramesh asked us to accompany them. We all got onto one bike each and decided to meet at the tea stall after checking out the available options separately.

The broker I was with was quite a talkative chap. He spoke mostly in Haryanvi, which I found quite hard to decipher. After we had checked out five horrible places, he stopped in front of a two-storeyed house. "This is the last one. God help you after that," he said looking at me disgustedly.

He got a phone call and gestured to me to press the doorbell. I read the nameplate DALALS and pressed the dirt-stained lemon yellow bell button. Within seconds, a fair Cinderella walked out in a Fido Dido t-shirt and a pair of ultra-short checked shorts. She wore bangles and bracelets up to her elbows and her legs were freshly waxed. "Yes?" she asked.

I turned to the broker. He'd moved a few yards away from the house and was abusing someone on the phone. The hottie smiled as I tried to get the man's attention. He turned and gestured to the lady that I was a prospective customer... I mean, tenant. I ogled at her shaved armpits while she conversed in sign language with the broker. Suddenly, a silver WagonR stopped near the gate. A short and fat fellow with grey stubble got off and walked towards us. He threw open the latch of the gate and barked curtly, "Savita, go inside!" The beauty cat immediately ran inside the house.

"Yes? What is it?" the fellow asked me rudely.

"I'm looking for accommodation," I said.

"Has that man brought you here?" he asked pointing a finger at the broker.

"Yes," I confirmed.

"Come, I'll show you the room," he said in a softer tone.

He took me upstairs to the first floor. It had a single room. Inside was a fellow in a torn vest reading from tomes fatter than M.L. Khanna. He banged the door shut as he noticed me peep inside his room. We crossed a dingy gallery to reach two facing doors, both locked. There was a tiny bathroom wedged between the two rooms. The owner unlocked one of the doors and we entered a twin sharing room with all the basic necessities, except a fridge and a television. I checked the attached bathroom and found it satisfactorily clean. Unfortunately, it had a European style toilet. I stepped into the balcony (quite narrow to be called one) and, blimey, a damsel in a nightie was reading something in the verandah of the adjacent house. I love this place! Beautiful women everywhere, I thought to myself.

"Who stays here?" I asked looking at the army green bermudas and the orange t-shirt hanging on a rope tied diagonally across the room.

"Joydeep. He works at Oxyopia. Nice fellow. Must have gone out somewhere."

I enquired about other details like rent, food, water, cleaning, electricity and power backup. Everything was included, except food, which we had to manage on our own. I decided to seal the deal. I gave the owner five hundred bucks as token money and promised to return with my Dad in another fifteen-twenty minutes.

The owner introduced himself as Gagan. The woman I met at the gate was his wife. His parents were gone to the doctor right then. But he promised to introduce me to them once I moved in.

As Gagan walked out to chat with the broker, I knocked on the door that had been shut on my face. Nobody responded. So, I knocked it again. "Who's it... sisterfucker?" came the reply. I was shocked.

I knocked yet again. "Coming," said a gruff voice.

After two minutes, the door opened. I came face-to-face with a short fellow who had a thick moustache and curly hair. "Yes? What is it? What do you want?" he asked as he tried to cover up his torn vest with a frayed hoodie.

"Hi. I'm Rishabh. I'll be moving in this evening," I said proffering my hand.

"Great to have you, sir," he responded, scratching his armpit and ignoring my proffered hand.

Oh man! It's really hard to start a conversation with such people.

"How do you find this place? Is it okay? Mr Gagan said everything was inclusive except food so I just wanted to know..."

He guffawed before I could finish my sentence, "Yeah, everything is inclusive. They even supply girls!"

I returned the smile. "What's your opinion?" I asked again.

"Look dude. You'll be paying rent. So, you've to make the choice. What can I say? The only thing I can say for sure is that this PG is very centrally located. Whatever else has been promised to you is all false. The rest is your decision, your money and your destiny. Now if you can excuse me, I need to get back to my books. We'll meet in the evening," he said and shut the door on my face, this time a lot more politely.

Fuck man, what a guy! Very pragmatic, very studious, very straightforward and extremely rude.

We finalised the deal with Gagan a short while later and paid the brokerage. I unloaded my luggage from the car and put it in my room at the Dalal's before joining Dad for late lunch at Atul's house. Afterwards, Atul showed us my workplace before dropping me off at my new home. Luckily, the office wasn't too far from the PG.

It was six in the evening when I moved on from Lal to Dalal, I mean, from college life to corporate life. My roomie was still missing. I started unpacking my stuff to settle in my portion of the wardrobe. Suddenly, someone knocked. I opened the door to find two fellows staring at me. "Excuse me. Who are you?" said one of them.

"Your new roomie, Joy. Fresh from the Bay of Bengal," the studious guy yelled as he entered the common bathroom.

A hand came forward. "Hi. I'm Joydeep Biswas." The long-haired fellow introduced himself and sat on the other bed. He was in a 'regular fit' pair of denims and a baggy t-shirt.

"Hi, I'm Rishabh Agrawal," I said.

"Joy, tell him about your aunt. I loved her film," the studious fellow yelled out again.

The third guy who had been quiet till now laughed and patted Joydeep's shoulder. I couldn't hide my smile either. "Where are you from?" Joydeep asked, ignoring the remark.

"Lucknow," I replied and got back to arranging my stuff.

"Really? I love Tunday kababs. You must get them for me the next time you go back home," the studious guy ordered entering the room. He seemed to be searching for something. And then he snapped his fingers. Within a nanosecond, he'd pulled out a towel from under the pillow that quite clearly had been hidden and wiped his hands and face with it. "Use your own towel bugger," said Joydeep irritated. The third guy laughed and patted Joydeep again.

"I don't eat non-veg," I replied.

"Really? Then what are you living for? There's no life without non-veg!" preached the studious guy.

"I feel like puking when I see it," I said making a face.

"Dude, if you want to live longer, change your room. Your roommate eats fish 24/7, that too inside the room!" the studious guy said pressing his nostrils and making a pukey face. My face lost colour.

"What's your name?" I asked the studious guy.

"Me? I'm Sam."

"What's your full name?" I enquired.

"Why do you want to know? Are you interested in making me your Jija?" he retorted.

The third fellow laughed again. Even Joydeep started cackling. I got irritated and banged the door of the cupboard shut.

"Just joking dude. Don't take it seriously. My name is Sameer Sinha. Age – twenty-five officially, actually twenty-one. Hometown – Indore. College – DU. Profession – Advocate. Employed – Yes. Where – Shivaliks, an LPO. Experience – six months. CTC – Not your concern," Sam barked out his introduction in one breath.

That answered everything. I told you, he was very pragmatic, very studious, very straightforward and extremely rude.

"Are you a student or do you work somewhere?" the third fellow spoke for the first time.

I noticed his t-shirt as I turned to him. It unfurled the meaning of LIFE - *Looks Innocent Fcuks Extremum*.

"Tomorrow is my first day at work," I said looking at his punk style hair-do.

"Fresher?" all three asked in unison.

"Yeah."

"Where?" Joy asked.

"XLSL," I said expecting the very obvious next question.

"Does it have something to do with Microsoft?" The LIFE t-shirt guy asked, scratching his privates. His low-waisted jeans clearly revealed the seam of his Jockeys.

"No, it stands for XL Software Limited. It's a small service-based company that started two years ago. That's all I know about it. So please don't ask any more questions," I replied petulantly.

"That's it, my boy. That's what I like," Sam got up from Joy's bed and patted me on the back. He picked up the steel vessel that Mom had given me and opened its lid without asking. His eyes glittered as he saw a mountain of ping pong ball-sized laddoos stacked in it. He ate one and tossed two at his mates as if he was feeding pigeons. Fuck! I should have hidden it.

The third fellow got up offering a handshake. "Phani," he said.

"What's funny about that? I just told you what I knew," I said.

"No, my name is Phani. P H A N I," he spelt it out for me.

Both Joy and Sam laughed boisterously as Sam remarked, "Tell him your full funny name Phani sir."

"Bastard. Stop making fun of my surname," Phani hollered.

"What is your surname Phani?" I asked.

"Bhoski. Phani Kumar Bhoski."

Even I couldn't resist smiling.

"Listen, if my surname sounds like a damn abuse in your fucking language, I can't help it. It's my family name, so please be respectful," Phani begged.

"Okay Bhoski. I promise," Sam said touching his throat with a twinkle in his eye.

Joy purred and rolled on the bed as Bhoski… sorry Phani turned red.

"Where do you work Phani?" I asked him.

Sam answered on his behalf, "Monsieur Bhoski works as a management trainee at Lefebvre & Roux, a French company specializing in gas turbines. And, Biswas Babu works as a junior scientist at the world-famous pharma Oxyopia Labs. The best things about their companies are the incentives like lessons in French kissing and drugs from Saridon to Viagra."

Both Phani and Joy dropped their smiles and started abusing Sam. There was laughter all around. It brought back memories of my school days as at one point I felt Sam was Jingur's twin brother! He was damn good at screwing people. Someone you can never win in the war of words with. After all, he was an advocate.

Sam kept devouring my laddoos all this time, tossing a few to the other two as well. I had to tell him to stop, "Boss, don't eat much or you might get a bad stomach."

"Really? I don't think so," Sam said and squeezed another one into his bloody mouth.

I snatched the container back from him. "Okay that's enough. They belong to me," I spoke brusquely.

All three burst out laughing. "Haven't you ever lived in a hostel?" Joy asked.

"No, I haven't. Why?" I replied.

"You mean… you're a pappu," Sam said astonished.

"What? What did you just say?"

"I mean, this is the first time you've been out of home!" Sam cleared the interpretation of 'pappu' for me.

"Yeah. But there's always a first time."

"Dude, your first time is five years late," Sam said showing his stretched-out palm.

Phani changed the topic as things had started to become serious. "Stop it Sam. Rishabh, tell us about your family. What does your father do?"

Although I was irritated, I replied, "My Dad works for—" And the lights went out.

"These electricity guys are motherfuckers," Sam shrieked.

It was pitch dark. Phani broke the silence, "Yes Rishabh. Your father works for……?"

"The Electricity Department," I said in a soft voice.

I could hear stifled cachinnation from all three until Phani fumbled to switch on the backup CFL. All smiles vanished at once. The bastards enjoyed the joke until I asked, "What does your father do, Sam?"

"He's a doctor," Sam replied and started fiddling with his cellphone. "Give more details Sam," Joy said.

"Is he a vet?" I asked.

Sam didn't answer, but Phani did. "He looks for problems in places where the world looks for fun. He's a gynaecologist!" Sam looked for something to throw at Phani but got only a pillow.

We chatted for another hour or so. Phani was half Kannada-half Telugu and was from Hyderabad. He spoke very well and seemed to have a cultured background. He was in Gurgaon on deputation for two-and-a-half years. I got interested in visiting Hyderabad with him as Ruhana was soon to be there.

Joy was a sangfroid kind of a fellow who hardly reacted to any leg pulling. He was from Dhanbad and proud to be so, not just because it was his hometown, but because it had an IIT affiliated college. Sam of course, doesn't warrant an introduction. An introduction needed him more than he needed it.

It was 8 o'clock when the power was restored and I was famished. Thankfully, no abuses to electricity guys this time around!

"Where do you guys eat?" I asked.

"Lakki Da Dhaba on weekdays and Andhra Mess on weekends. You can join us... we go Dutch. We split the bill," Sam explained rubbing his stomach.

"I don't like South Indian food. Can we go to that dhaba you just mentioned?" I asked.

"Dude, those guys make lovely non-veg. Just try once. You'll definitely give up all these grass-eating habits," Sam urged in his own style.

After a bit of pleading, Phani relented.

Soon after, Joy changed into his green bermudas and the orange t-shirt hanging on the line right across the room. Man, he was an extremely hairy fellow, a clone of a popular hero from Bollywood. He had organised for a tiffin service to deliver food to him so he didn't come with us. I was happy not to have to see fish on the first day itself.

We reached Lakki Da Dhaba tripling on Phani's bike. Sam made me sit in between and sat so intimately that I could feel his privates rubbing against me. Lakki Da Dhaba was a roadside eatery full of bachelors like us. Boys aged ten to fifteen, each one addressed as Chhotu, took our orders. We ordered kadhai-paneer, yellow dal and mixed veg along with a dozen tandoori rotis.

Phani's cellphone rang as we were waiting for the food to arrive. He stared at it for a second and then got up to take the call.

"Girlfriend," clarified Sam to me.

"Really?" I asked.

"Yup, long distance relationship. He talks for hours and hours."

I became silent thinking of how I'd loved one girl all my life and had had sex with another.

Phani returned ten minutes later as our order arrived. That first meal made me aware of the wolfish rapacity of those human dinosaurs. Either they shat out everything the next morning or were born ectomorphs.

I woke up the next morning to find both the bathrooms occupied. Sam kept kicking the door and abusing as Phani had crossed his time limit. Yes, there were time slots for the toilet! If you crossed the limit by more than two minutes, the next in line had the right to abuse and curse you or even break in. I looked at the clock. It was quarter past eight. I had slept at least an hour more than I should have. I knocked on the door of the bathroom inside my room. "Joy, how much more time will you need?" I asked.

Joy closed the tap and screamed back, "I'll take a minimum of twenty minutes. I've just come in."

I went to the other one as Sam shrieked, "Bhoski! Open the door, you sisterfucker. I'll puncture your bike if you don't come out within a minute."

"Sam, please let me use it. Today is my first day in office," I begged.

"No way Pappu. It will be my last day in office if I'm not on time. My boss is a big motherfucker. He comes at eleven but wants me to be there by nine-thirty," Sam banged on the door hard.

Phani emerged semi-naked from the bathroom. A gush of stale smelly air hit our nostrils. He laughed like a monster and greeted, "*Bonjour, monsieur l'Avocat!*" Good morning, Mr Advocate!

Sam replied catching Phani by his towel, "*Obtenir perdu, trou du cul.*" Phani removed Sam's hand from his towel and ran towards my room's bathroom. He knocked with a whistle and Joy opened the door. He hopped in and bolted the door with huge screams of 'Baby, baby, baby…'

Fuck! Faggots, I thought.

"Bloody gays," I heard Sam mumble.

"What did you just say to Phani?" I asked him.

"Get lost asshole," he replied.

"Hey, mind your language," I warned, offended by the comment.

Sam smirked and said, "That's what I said to Bhoski. But if you like it, keep it for yourself."

"You know French?" I asked surprisingly.

"Only abuses," Sam clarified and started going into the bathroom covering his nose as if entering a heavily putrefied morgue.

I begged him again, my eyes brimming with tears, "Please Sam. Please. It's my first day at work. I beg you."

Sam relented, "Only ten minutes. Just dry-clean, don't bathe. Also shit in office under the air-conditioner. This Bhoski has already exploded an atom bomb. I don't want another. If you don't come out in ten minutes, I'll bolt the door from outside. Then Nawab Sahib would have to take a train back to *Nakhlau* this evening itself."

I thanked Sam and freshened up in the quickest possible time of my life. I vacated the bathroom in precisely eight-and-a-half minutes.

I reached office sharp at nine. Although it had a princely entrance, the cubicles were congested and quite strangely, there was no canteen. The staff strength was somewhere in between eighty and hundred. The weirdest thing was that there wasn't a single woman in the office – from the CEO to the peon, everyone was male, even the receptionist! After completing the joining formalities, the HR introduced me to the team I was supposed to work with. Most of my colleagues looked at me suspiciously when they heard I was a fresher. XLSL had never visited any campus, nor had it conducted any walk-ins in the past six months. I tried my best to fudge the remaining enquiries. My boss was just about ten years older than I was and wasted no time in giving me a lecture on .NET, a programming language I'd just heard about from Aarti. I was allotted a workstation and my task for the week was to go through the project code. I sweated under the chilly air-conditioner thinking about what I'd do next week when I was pushed into the project head on. I had a strong premonition that I'd sooner or later be kicked out of XLSL. Sam's prediction of my catching a train to Lucknow seemed to be coming true pretty soon.

It was blissful at the PG and stressful at office. Within a month, I was moved to IT services looking at my extraordinary skills with the code. My job was to install/uninstall programs on employee workstations and do some wiring stuff in the server room. The only good thing was that I had unrestricted access to public mail services which helped me connect with Ruhana. She'd joined work at Hyderabad and was at a training program. She was enjoying her professional life, but she said she missed me a lot, a lot more than I did. We exchanged phone numbers and I fed it into my not-so-great new cellphone.

During this time, I'd also learnt a few other things about my new friends. Unlike me, each of them had a specific goal in life. My life was aimless. I only wanted Aarti but that too got messed up.

Joy wanted to buy a car and a home for his parents. He'd seen them sacrifice a lot and was determined to do this for them. He also paid his cousin's tuition fee from his salary. I was too selfish to even think about something like that. Phani came from a decent financial background as his father was a scale five officer in a nationalized bank. His goal was to become an entrepreneur and if possible, kiss his girlfriend atop the Eiffel Tower! Sam wanted to become a youth icon. He chose law because his father had lost their ancestral land in a family dispute. Sometimes strong feelings of revenge can take you places. That boy had a spark and I was already his fan.

▼

I'd been living with these guys for about eleven months now. I'd even brought my bike from Lucknow so that we could go to places in Delhi as well as commute within Gurgaon. Public transport was hell in the city!

Joy requested me to shift temporarily to either Phani or Sam's room because he was expecting his parents. I agreed only on one condition – that he treated me to two movies and introduced me to his three hot friends about whom I fantasized! He agreed to the movies, but reduced the girl count to just one. Huh!

Joy's parents were to arrive on Sunday. He'd cleared up the room and hidden all the illegal stuff, which was mostly mine. I moved into Phani's room. He talked on the phone till almost one in his native language while I surfed porn on his laptop. I also snuck into his private folder to catch a glimpse of his mysterious girlfriend. Fuck! She was hot. I cursed Phani's good luck and got back to my favourite pastime. He finished his long-distance call, guzzled half a litre of water, put his phone on charge and yawned like a buffalo. "Dude. It's time to sleep. Shut down the laptop. I'm switching off the light."

"Just ten more minutes. These chicks are amazing," I replied hiding the bulge inside my lowers with the pillow.

"Hey. Clean up all the cookies before shutting down. This is my office laptop. I don't want any trouble."

Just then I found an extremely hot babe with three men. I turned the laptop towards Phani, "Just look at this. I'm jealous of these guys."

Phani looked at it for a while and yawned once again, "I'm sleepy dude. You enjoy yourself." He then did the unimaginable. He stripped in front of me.

"Fuck man! Can't you change in the bathroom!" I shrieked.

"I don't have that much energy left. And what's the big deal. You've the same thing too," he said coolly.

"Fuck you, bastard. You filthy asshole! Get your clothes on," I said pulling off my gaze from Phani's privates.

Phani laughed and dived into the bed pulling up his lowers. I switched off his laptop after cleaning up the cookies and the recent items list. The bastard had totally spoilt my mood.

Joy's parents arrived the next day. We trooped into the room sombrely and introduced ourselves, giving an impression of being extremely cultured boys. Joy's Mom was silent most of the time as she only understood Bengali. We just smiled at each other whenever our eyes met. Joy's Dad had stayed in Delhi when he was young, so his language was okay. He was tall, dark and unbelievably, miles away from baldness. He was an interesting person to interact with.

He asked Joy openly if he had a girlfriend, "Joy, it's high time son that you go out on dates. When will you have fun? At my age?"

I'd have screwed every girl in town had my Dad been so liberal. Joy kept nodding as his Dad lectured us on how to woo girls. Joy's Mom got quite uncomfortable with her husband's salacious speech and made an excuse about wanting to meet the landlady. I shifted to sit on Joy's bed next to Uncle to escape Sam and Phani's bum-pinching. All this time, Joy was leaning on the bathroom door as he was about to take a bath. But the fear of what we'd say to his parents had kept him waiting. Soon, the topic of cricket came up. Sam was a huge buff who followed each and every match being played anywhere on the planet, thanks to his newly-purchased portable TV. He turned into an encyclopaedia blessing us with CNN type coverage of international and domestic cricket, of both the men's and women's teams. Thankfully, gully cricket was spared.

Joy's Dad said, "I tell you boys, Ganguly is going to make a strong comeback."

"No way Uncle! His days are over. He's history," Sam remarked.

"History? Son, he's the best captain India has ever had. He's just become a victim of some ugly internal politics. I'm sure he'll come out crushing all conspiracies."

"Huh. Have you seen the advertisements? He's literally crying, asking people not to forget him. His career is screwed. You cannot live in Rome and fight with the Pope. He fingered the management and they've caught him by the nuts," Sam didn't mince his words.

That statement fucked up everything. Sam had done what he shouldn't have. First, he insulted an undoubtedly top notch sportsperson. Second, he did it in front of his most loyal supporter. And third, he broke our tacit agreement of no vulgar speech.

There was pin drop silence in the room for about five seconds. We suddenly heard the tap pissing into the bucket. Joy had smartly tiptoed into the bathroom sometime during this heated conversation. Phani picked up a women's magazine and hid his face behind its pages. Sam, the culprit, pretended he got a call, "Hello, hello, your voice is breaking... wait, let me go up to the roof," he screamed over his phone and left the room. I was the only one left.

Uncle looked at me, "Is this the kind of language you guys use? I thought you all belonged to good families. I'm going to take Joy out of this PG. You all will spoil my innocent boy."

He continued, "And for your information son, Ganguly is a player of unparalleled class. He is a prince. He made careers of nobodies and taught us how to be aggressive. He's a gem whose glitter hasn't gone well in the eyes of some idiots."

I nodded in shame and apologized on Sam's behalf, adding superlatives to Ganguly's portfolio. Phani kept hiding behind the magazine, but I could sense his sniggers. As we left the room fifteen minutes later, Uncle gave his final blow, "Phani, Bengali books are read like all other books. We don't read them upside down."

Phani didn't answer as we rushed out of the room. Joy was still having a bath – probably the longest bath he'd ever taken in his life. Sam the bastard, the fucker, the... in short, all abuses bundled into one was rapping "Remember The Name" at the top of his voice in his room. We barged in, bolted the door and made Sam forget his own bloody name.

That night Phani stripped again. I was very uncomfortable, even though I knew that he was straight. He was just taking advantage of my not being a hosteller ever. So, the next day I moved out of his room and took refuge in Sam's den. Sam, surprisingly, had a very strict schedule when it came to studies. Two hours of night study was mandatorily mandatory, no matter what.

Sam commenced his night activities with the newspaper, devouring it in fifteen minutes flat, ten of them spent on sports.

This was followed by five-minute high-pitched chat with his family, followed by a few short calls to three randomly selected friends. Sam always believed in remaining connected. The telephone calls were succeeded by ten minutes of fusion music which Sam claimed charged up his batteries and cleared his head, although it drained mine. And then started his two hours of focussed study shrouded in graveyard silence. I wasn't allowed to switch on the TV, cough, sneeze or even fart.

I checked Sam's phone while he was studying something called *ad valorem* tax (VAT). His contact list was endless. I had not met as many people in my life as there were in his contact book. All the girls were saved under the group 'Cutiepies' with all the names in code. Only a bastard like Sam could do something like this. I checked for my name. It wasn't there so I switched his cell to silent mode and called from my phone. Two words flashed on the screen – 'Pappu calling.' Cursing him, I updated my name to Pappa. I hope his Dad didn't get offended.

Two hours later, Sam slammed down his fat book and exclaimed loudly, "Adjourned. Time to sleep." He jumped into bed, taking off his hoodie to reveal yet another torn vest.

"What are you smiling for? Did I miss a joke?" Sam asked seeing me dimple as I read the newspaper.

"Just go through this article," I replied passing on the paper to him.

Sam scanned it in a jiffy and abused in a deafening tone, "You're fucking sick. An innocent girl gets gang raped and you think it's worth smiling. Shame on you Pappu. Shame on you!"

"Hey, I was just appreciating the author's writing skills," I said.

"I see the traits of a rapist in you. That smile of yours clearly reflects that. For you, women are nothing more than objects of pleasure," he said looking disgusted with me.

Before I could defend myself, he added, "As for the writer, I think he's a pervert too. Instead of being sensitive about something so serious, he has sensationalised it by intentionally using erotic language with elaborate descriptions to titillate people like you. Just look at this supplement too. Full of nude firangs and their sexual exploits. These... these are not newspapers. This is soft porn. I think all you people – this asshole journalist, his bloody editor and you – should all be prosecuted. You guys are no less than rapists."

Sam crumpled the newspaper and tossed it into the dustbin. "Great speech, Mr Advocate. But I think you're overreacting," I said as soon as I got a chance to speak.

"Overreacting? You really think so? Suck my dick, you loser," Sam shot back.

"Fuck you, asshole. Enough of your moral science lecture. Just because I'm not saying anything, it doesn't mean you can cross the line," I retaliated.

"Okay okay. Cool down. I'm sorry for that filthy comment. That was impulsive. But I still don't think I overreacted. Sexual assault is not just an act of violence – it's a heinous crime. If given a chance I want to be an amicus in this case. I'll get the section 376 amended. The guilty should be chemically castrated. A man loses all the battles inside him if he loses his masculinity. Death is too easy for these bastards. The punishment should be mentally agonizing and humiliating for life. Once castrated, these buggers should be incarcerated for fourteen years with no clemency whatsoever. Any organization that fucks around asking for amnesty on humanitarian grounds should be heavily penalized. Only such hardcore judgements can set things right and provide what I call true justice."

I turned my eyes onto the ceiling fan as Sam stopped.

"Pappu, look here. Listen to me. This is free advice... start respecting women or else you'll never be able to become a complete man," Sam said putting his arm around my shoulder. I couldn't gather the courage to look into his eyes. So, I just nodded. A short silence ensued.

"Okay man. Let's change the topic. Don't make my room a graveyard. Tell me, why did you leave Bhoski's room?" Sam quickly changed the topic of discussion.

"I wasn't comfortable there," I finally broke my silence.

"Why? Did he do something to you?" Sam said, his eyebrows knotted.

"No, nothing like that," I said hiding the tale of his nude shows.

"Whatever the reason, you've come on your own to my room. And now because you've got asylum, I need you to show your gratitude. Will you pay in cash or in kind? *Quid Pro Quo*, you see," said Sam winking.

"Bastard! Get your hands off me," I howled removing his hand which had started to roll down my stomach.

"Oh, come on! Don't act like a typical Indian housewife. Not tonight, darling. I'm not in the mood. I'm tired... blah, blah, blah...," Sam gripped my shoulders extremely hard.

"You bastard. Let me go, you sisterfucker!"

"Hey, come on, be my mate tonight. I promise you won't be disappointed. Just give me one chance," Sam said puckering his lips as he came close to mine.

I kicked him in the shins. "What happened? The gang rape news was fun, but this isn't?" Sam said holding his leg.

"So, you're trying to teach me a lesson!" I shouted.

"That god will teach. I'm just trying to lighten up the mood. If you don't want to, please leave. This is my room, not yours."

I had no option but to compromise. For the next five days, I slept in his smelly embrace. Thankfully, he was neither homosexual nor a rapist. He just enjoyed life and made complete use of the slightest possible opportunity to have fun.

Once Joy's parents left, I forced him to keep his promise. He took me to two Hollywood movies and introduced me to one of his hot friends. Somehow, she didn't give me much attention which Joy claimed was primarily because I wasn't hot enough to waste time and body on.

▼

It was Joy's birthday and my first job anniversary. The bastard hadn't told me the previous year as I was new and no one wanted to invite an unknown person to a party. He treated us to dinner at Get Bowled, a resto-bar with the ambience of a cricket ground. The waiters were dressed in jerseys of the Indian cricket team and the cashier sported an umpire's outfit while the menu card had cricket crazy names. Sam ordered everything non-veg, special mention – Australian keema, while Phani ordered everything alcoholic, even the appetisers! Joy dolefully calculated the expected bill while I wondered what to order. "What happened? Feeling bad for the chicken?" Sam asked.

"Why didn't you order something veg?"

"Come on Pappu! Eat it for Joy. You'll definitely like it," Sam requested in his signature style.

"And drink as well. Just do it man. Do it for Joy," Phani added.

Joy shrugged and then put in his half-hearted appeal too. Both Sam and Phani kept cajoling me until I agreed. Thankfully, they didn't ask me to smoke. Assuring me that it was chicken; those bastards tricked me into nibbling lamb, the gentle animal whose poem I recited in kindergarten. What happened next was the second-best dysentery of my life (the typhoid one still scored the highest). That historical night, I tipped the barman five hundred bucks. After all, I'd just had a 'Sehwag Cracker' followed by a 'Murali Doosra' complemented with two 'McGrath Snorters'. Quite apparently, I just *got bowled*.

▼

They say once a tiger tastes human blood, it becomes a man-eater. I'd tasted animal meat and now nothing in the universe could stop me from becoming a rapacious monster! As far as my friends were concerned, Sam was delighted to have transformed a Pappu's life. Phani was glad to have found a drinking mate. Joy was also happy to be free to eat his meals in my presence. But soon, his happiness turned to misery as I used to gobble up his fish curry whenever he wasn't home.

I also started accompanying Sam and Phani to Andhra Mess for non-veg meals. Earlier on, I was offended when Phani called out 'Pappu' publicly, but then I learnt that dal is called 'pappu' in Telugu. Sam, the established bastard, made full use of this golden opportunity. Whenever the servers would bring the dal to us, he would ask me in front of them, "Pappu, you need pappu?" I stopped going to the Mess until Sam swore not to call me by that name to deliberately insult me publicly.

Diwali arrived and I took leave to go home. Mom was happy to see me four to five kilos heavier than I was when she saw me during Holi. She thought I was eating well. But the fact was that I was eating everything that came my way. I was blindly following Sam's ideology about not letting other species take over this planet and bringing them to the dining table instead.

Orkut

The results of the first appraisal of my professional career were out in April 2007. I got a miserly four percent hike after being rated 'satisfactory'. It was extremely demotivating. I got even more upset seeing the hikes of Phani and Joy. But there was one more person who was hyper-dejected. It was Sam. He didn't get a raise at all.

All this while I was constantly in touch with Ruhana. She was happy that she'd got a handsome seventeen percent raise. I missed her, but probably not as much as she missed me – maybe because my PG mates had filled my life with fun. But yes, I sincerely craved the sex.

▼

Life moved gaily until an office colleague introduced me to Orkut, a widely popular social network. I joined it right away to connect with friends as well as to try my luck in trapping some hot chicks. I was excited to find many of my childhood buddies already registered on it and added everybody, irrespective of whether I liked them or not. Ashu had made it to MIT and was now employed with a US MNC called Romano & Schieffer. Jingur was with HSBC Singapore while Sarah was doing her MD from Pune and quite sadly, her relationship status said 'Committed'. Karan rejected my request while Kaddu, Aarti, Ben and Priyanka from DST were untraceable. I called Ruhana to update her about this awesome discovery, but she lectured me on how it was a total waste of time and I should not get into it at all. She had joined and deleted her account ages ago. I promised her that I would, but soon forgot about it.

Phani was already on Orkut, but never mentioned it to us, probably because his girlfriend was also on it and he didn't want us to communicate with her. Sam and Joy also joined the networking site and Sam created a group called 'Dalal's Gay PG'. As was expected, none of us joined the group till he agreed to rename it 'Dalal's Great PG'.

Joy was shrewd – he would write and receive scraps in Bengali so that we couldn't understand what they were about. He scrapped a lot with someone called Oiendrilla. He told us that she was a childhood buddy and nothing more. But we were quite sure there was more to it because his phone was almost always unusually busy. He then started spending weekends at some previously unknown Uncle's place in Delhi. We tried to find out more but he kept all his call records, inbox, drafts and reminders empty. There was no Oiendrilla either in the picture gallery or on the contact list. All this bullshit was getting on our nerves.

In the meantime, I went on two blind dates, which, in hindsight, were a total waste of time and money. But yes, I did have to bear two SRK movies because the girls loved him a lot.

▼

It was a life-altering morning. Yes, it indeed was. I'd received a friend request from none other than Aarti. I was reluctant to accept her request, but then temptation took over, and I spent the rest of the day going through her profile. Aarti was married to someone called Rajat Java who also happened to be an IT guy (both by profession as well as the family name!). They were settled in the US, that too in the Silicon Valley, a place responsible for the software shit around the world. I was just happy that Aarti wasn't with that bastard Imran. She'd been married for the last one year or so and her profile showed her marriage pics. Her husband was handsome and looked extremely studious. I felt a tug at my heart seeing her with another man and thoughts of becoming SRK of *Darr* came to my mind. But then I remembered the tragic ending of the movie.

I badly wanted to write Aarti a scrap, but couldn't muster up the courage to even say hi. That night I went to sleep thinking of Aarti and all that had happened between us.

The next day I received a scrap from Aarti saying – *Hi Rishu. Where have you been? It's been a long time. I've missed you a lot.*

Her scrap led to a long list of scraps from others I called friends, each one enquiring who the hot chick was and why she was missing me like hell. I was really embarrassed and deleted them all. I sent Aarti a private message instead –

Hi Aarti. I'm fine. It's nice to see you married – your hubby is very handsome. I'm sorry for asking this, but what happened with Imran? I thought you were a couple.

Aarti replied the next day.

Thanks a lot, Rishu. Let's catch up sometime when I come to India. I'll inform about my plans beforehand so that we can meet. And let's not discuss my past please – Rajat is my present and my future. He's a great guy and I love him very much.

I understood that something must have gone terribly wrong between Aarti and Imran. That's why she wasn't comfortable to even mention him. I hope she and Imran hadn't crossed the line like Ruhana and I had.

A week later Aarti posted that Jackie, her horrid dog, had died. I celebrated the news with a quarter bottle of Old Monk later in the evening.

Our e-conversation continued for days, but neither of us tried to exchange numbers. There wasn't any point starting it all over again, that too at ISD rates. I was satisfied with my current life while Aarti too appeared cheerful and quite possibly, satisfied.

▼

It was a balmy evening when I received a call from Ruhana telling me that she was engaged and was to be married in three months and move to Dubai. I congratulated her and promised to attend the ceremony for sure. Ruhana expressed her desire to meet me one more time before she got married. I too wanted to see her as Aarti's virtual presence had made me quite twitchy. I just wanted to crawl into her arms, even if it was for a day.

▼

Phani's deputation got over in April 2008 after a short extention of three-four months. He was to leave the PG soon. We were all feeling lousy at our group disintegrating, but Phani promised to be in touch. But the fact was that he was leaving permanently in a day or two.

I decided to take the opportunity to see Ruhana in Hyderabad and booked my air tickets along with Phani's. He was happy that I was accompanying him to his hometown. Of course, he didn't know the actual reason. Phani was given a grand farewell with tequila shots and grilled duck. The next morning, Phani and I took the Kingfisher Red flight from Indira Gandhi International Airport. Though the flight attendants were implausibly hot, the journey was distressingly turbulent. I finally confided to Phani that I was actually going to Hyderabad to meet a female friend one last time before she got married. Phani was shocked and started asking many questions. I answered all of them without mentioning Aarti even once. Phani promised to arrange for a place for me to meet Ruhana in private, when he was satisfied with my answers.

From the swanky Rajiv Gandhi International Airport, we headed straight to SR Nagar to Phani's house. His parents were very happy to have him back and also took very good care of me. The only problem was the overuse of the word pappu while we all had our meals.

After a post-lunch afternoon nap, Phani and his younger brother Mani took me out for a city tour. Hyderabad was pretty much like old Lucknow, but the biryani tasted far better. And Karachi Bakery's *dilkush* was straight from heaven. I called Ruhana later and told her that I was in Hyderabad. She didn't believe me until I called from a PCO. She got desperate to see me, but I managed to convince her to meet up the next morning.

The next day, Phani took me to East Marredpally and handed me the keys to his Uncle's villa. His Uncle lived in Vancouver and had recently decided to put the house on sale. While I took a round of the lavish dwelling, Phani removed the sheets from the sofas. It was twenty minutes past one and I was supposed to return by four as my flight was at eight in the evening. I called Ruhana and got Phani to explain the directions to the villa. Before leaving, Phani said, "Dude, I know why you're meeting this girl here. Keep this – you'll need it!" and he slid a packet of condoms into my chest pocket.

I crimsoned but didn't say anything. Ruhana called back ten minutes later. Although Phani wanted to see Ruhana, I begged him to leave so as not to embarrass her. The bastard left only after I promised to click some of Ruhana's pictures for him to see.

Ruhana walked in five minutes later. She was dressed in a psychedelic flowery maxi dress and had a coffee-brown purse slung on her shoulder. Quite surprisingly, she was wearing glasses, which suited her personality quite a lot. Somehow, she looked thinner than before. Either her job demanded a lot from her or she was dieting to look good on her first night. Whatever it was, she was looking beautiful. The only thing that hadn't undergone change was her hands. They were as delicate and pretty as I remembered them.

Ruhana was so excited to see me that she made it extremely difficult for me to even bolt the door! She embraced me from behind and kept kissing my shoulder until I said, "Okay, okay. I got it. You missed me a lot."

"Yes, fatso. I missed you a lot," Ruhana said kissing my cheek.

"You called me fatso?"

"Of course. You're almost twenty kilos heavier than you used to be," she said.

"I'm eating well, but I'm not fat," I said pretending to be miffed.

Ruhana smirked and said, "Whatever it is, I still love you, my teddy bear."

I turned around and hugged her hard. Emotions were pouring out of our bodies. We looked at each other and then, without saying a word, our lips entwined. We kissed passionately for a while until Ruhana drew back. "Is this what you've called me for?" she asked.

"No," I replied abashedly, although the reason was yes.

Ruhana took my hand as we settled on the sofa. "Rishu, I wanted to meet you before I started a new life. I really wish that life was with you."

"Me too," I said sliding my other hand around her waist.

"Hey! Stop it," Ruhana removed my hand from her waist.

"Oh, come on! Don't tell me you don't want it to happen," I said grabbing her waist once again.

"No, not at all! I'm engaged and getting married next month. That would be cheating," she said showing me her engagement ring.

"Tsk. Don't spoil the mood. Come on, be a sport. No one will ever get to know about it," I said and started kissing her on her chest. I then quickly slid her maxi up to her thighs and started to tug at her panties.

Ruhana slapped me back. "You're insane Rishu. Insane! I thought we were each other's support. That is why I came to meet you. But I was wrong. All you need is sex. You're such a pervert. Get away from me," Ruhana pushed me away looking devastated and got up to leave.

My craving for a woman's body had made me a beast. I couldn't let go of one when it was so close to becoming reality. I caught Ruhana's arm and tried to make her sit back on the sofa. When she resisted, I got up and caught her by her hair. "You're not going anywhere until we do it. Do you hear that?" I roared and pushed Ruhana hard onto the sofa. Her glasses fell on the floor and broke.

"Let go of me, you scoundrel," Ruhana shrieked.

I covered her mouth with my hand and sat astride her. Ruhana resisted hard but I was out of my mind. Within seconds I'd ripped off her panties and pushed myself in the tangle of her naked legs. Ruhana cried for mercy and begged me to let her go. She tried to push me aside, but I was too heavy. I kept doing what I'd to without even bothering about any protection or someone coming in on hearing her cries. I knew it wasn't consensual, but the feebleness of mind had made me a monster. After five minutes of fiery pounding, my grunts ceased and I rolled off her with a satisfied smile on my sweat-soaked face. Ruhana lay beside me, tears trickling down her kohl-rimmed eyes. "O Ruhana. You're a damn good fuck. I feel like a man everytime I stick it in you," I sighed as I got up to wear my clothes.

Ruhana was lifeless. Her eyelids weren't fluttering. But her chest was going up and down. At least she was breathing. When she didn't move for a while, I got a bit worried and crouched down to check on her. I clapped my hands and snapped my fingers to draw her attention. But she didn't react. So, I touched her face and then her chest. She didn't respond this time either. She'd probably gone in a state of shock. I got perturbed. My head was between my hands. I had no clue on how to revive her. My pulse went awry as the clock ticked on and on and Ruhana showed absolutely no signs of recovery. She just lay motionless on the floor. But I had to bring her back to normal. I thought maybe a second shock might work. So, I got down on the floor and positioned myself on top of her once again. The moment I entered her, her eyes blinked. She rotated them around until she found me. I gave her a smile of relief. She just stared back in an unusually sinister sort of way. And then without the slightest hint, Ruhana punched me on the face. I immediately moved out of her. Before I could understand, Ruhana sprang up on her feet. She picked up an ashtray and then pounced on me like a wounded tigress. I got hit a couple of times on the face. They were strong meaty blows. Consequently, everything in the world went numb! My skin opened up to make way for a meandering current of blood. I fell to the floor, holding my head. Ruhana watched as I writhed in pain. She threw the ashtray onto the floor and corrected her tattered clothes.

"You're not the person I loved. You're a filthy pig. A bloody sex-starved animal. I always thought you understood me. Maybe even loved me. But I was wrong. All you ever wanted from me was sex, and only sex. What Aarti did to you was absolutely right. You don't deserve a woman. You're just a fucking loser," Ruhana howled at me between her sobs.

She was hysterical. She clicked pictures of my nakedness on her phone. I could do nothing to stop her from doing that. Her blow had almost paralysed me. I was still struggling to sit up. There was blood all around and my vest was stained to a great extent by now. I was feeling nauseous and dizzy with every passing moment. Ruhana picked up her purse and broken glasses and opened the door to leave. "Just in case you try to contact me or harass me further, I'll put these pics on the net. If needed, I'll even go to the cops," she threatened, wiping the tears rolling down her face.

"Ruhana, please forgive me. I didn't want to hurt you," I cried, my hand still nursing my head.

"You don't deserve forgiveness. You don't deserve anyone. People like you who see women as commodities don't deserve to be loved. If my god is hearing this, I call upon him to give you a destitute life; a life where your dear ones will desert you. May my curse befall this man *al-Malik*," Ruhana looked up at the ceiling closing her eyes momentarily and then left the house slamming the door hard.

I kept lying naked on the floor as thoughts of remorse crept up on my mind. I had never intended to do what had just happened. But now what had been done couldn't be undone. I had made an irreversible mistake. I'd actually raped Ruhana – committed a felony beyond absolution. As I cursed myself again and again, the phone rang. It was Phani.

"Dude, why're you sounding so low? What happened?" he asked on hearing my sombre hello.

"Nothing, these girls talk so much emotional stuff," I lied.

"So, you guys didn't do it?" Phani asked.

"No, she just wanted to see me. I'm very disturbed right now. I'll be back in an hour or so. See you then," I said and disconnected the call.

Phani's call made me quite nervous. I'd already lost a lot of blood and didn't want him to come over and worsen the already ballsed up situation. So, I picked myself up from the floor, took off my vest and tied it around my head to minimize the blood loss. It took a lot of effort for me to wear my clothes back. I got out of the villa taking care not to let the blood drip around and then took an auto to the nearest clinic. And guess what, I got three stitches – just like Aarti and Karan had. I think we're even now.

An hour later, I went back to the villa after purchasing a few toiletries along with a rag and a floor cleaner. I was too afraid to leave evidence behind. Afterwards I made a quick inspection to ensure that everything was put in place just the way it was when I first entered the house. I carefully locked the front door and then walked two kilometeres to dump the remaining stuff of my purchase into a faraway roadside bin. I hailed a taxi to Phani's residence.

Phani and his family were shocked to see the bandage on my head. Phani had lied to them that I'd gone to visit one of my college seniors. I added to that lie by saying that my auto met with an accident while I was coming back home. That is why I had to take a taxi. Phani was still sceptical. He kept asking what exactly had happened, but I couldn't get myself to tell him the truth. I took a false oath on my mother to assure him that I wasn't lying. I even returned the condoms in an intact condition just to exonerate myself of any wrong-doing.

I couldn't gather the courage to call or message Ruhana to apologise before I left Hyderabad. She had my pictures and I didn't want to risk being humiliated publicly or beaten with batons in a jail cell. Whatever humiliation happened, it happened behind closed doors, all to her and nothing to me.

After my return to Gurgaon, I narrated the same made-up story to Sam and Joy as well as to anybody who asked me about my injury. I was actually worried about two things – people getting suspicious if my story had variations, or worse, Ruhana taking me to the court of justice. I even stopped reading the newspaper because there were reports of rape and molestation almost every day. It was total anarchy and NCR had suddenly become the rape capital of India, I being one of the free-roaming assailants.

▼

Five months passed. All this while, Sam was busy muguping his new tome in Hindu Law by Mulla, Joy dallying with his secret Orkut friend and Phani singing love songs to his girlfriend almost a thousand miles away from us. Friends who'd once made life rocking for me suddenly seemed to have drifted oceans apart. Life at office also sucked. No leaves were being sanctioned because attrition had touched an all-time high. I was homesick, but couldn't go home. Though my fears had lessened, Ruhana's curse haunted me every now and then. On top of that, Aarti's sentimental messages had made my life hell.

One day, Aarti went missing from Orkut. Her status updates dried up. Her personalized messages stopped coming. Even her album uploads froze. I don't know what happened. I hoped she was okay.

Goof–up

It was Diwali vacations and I was seeing my family after a very long time. Mom was surprised to find me leaner this time. All the result of the taxing time I'd undergone in the past few months.

On Diwali day, Dad called me to his room and said, "Rishu, we've received a few good marriage proposals for you. Your mother and I have shortlisted three of them. Take a look." He handed me an envelope.

I became very self-conscious and said, "I don't want to get married now. It's too early. I'm only twenty-six."

"Look son. It takes time to finalize things. We need to start now – because it will take almost a year to get things done," Dad tried to convince me.

"Even then…"

He cut me short, "Just go through these profiles. I've invited the parents to our house tomorrow and the day after."

I opened the envelope and took out a photograph to look at. "Take them to your room for a better look. Let me know which one you like," Dad said.

It was extremely awkward. What was there to look at 'better' in those sari-clad girls who were smiling as if they'd bagged a movie

160

role? Still, I took them to my room and looked at each of them *properly*. I liked two of them, basically because of their figures.

During the next two days, I was showcased in front of three sets of unknown people. They all had one thing in common. Apart from extracting other personal details, everyone wanted to know about my take-home salary, annual hikes, onsite options and office timings, as if I was an HR executive offering a job to their daughters.

Later at night, Mom and Dad had lengthy discussions about the 'prospective parties'.

Nothing happened till the time I was at Lucknow. Two days after coming back to Gurgaon, I got a call from Dad. He asked me to meet up with a girl who also happened to be working in Gurgaon. She was one of the two girls I had liked in the snaps. But I couldn't exactly remember which one! Dad gave me her number and asked me to fix a meeting place.

I was mortified. Calling an unknown girl and asking to meet up to judge our mating compatibility was quite a weird feeling. I searched for her on Orkut, but couldn't trace her. There were hundreds of profiles with the same name. I finally dialled her number with trembling hands. "Hello," answered a sweet voice.

"Hello. My name is Rishabh. I got your number from my Dad which he probably got from your Dad. I'm sure you know why I'm calling at this hour of the night," I said.

The girl chuckled at my statement and said, "Oh hi Rishabh! Yeah, I know. Marriage proposal! So, where do we meet?"

Fuck! This girl is quite open! I thought and said, "Will Ambience Mall be okay?"

"Yeah. That's okay. Tomorrow, 7 p.m. Alright?" she asked.

"Yep. Come directly to CCD. I'll meet you there," I said. CCD was still in my blood.

"Okay bye!"

"Bye!"

The next evening, I reached Ambience Mall dressed in the most decent clothes I had. The mall was brimming over with good looking babes. Suddenly, a buxom beauty in a knee length pink skirt and sleeveless white top crossed my path. I got a strong urge to shag her as she flicked her romantic tresses back from her face. Wonder which lucky bastards get such sizzling bods! Two minutes later, my cell rang. It was my date calling to ask my whereabouts. I picked up and said, "Hi. I'm already here. Just next to CCD."

"Me too. What are you wearing?" she asked.

"Clothes!" I said idiotically.

She laughed at my glib response. Just then I felt somebody tap my shoulder from the back. I turned around to come face-to-face with the pink skirt hot chick I was fantasising about.

"Rishabh?" she said as I got lost in her beauty.

"Excuse me, are you Rishabh?" she asked again.

"Yeah... yeah, I'm Rishabh," I stammered covering the mouthpiece of my phone.

"Hi, I'm Priyanka," she said proffering her hand. Fuck man! She was the girl I was being asked to marry. I mentally made children with her that very moment.

I took her soft hand into my dark hairy hand. We shook hands and then grabbed a table as the boys in the vicinity drooled over her.

"What would you like to have?" I asked passing her the menu card.

Priyanka put her huge white purse along with an expensive looking cellphone on the table and took the menu card from me. Her phone somehow slipped and I heard a muted "Oh shit!" as I bent down to pick it up. Unintentionally my eyes fell on her legs. Fuck! She'd a flawless pair of waxed legs, something that made me remember Sarah. I scanned them for a little bit longer than I should have and finally sat up to return her phone. She checked it out like a concerned mother. "Is everything alright?" I enquired.

"Yeah. Absolutely."

"Good. So, have you decided what you'd like to have?"

Priyanka took the names of the things I was aware of. Thanks to my CCD days with Aarti.

"What about you?" she asked.

"Same as yours," I replied.

Priyanka gestured to the waiter and ordered for both of us. We looked into each other's eyes but said nothing. Her hot-pink nails and neon pink lipstick were gradually turning me on.

"Don't look at me like that," Priyanka grouched as she blushed.

"I'm so sorry. I don't know what to talk about," I said and started to look inside the menu.

"Oh, come on! You have a beautiful girl sitting with you and you're saying you don't know what to say!" Priyanka was very direct. She knew she was hot and flaunted it well.

"You look great. I never imagined I'd ever get to talk to a girl like you," I replied feeling shy.

Priyanka chuckled, "You're embarrassing me. I'm not that sexy!"

Fuck! She was too bold, too frank. Even Aarti was nowhere near her.

"What qualities are you looking for in your spouse?" she began.

What kind of a question was that? Something that guys can never define... because they just focus on the physical attributes before marriage... of which this girl was well in possession of.

"She must be good," I replied.

"And how will you know that?" Priyanka asked resting her chin on her palm.

"Aaaaa...," I wanted to say by sleeping with her but restrained such vulgar talk. Just then, our order arrived.

"Okay, leave it. Do you have a girlfriend?" Priyanka asked looking into my eyes.

"What?"

"These days everybody has a girlfriend. Tell me. I'll not tell your Dad via my Dad," she giggled.

"No, I don't have any," I said nervously tapping the spoon on the saucer.

"I don't believe you," Priyanka said raising her hands.

"That's not my problem," I replied rudely.

"Okay, I'm sorry. But I want you to know something. I've had four boyfriends till now, but right now I'm single," Priyanka shared her glorious past with me.

Shit man! I couldn't handle it. Four boyfriends! Please god, don't tell me she is not a virgin. I became grim and started to stir my coffee. I know that was mean but... all men want virgin wives, no matter how characterless they themselves are.

Priyanka snapped her fingers in front of my face, "Hey! What happened?"

"Nothing."

"You shouldn't feel bad about that. I didn't sleep with any of them. It was just..."

"You're very frank Priyanka. I've never met such a straightforward girl in my entire life," I interrupted.

"Thanks for the compliment. I just wanted to tell you that I'm not a bad girl. You must have thought dirty things about me seeing my clothes," she continued.

Fuck! She knew that all beautiful girls who look inaccessible are termed 'loose' by losers like me.

"No, I..." I stammered.

"It's okay. It's your decision. My Dad wants me to marry you because he found you honest and good."

"What do *you* want? That's what matters. I know I'm not as good looking as you are or maybe your ex-boyfriends were, but please don't choose me just because your Dad wants you to. I don't want you to take pity on me," I said like a Mahatma, although I was a big asshole.

Priyanka became emotional and put her hand on mine. I retracted my hand immediately. She touched it again, "Rishabh, you seem to be a genuine person to me. Someone who thinks from a girl's perspective which none of my exes or the ones I met for matrimony thought. I think... umm... I might go with my Dad's decision."

Fuck! Fuck! Fuck! I couldn't believe it. Priyanka liked me. I felt like kissing her full lips and going forward with all that right away. But then, she was still a stranger and I didn't want to reveal my true identity yet. We talked about a lot of things, our hobbies, movies, jobs and some other personal stuff. I offered her a lift back home, but she said it was too early to become friends.

That whole evening I fantasized about my honeymoon with Priyanka.

At night, Dad called to ask, "So, did you like Priyanka?"

I kept silent. There are times in life when saying yes feels like a crime. Dad asked again, "Should I say no to Guptaji?"

I responded immediately, "No, I... I mean..."

Dad guffawed like never before. "I've got my answer, beta. I'll ask Guptaji to arrange for us to see Priyanka too," he said.

I said nothing once again as faltering had worked well for me earlier. My neuron activity became hyperactive realising what was about to happen.

▼

The next weekend, Mom and Dad met Priyanka at her parents' place. They liked her very much and the 'deal' was finalized with the customary exchange of sweets, dry fruits, cash and gold ornaments. Three weeks later, we were engaged in Lucknow.

The wedding date was finalized for Rama Navami on the 3rd of April 2009, the day after my birthday. Dad bought me an Alto (thankfully without taking a loan and passing on the EMI to me), although Gupta Uncle, my future father-in-law, promised me a bigger car soon.

▼

The much talked about recession officially hit us the following month. Joy was its first victim. He was made to take a hefty cut in his variables. Sam became a bit more occupied with his work. I was loaded with work too, but my mind was mostly on Priyanka. Initially we scrapped on Orkut and chatted over the phone. But as the bill crossed a thousand bucks, I decided to take a more economical and 'opportunity-prone' route. I offered Priyanka a daily lift to her office to which she agreed in a flash! I think all girls like a free commute. Gradually, we started going to the movies and parks. Priyanka was quite lively and frank while I remained deceptively calm and 'good-boy' types. We did nothing more than holding hands or giving each other little hugs in parking lots.

▼

One foggy night, we were returning from Delhi after a party. I was driving. Suddenly, I swerved the car as I suspected a massive pothole in the center of the road. Priyanka lost her balance and hit her head on the window. She was furious, "Stop the car," she screamed, rubbing her head.

I stopped the car and killed the engine as the other vehicles hurtled by.

"What happened? Are you alright?" I asked with concern.

"Only till this point. If you want both of us to be alright, let me drive or else you'll get us both killed," she said.

"I'm in full control. Don't worry," I said looking into her eyes.

"No, you're not. Move out and come from the other side," she said removing my seat belt.

"I'm not going anywhere," I said arrogantly.

"Listen. You're not in your senses. You're high. Let me drive."

"Nopes."

"Honey, there are times when we need our partner's help. That's what family is. Let me take the wheel, please," she pleaded.

"Family? We haven't even kissed!" I said and honked to confirm.

"Oho! Family isn't just about making babies. It's about love," Priyanka soft-pedalled.

"Love? Have we even proposed to each other?"

"Tsk... Okkkay... fine. Let's do it. But then, I'll drive."

"Alright sweetie. That's a deal. We'll propose right here in the car. Whoever's proposal is better will drive," I said sulkily.

Priyanka agreed, "Okay, you go first."

"Priyanka, my darling. I love you, I love you, I love you," I brayed and pecked her on the cheek.

Priyanka giggled and said, "That's it? That's your proposal?" You should have had at least one girlfriend.

"Ha ha! Let's see what you come up with. Your turn now. After all, you have much experience with four hunks," I said challenging her.

Priyanka drew close to me, looked into my eyes and said, "Fantabulous Adorable Mister I Love You. That's what family is." She then did the unimaginable. She pulled me by the tie and smooched me with her lipstick-laden lips. The alcohol inside me evaporated in a flash. We smooched again and this time I tickled her tongue with mine. Priyanka retracted. "Looks like you made up that 'no girlfriend' story," she said looking surprised.

I smiled sheepishly and then said confidently, "It's only you my darling! It's only you. You're my first one as well as the last one."

Priyanka was so excited to hear my lie that she started kissing me all over my face.

After two minutes of fervid kissing, she moved onto my lap. Her knees were around my hips and eyes submerged in mine. We kissed again, this time even more intensely. Emotions were extremely high so I slid my hand inside her top and grabbed her left one. Priyanka shoved my hand out and slapped me half-heartedly.

"What the hell are you doing?" she said visibly appalled.

"Come on baby!" I said running my fingers over her arm.

"Are you mad? Not before marriage."

"Oy Miss Pure! Don't tell me you're fresh," I said running my nose through her hair.

"Fresh? How cheap? You're the first one who has made it this far," and Priyanka slapped me real hard this time around.

I was embarrassed at being slapped by my future wife. "I'm so sorry Priyanka. I shouldn't have said that. Please forgive me. I've gone out of my mind. Please get off my lap. I'll sit at the back. You drive," I apologized for my words as Priyanka had taken off her engagement ring by now.

Priyanka's face was flushed with all the kissing, but she still had control over her emotions. She wore her ring again and issued a verdict adjusting her hair and top, "We're not going out from tomorrow. I'm deeply hurt."

"I'm sorry Priyanka. It was a mistake," I pleaded.

"No, it was the truth. That's what you think about me. For you, I'm a bloody slut who has slept with the whole of Gurgaon. And now I'm trying to get away from my dirty past by marrying an innocent boy like you," Priyanka put into words what I partially thought about her.

"No, absolutely not! You're taking it all wrong. I trust you now more than I trusted you that day. We're family. I'm deeply sorry for what I said. I know you're pure. Please. Please forgive me. I love you baby," I came up with the best lies I'd ever mouthed. The primary reason I was marrying Priyanka was her physical beauty. Had that not been the case, I'd have termed her a whore on the first day itself when she told me about her four boyfriends.

Priyanka calmed down, looked into my intoxicated eyes and then out of nowhere kissed me like a sportsperson kissing his winning trophy. The violence in that kiss made me realise that Priyanka was head over heels in love with me. But this time I didn't try to touch her. Not even her toenail. Priyanka took the driver's seat while I straggled over the backseat for a pretend nap.

▼

It was my wedding day. By this time, Priyanka had infallibly started to treat me like a god. I too had started to like her, but wasn't sure if it was love. Unfortunately, our brief and intense courtship hadn't progressed beyond kissing. But now the moment of pleasure wasn't quite far away.

I was happy to have Sam, Joy as well as Phani making it to my marriage despite the global recession and the risk of them losing their jobs for skipping work. Roshini didi, Jijaji and my five-year-old nephew Adit had also arrived. It was the first time I'd seen so many relatives, meeting some of them for the first time ever. Even

Priyanka's family and relatives were there on the same premises. We had booked two floors of the same hotel. I was tired of all the rituals and was trying to take a nap in the afternoon when my phone rang. I was in no mood to answer it. But the caller was persistent and kept calling back. Out of irritation, I finally checked my phone. It was an ISD call. I wondered who it was.

"Hey Rishu! Congratulations my dear. I'm so happy for you," said a female voice.

Fuck! It was Aarti. I couldn't believe my ears. I thought I was dreaming. I asked, "Who's this?"

"Idiot! It's me. Aarti! You've forgotten my voice! Bad boy!"

"Oh, hi Aarti! Sorry, I didn't recognize you," I said.

"Why should you? Now that you're getting married to a beautiful girl... who the hell remembers old friends?" Aarti giggled pulling my leg.

I too imitated a laugh and asked, "Where did you get my number from?"

"Police station."

"You haven't changed at all."

"Arrey baba. It was on your wedding card. I visited your profile to leave a birthday message and just by chance came across the card in your album. You didn't even bother to invite me. How mean is that!" she complained.

"I wanted to invite you, but you just stopped replying since around last Diwali."

"Oh Rishu! There's some good news for you," Aarti said.

"And that is...?"

"I became a mom six months ago!"

"Really? Boy or girl?"

"Boy."

"Single, twin, triplets, quadruplets…"

"Okay, that's enough. One child only," Aarti asked me to stop before I reached offspring bearing capacity of animals.

"What's his name?" I questioned.

"Still searching. But I call him Rishu sometimes," she said giggling.

"What nonsense?"

"You don't have a copyright to that name. I can call him whatever I feel like," Aarti giggled harder. "But Rishu, seriously… I can't tell you how much I miss you. How much I miss our school and college days. That time was so good."

I fell silent as I felt the love in Aarti's voice which I always wanted to. She continued, "I'm so stupid. It's your wedding day and I'm getting so emotional."

"No no, it's okay. I also miss you. You can keep your kid's name Rishu. At least you'll remember me that way," I said.

"Oh! I'll never forget you Rishu. Never ever in my life," Aarti replied in a teary voice and fell silent.

"What is it Aarti? Tell me. Are you crying?"

"No, just… I just became a little senti."

"Are you happy?" I asked.

"Of course, you stupid! Why shouldn't I be? Now tell me about Priyanka," Aarti replied.

"How do you know her name?" I was surprised.

"Bond… James Bond!"

"Tsk. Tell na."

"Wedding invites usually have the names of both the bride and groom!" Aarti said sarcastically.

"Oh yes yes. How stupid of me!"

"As always."

I didn't respond, so she continued, "Earlier I thought she was Priyanka from our DST days, but then going through the card I realised she's a different girl. I'm sure she must be as hot as the Priyanka we both knew. Right?"

I grinned over the phone.

"Come on Rishu! Answer me. Is Priyanka hot and sexy?" Aarti poked me.

"Yeah, she's hot but not more than you. You're still my favourite," I replied.

"Hey! Don't you flirt with me or I'll knee you down."

I grinned again. Aarti carried on like she always did. "Rishu, you're the best person I've ever met in my life. Priyanka is the luckiest girl in the world to have you as a husband. My best wishes to both of you."

"Thanks a ton, my dear," I said.

"I'll catch up with you guys on my next trip to India. And yes, I'll definitely tell Priyanka what you used to do on your computer," she teased.

"Hey, that's cheating! I'm going to kill you. You can't do that!"

"You already have."

"What?"

"Nothing."

"No, you said something about me killing you," I asked quite taken aback.

"Just a slip of the tongue. Okay, I'm hanging up now. Enough of my nonsense. My best wishes once again. Live a happy life my dear friend," and she hung up.

I went numb. I felt as if I'd just been woken up from a dream. Aarti had called after five long years and said nothing about our fight. I could tell that she missed me like hell since she had named her kid after me and even tried to hide her tears. But why did she say I had killed her. All these thoughts made my head spin. I grabbed the whiskey Phani had brought for me and took a long swig.

Though I liked Priyanka and was about to marry her in a few hours, but the fact was I had never loved her the way I should have. Aarti was the only one who'd made her way to my heart. And that call from her had rekindled all that I felt for her.

I kept swigging down the whisky, replaying my conversation with Aarti over and over in my head. Emotions swirled as the booze took over my senses.

"Rishu, what are you doing? You're drinking! I didn't know you drank," Dad asked taking off his specs, his mouth agape. He'd just entered the room cracking jokes with one of my uncles and his elder son Himanshu. They were all shocked to see me reclining drunk on the chair, that too on my wedding day.

"I do a lot other things that you don't know about, old man," I answered disrespectfully, trying to pick myself up from the chair.

Himanshu ran immediately to fetch Mom. Minutes later, everyone was trying to calm me down. But by now, my mind and heart had stopped talking to each other.

I stumbled out of the room holding the whiskey bottle. I reached the hall where shaadi songs were being played. The guests were busy grabbing snacks and cold drinks. I staggered to the centre of the hall, gulped another shot directly from the bottle and screamed, "Stop eating, you pigs! Stop this celebration. I said stop it!"

A short shock-induced silence prevailed. Nobody moved. Then Jiju stepped forward. He tried to tug me back to the room. But I pushed him away. And then smashed the bottle onto the floor.

"Listen clearly you morons. There isn't any marriage happening over here. Get lost or I'll screw your mothers," I hollered, pulling the cloths off the tables and food stalls.

"The groom is out of his mind. He's drunk," remarked a guest.

"Who said that? Come out you sisterfucker. I'm not drunk. I'm in love. In love with Aarti. I love her more than anybody else. Since she couldn't be mine, there's no point in getting married," I hooted like an owl and picked up a shard from the floor. Himanshu lunged at me. He forced open my grip and threwe the shard down. What followed was a loud smack, a furious-insulted look, and then an awkward tussle. I remember the thud against the floor. I remember a man knelt across my chest. I remember the taste of his knuckles. It was about then that I passed out.

I don't know for how long I slept. When I opened my eyes, I saw Mom weeping as if I was lying in a morgue. There was pin drop silence in the room and my jaw hurt. I looked at the clock. It was eight in the morning. The storm of insanity was over and so was my wedding. Dad was inconsolable. His red eyes clearly reflected how much he'd wept last night. Roshini didi was more or less the same as Dad. Sam, Joy and Phani stood in one corner like corpses. Himanshu simply walked out of the room. Nobody talked to me. Not even my friends.

I rushed to Priyanka's floor. But her family had already checked out. I tried her number almost a dozen times, but her phone was switched off. So, I went to her house. Her grandfather opened the door.

"We come from a respectable family, Rishabhji. Our daughter is not a toy that you can play with whenever you like to. Please leave us alone," he said folding his hands before me and then closed the door.

I could understand how much humiliation Priyanka's family faced because of me. I had ruined her life for no fault of hers. Nobody wants to marry a girl whose marriage gets cancelled on the day of the wedding. People make up all sorts of stories about her character.

After my return to Gurgaon, I went to Priyanka's PG as well as her office. I just wanted to meet her once. But she'd already left her job and PG by now. It was all because of me. I went online to check her Orkut profile. It was active, but I wasn't on her friend list anymore. All I could see on her public profile was a pic carrying the message, 'It's Over'.

I'll never be able to forgive myself for what I did to Priyanka. My unfulfilled love had made her lose the love of her life too. Ruhana's curse had come true.

My First Love Letter

The recession took away all my grief as it brought along its own pain. After much defamation at my PG, office and the rest of society, I got busy with my office work. Life had taken a serious turn and fun was a thing of the past. I sold my Alto, changed my phone number, deleted my Orkut account and kept a very low profile, focussing only on my everyday work. Mom and Dad hardly spoke to me. For them, their son was all but dead. Joy and Sam were still part of my social circle, but we hardly interacted on personal matters. They understood my agony and I appreciated that a lot.

Six months later, Joy broke the news about his marriage to Oiendrilla in January. He changed his job just before his wedding and shifted to Kolkata. Sam and Phani made it to the wedding, but I gave it a skip. I didn't want to remember my past. Joy was upset about it, but Sam managed to pacify him somewhat. It was really nice of him to send back some sweets and gifts for me with Sam.

My concentration on work grew exponentially as the days went on. My boss was extremely happy at the change in attitude and gave me a promotion – without a hike!

By this time, the world had moved from Orkut to Facebook as yet another means to waste time and energy. I didn't bother to get on Facebook as Orkut had left me with bitter memories. My aim was to get so involved in work that I wouldn't have any time left to think about anything else in life. And that's how it was.

After a year, Sam moved to Mumbai as the recession clouds lifted and the job market opened up. He was now working for a financial institution. All this while, I got new roomies, but none of them was worth striking a friendship with. The day Sam left Gurgaon, I gave up non-veg. Non-veg tasted like veg only with him.

After a month of Sam's departure, I got a new roomie, the kind you pray you don't get. He had really peculiar habits. He would apply a whole lot of cheap cosmetics on his pimple-laden ugly face and keep asking if it looked okay and bugged me till I told him that he was looking super sexy. He kept a scary red bulb on all night and often screamed for his mother in his sleep. I bore that bastard for about a month before managing to move out of Dalal's place.

This time I took up a single room with no one to disturb my privacy. I was lucky to find one with a nice family who valued human relationships more than money.

A few months later, Sam and Phani got married in quick succession. But I skipped their weddings too. Marriage invitations had started giving me sleepless nights.

The annual appraisal happened and I got another promotion. With it came a laptop along with a data card and a hike of almost fifty percent. I watched movies and surfed the net almost every night. And then one day, I joined Facebook – probably the best thing to while away your time on when you've nothing else to do in life.

The biggest problem with networking sites is their bloody algorithm of 'suggesting' friends. Aarti found me yet again and we helped each other add one more friend to our respective friend lists. She asked me why my relationship status was 'single'. I avoided answering her for a few days, but had to finally because Aarti wasn't one to let go so easily. I made up a lie and told her that Priyanka had run away an hour before the ceremony. Aarti sympathized with me, "Don't worry, you'll find someone better than that bitch." I can't tell you how bad I felt for Priyanka. She was so unlucky to have once had me in her life.

I looked at each of Aarti's albums on Facebook. She was maturing elegantly. Her dressing style was urbane and jaunty. None of Aarti's pictures showed her in her mangalsutra or vermilion to certify her marital status. Her lively brown eyes always smiled and made her look the confident modern girl she was. Apart from her childhood red coral, a diamond ring sparkled on her left ring finger. It was her wedding ring which I wish I had given her.

Aarti had put on a little weight, but that was quite normal. After all, she'd had a baby. The important thing was that I was still in love with her. There were albums of her son too. He was really cute, with his Mom's eyes. I wondered what he would have looked like had he been my son. His biological father seemed a much better choice. I hope he loved Aarti much more than I did.

Aarti always commented on my posts and even sent chat messages, but I never replied. I'd stopped responding after I badmouthed Priyanka. I was happy to be a silent observer of her life via her pictures and posts. Her status and album updates were more than enough to keep me in good stead. I just 'liked' whatever she posted. That's the best thing about Facebook. You can 'like' a girl's photograph and her status message and she likes it too – without even realising that you actually like her. The last thing I did every night was to check Aarti's profile. I followed her like a dog's tail. Be it eating Maggi at midnight or watching SRK's heavy budget superhero science fiction – I did it all. I downloaded and listened to the *Dildaara* song on loop all through the night. In short, whatever Aarti did continents apart, I imitated without a thought.

I leapfrogged professionally, but lived in solitude for a little under three years. The only mentionable things that happened all this while were India's cricket World Cup victory and the re-release of *Titanic* as a 3D movie. Coincidently, both happened on my birthday and around it. But this time around, I connected with the emotions I saw in the movie.

And then, on one dreary December evening, the planets changed direction. I was jaywalking when a rich man's twenty-something jumped the signal and rammed his SUV into me. He fled the scene before anyone could react and the last thing I remember before blackout is being peered down by a group of unfamiliar faces, a few curious eyes, a few hollering mouths, and a few flashing phones.

Who am I? Where am I? And why?

Those were my first conscious thoughts. The light was blinding and it forced tears to sprout from the edge of my squinted eyes. My head pounded and my chest ached every time I inhaled air, although I had the liberty of an oxygen mask.

"He's back. He's back. He's out of coma," I heard someone roar. And it resonated a couple of times. My ears hurt. Felt like an earbud drifting far too deep. Why do people have to be so loud?

This was thirty hours after I was knocked down unconscious. I'd had four limb fractures, two broken ribs, a dislocated shoulder and a severe traumatic brain injury (TBI). Luckily there weren't any blood clots. Just a swelling of the brain. Though I was fortunate enough to escape all forms of surgery, but still, the pain down my spine was unbearable. Even worse, I was so disoriented that I couldn't recognize my own parents.

Two days later, I was transferred to a specialized trauma care unit. Initially I suffered from post-traumatic amnesia and had trouble brushing teeth, getting out of bed and eating. But the rehabilitation team took good care of me. Somehow, my ears kept ringing. Every little sound felt like a hammer striking a gong.

Weeks later, I got fully recovered from the basic cognitive issues. It was then that I met my first batch of visitors, my colleagues from XLSL as well as my landlady. Sam called, so did Phani and Joy. But the ear-ringing hadn't stopped. The doctor said it was called tinnitus and it'd take some time to fade out.

After a fifty-day-long and painful treatment at the hospital, I moved to Lucknow where most of my time was spent sleeping. At times, I watched TV and even surfed the net. I was under strict medication and a physiotherapist used to come to our house six days a week. I also had to visit a neuropsychologist once a week as TBI had left me with problems like tinnitus and insomnia. Maybe my melatonin levels had gone haywire.

Every night I used to toss in my sheets and gaze at the ceiling, pining for Aarti. At times, I even thought of Ruhana and the words she once said - *it's extremely hard to stop loving the person who means everything to us.* I guess, she was right. I just couldn't stop myself from thinking about Aarti.

Though I regained physical health with time, but somehow, I did develop catatonic symptoms. I used to stare aimlessly at the walls and at times hallucinated about death in Aarti's arms. The anti-depressants were no medicine for a soul whose love was incomplete. I just wanted to end the misery.

But before that, I wanted to tell Aarti how much I loved her. So, I penned my first and last love letter putting in all the pain I'd been in over the last few years.

Forgive me Aarti, please forgive me.

I lost the right of being called your friend the moment I voiced those pathetic thoughts of mine to you. You might have forgotten them, but I remember those moments when you dispelled me from your life. I hurt you, your feelings, and your trust — just because I was jealous to see you happy. That day, I not only lost my best friend, but my life. It's not been easy ever since. Please forgive me. Please have mercy on me. I beg you... do me a favour and set me free. I can't live with this burden anymore.

The day you left me on that pavement, I died. Your spit fell not on my face, but on my life. I didn't know what to do, where to go. And I'm still searching for those answers. I'm a living corpse, a stinking garbage pile, a monumental liability — not only to my family, but also to the society.

That day you judged me right. I'm a loser — a loser with no guts. But today I want to break free. I don't want to be a wimp anymore, a chicken that's born to gratify a famished soul, a movie that's watched and forgotten. I want to say what I always wanted to — since our school farewell when I brought roses for you.

The world has moved on, but I still live in those days. Each day of my life I think about your first 'hi'; those countless bus chats; that ball dance and everything else we did together in school. I miss that trigo tutorial, those DST days, those driving lessons, those CCD treats, those drives to and back from college, those C tuitions, those mild rebukes, and most importantly, you.

After all these years, I sit alone, walk alone, and drive alone. I've nobody to share Maggi with or to argue endlessly with. Each time I visit Lucknow, I go to our school and to our college. I loiter around in the campus and I tell you, each time a flood of memories hits me. I sit at CCD and order the stuff you used to order. I look for you in every corner of the city. You're my world, no matter where I go.

There isn't a day when I don't go through your pictures. I talk to your eyes. I touch your lips, your dimples, your lovely hair and the faint little scar over your temple. Each night I see you smile at me through the clouds. I go to bed thinking about you, about the days we breathed together, about our embrace when you got your first job and about the accidental kiss we shared once. Each morning I get up, I hug my pillow imagining it to be you. I feel you in my heart, in my soul, in every blink of my eyes. You're always on my mind, running through my blood every second of my life.

I miss seeing you, your sweet smile, your ankle thread, your blue capris, your cute phone and everything else that ever belonged to you. I miss you more than I miss myself. You're the best thing that has ever happened to me. If god granted me a wish, all I'd ask for is you and nothing more. You're the only one who can bring together the pieces of my heart. You're the true panacea of my malady. I'm never gonna make it without you.

I'm sorry for being a part of your life. I'm sorry for bruising your heart. I'm sorry for not understanding you. I'm sorry for writing this mushy letter after so many years. I'm sorry for everything that ever annoyed you. I just want to say this before I close my eyes.

I loved you yesterday, I love you today and I'll love you till the end. That's the way I love you.

P.S. In all these years, everything that I did reminded me of you. You were always in my life, even if I wasn't. You were always the one I thought about, the one I pined for. That's my penance, my atonement. That's what I deserve.

Goodbye forever.

Rishu, your loser friend who fell in love with you.

I went to Aarti's profile and was surprised to see that she still used her old mail account – aartiraisinghani18@rediffmail.com. I mailed her my impromptu confession of love and locked the door for my final journey. I took out the blade I'd stolen from Dad's shaving kit and prayed for strength for my parents to bear this pain. Beads of sweat surfaced on my brows as I felt the blade's edge over my skin. My hand started to twitch. I couldn't build up the courage to slit the twin pipes protruding from the back of my wrist. But I had to. I closed my eyes. Images from the past flashed in my head. The fight with Aarti, the assault on Ruhana, and the disposal of Priyanka. I felt ashamed, sorry for everything, said it to the barren walls, and raised the blade for the final act!

"Rishu, open the door. What are you doing so late at night?" I heard Dad's voice. He was knocking at the door, urgently.

I didn't answer. He started pushing the door, trying to break in. I gave up, hid the blade and unlatched the door.

"Why did it take you so long to open the door?" Dad asked angrily.

"Nothing. Just doing something on my laptop," I lied.

Dad scanned the room and said, "I had a very bad dream. So, I came to check on you."

"What did you see? Did you see me dead?" I asked.

"Don't you dare say that again. I'll die before seeing that day," Dad said and hugged me close and tight.

He left only after I promised to get into bed in a few minutes. He asked me not to bolt the door so I moved to the drawing room with my laptop. Committing suicide is not an easy job when people dream about it before you actually do it. I checked my mailbox with mixed thoughts – whether to die or to live. Surprisingly, there was an e-mail from Aarti.

Rishu
You idiot! Give me your phone number.
Aarti

Before I could think of anything else, another mail entered my mailbox. It was Aarti again.

Rishu
I know you're online. Give me your phone number. I'll call. I want to talk to you. Please do me this favour.
Aarti

I didn't reply and started to wonder what Aarti would say if I sent her my number. Another mail popped up a minute later. This time Aarti wrote —

If you don't reply in the next two minutes, I'm going to post what you just sent me on your FB wall. And if you're thinking you can 'block' me, I'll put it on mine.

Fuck! Aarti was angry and I didn't want public defamation, even after suicide. My reputation had always been dear to me, though I wasn't a celebrity or someone high class. With vials of fright transfusing into my system, I mailed my number to Aarti and stepped out into the balcony.

After two minutes, an ISD number popped up on my cell. I kept staring at the screen, but just couldn't get myself to pick it up. It got disconnected. Then rang again. This time, I picked it up.

"You bastard! You idiot! You… you… why didn't you say all this before?" Aarti was fuming.

"I… I thought you loved Imran," I replied.

"That Imran was a bugger. He never loved me. He just wanted to sleep with me. You were always right about him. The day he tried to force himself on me, I understood your true worth, Rishu. I realised your love, your care, your respect for me. You never tried anything with me, no matter what. I'm so sorry. I never understood your feelings, your unconditional love. Please… please forgive me for all that I did to you," Aarti said.

I was silent. "Rishu. Are you there? Hello…"

"Yeah. I'm listening."

Aarti continued, "I tried every possible way to reach you after that Imran episode. I mailed you for almost six months, but you never replied. I called your house many times, but Aunty told me that you didn't have a phone. I even went to your place but…"

"But what? Did Mom say anything to you?" I was totally taken aback by the revelation.

Aarti was silent. "Tell me Aarti. Tell me. Pleeeease," I pleaded.

"Aunty said she wouldn't let me enter her house even if I was thinking about it," Aarti said hesitantly, her voice shaky.

I was furious and yelled, "She has no right to take decisions on my behalf. I'll never forgive her."

"No, Rishu. No! She's your mother. She owns you more than anybody else on earth. Promise me, Rishu… you'll never tell her that I told you this. Just remember that I love you as much as you love me," she begged.

I controlled my pulsating anger and said, "I want you Aarti. I need you. I can't live without you. I've died every day waiting for you. Please come back to me."

"Rishu, it's too late. I have a family now. Even if I want to, I can't do it. I can't cheat on my husband," Aarti replied.

"What about me? I've loved you since our school days and… and I just can't stop loving you," I cried.

"Try and understand. It's not only about you and me. It's not a movie. It's life."

"For me, it's only about you and me. You're the only one I want. And I don't care what people think."

"Rishu, Rishu, Rishu… why don't you understand. Nothing can be done now. You're simply wasting your time trying to pull me in. It's not gonna happen. Accept the reality. Be mature. Move on. Get married."

"Huh… get married? If I can't be with you, I'm not going to get married."

"Listen… just listen to me. You get married. A partner will help you forget me."

"I don't need a lecture, understand?"

"It's not a lecture. It's about you, your life. We can't be together, not at least in this life."

"Then I'll end it," I threatened.

"You'd better not do that. Or I'll never be able to look at myself in the mirror. Please listen to me. Isn't it enough for you to know that I love you too?"

When I didn't reply, Aarti started to cry. I could hear her son asking in his American accent, "Mommy… Mommy, why are you crying?"

"Rishu, you'll find a good girl. Someone who'll love you more than I ever could have. If you want to see me happy, please do it for me," Aarti spoke in a heavy voice.

"I tried to get married once. But I just couldn't go through with it. I don't want to spoil another girl's life," I said.

"What? Priyanka didn't run away?" Aarti asked surprised.

"No, she didn't dump me."

"So, it was you who called it off? Oh… shit… O… Oh my god. I spoilt your marriage. I shouldn't have called that day. I'm feeling so bad about Priyanka now. I've ruined her life too," said Aarti and started to sob again.

"It wasn't your fault," I tried to console her.

She kept crying with huge sighs. "I want you back Aarti. If you can't come, I'll live like this. I deserve this life," I said.

"I want a promise from you," Aarti croaked.

"Don't ask me to marry someone."

"You just come to my funeral."

"No, no Aarti. You're not doing anything foolish," I said immediately.

"You've left me with no choice," Aarti said and disconnected the phone.

My mind went numb. I didn't know what to do. Just a while ago I was planning to commit suicide, but now I was trying to convince someone not to do so. I called Aarti back, but there was no answer. I added her number to the phone's contact book and sent her a WhatsApp message. But she didn't respond. I then rushed back to my laptop and wrote her a quick e-mail. No response again. I started getting very nervous. I called her number again and again and kept sending messages and e-mails over the next half-an-hour, but all in vain.

I knew deep down that Aarti was okay and this was just a pressure tactic. But what if not? What if she actually took an unthoughtful step? What if she already had?

They say love is blind and so was I. I acceded to Aarti's emotional blackmail and wrote her an e-mail promising that I'd do whatever she asked for. All I wanted at that time was to hear her voice once again.

Aarti called back five minutes later. She made me vow that I'd make every possible effort to find myself a wife. I agreed to everything that she demanded. But then, I made a promise to myself that I'd never love another woman, ever.

Salted Wound

It was an endless night. It wasn't just Holi, but a lot more than that. The emotional jolt had disturbed my sanity, but I still had a few things left to do.

First – Settle scores with Mom. Dad stood as a spectator as I cursed her for ruining my life along with a lot of other things that were totally out of context. Mom used a woman's most lethal weapon – tears. But I didn't budge.

Second – Giving up all thoughts of committing suicide, which had already become feeble post Dad's and Aarti's emotional acts.

Third and most important – Searching for Imran the bastard. I found him on Facebook. He lived in the US and accepted my friend request within minutes. He was married and had a daughter. I wrote all that I felt about him on his wall, calling his wife and his daughter filthy names. As expected, Imran 'unfriended' me just as quickly as he had accepted me! I'm sure he blocked my profile and reported 'abuse', but I was too angry to care. For me he was an asshole and would always be.

Aarti called me regularly over the next few days to get me to find someone else to get married to. Though uninterested, I endured her lectures just because I was getting a chance to speak with her.

During that time, I learnt a lot about Aarti's life post college. How she broke up with Imran, the emotional turmoil that she went through, how she got married, moved to the States and so forth. She praised her husband for being an extremely supportive guy. She talked about her son, her job, her car, her house, her travels and everything else that I asked about. But she never forgot to mention that it was time for me to move on.

Our drama went on for a little over two weeks until we mutually decided to put an end to these nudging and nagging calls. There wasn't any point in hearing the same stuff day after day, over and over again, especially the line, "Rishu, I can't be yours."

▼

"Dad, I want to get married," I said while we had lunch on my thirty-second birthday.

Dad was sprinkling pepper on his salad. His hand froze mid-air. Mom's ears were always flapping, no matter which part of the house she was in. She scuttled out of the kitchen and said excitedly, "I'm so happy to hear that Rishu. This is the best day of my life."

A week later, Dad put an ad in the matrimonial sections of all the leading dailies. He even got me to create paid accounts with three of the matrimonial websites. I was amazed to see the response pouring in for a thirty-two-year-old. The reason was but obvious. Fat pay package. Thanks to my donkey work at XLSL.

I learnt a lot about arranged marriages in that time. The first thing a girl's family looks for is the boy's financial stability. This is followed by finding out how many heirs the boy's father has, which in turn is followed by whether the son would be living with his parents or not.

From the perspective of the boy's family, two interdependent factors drive the show. First, the budget of the opposite party, and second, the physical attributes of the bride-to-be. Everyone wants an extremely fair daughter-in-law. She should also be 'beautiful, decent, well-educated, and most importantly, well-cultured' – overall a highly-endangered species.

I met a few girls, but everyone showed me the door. After exactly eight rejections, I met Shefali. She was from Kanpur. We met at Saharaganj – a gigantic mall that had sprung up at Hazratganj just after I left Lucknow to join XLSL. It was a Saturday evening and the area was buzzing with people. We had a tough time finding a place to sit. After a little chit-chatting, Dad asked me to take Shefali for a walk. Her parents nodded in agreement. Shefali was only twenty-five. She was slim and fair, had an average height and beautiful long hair. She wore a sari accessorised with minimal jewellery. She had her eyes downcast all through and was too shy to even look at me.

As Dad pushed me again, I left my chair and so did Shefali. We strolled out of the coffee shop looking in opposite directions, walking a feet apart from each other.

"How did you get hurt?" Shefali broke the awkward silence between us.

"It's a long story. But now I'm fine," I said. I was sick of answering the same question over and over again.

Shefali pulled out a PVR leaflet from the pile stacked inside one of the side-stands. "Do you watch movies?" she asked scanning the contents of the leaflet.

"Yup. Mostly Hindi, but at times English as well."

"What about these ones?" she smiled pointing to a Telugu movie name that was showing at PVR. Frankly speaking, I'd actually watched one called *Pokiri*, with Phani and the gang.

I shook my head to say no and then out of curiosity asked her, "Who's your favourite actor?" Our conversation was slowly turning into a Bollywood chat show rather than a compatibility check.

"SRK. Who else? He's been my favourite since I was five. Though he's almost fifty, he has real class. Even now I have a lot of his old movie posters on my walls at home," Shefali said animatedly, looking decidedly different from what she'd projected in the past half-an-hour.

I looked into her eyes for the first time ever and tried to find Aarti in them. She got embarrassed and looked down again.

"You're really shy," I said.

"I normally don't talk to boys."

"Really? Not even at work?" I was surprised.

"Only when it's required. And in school, that hardly happens. I just love being with children," she explained. Shefali was a junior level school teacher who'd done her Master's in Economics.

"You like children?" I asked.

"Yes, a lot!"

"What else do you like?"

"Music."

"Don't say classical, please," I begged.

Shefali laughed and said, "No, I like country songs."

I sighed mentally before she asked, "Do you drink, smoke or eat non-veg?"

"No, I'm a teetotaller in all the departments," I spoke the truth that was a lie till a few years ago. Shefali looked somewhat dissatisfied with my answer.

Neither of us spoke for the next two minutes.

"Mom will ask me about you. What should I say?" she finally said.

"Speak your heart. If you seriously want to marry me, only then say yes. I won't mind the rejection," I preached magnanimously.

"Rishabh, it's not about selection or rejection. It's just about... umm... aa... an instant connection; no no, I think..."

"Love at first sight," I dropped a hint.

Shefali chortled and said, "Maybe, but I'd call it 'click'."

"So? What's your opinion? Did I click?" I questioned.

"I don't know right now. I hardly know you. How can I decide in ten minutes whether you're the one or not?" Shefali was apprehensive.

"Then how else can you decide? Wherever you go, you won't get more than ten to fifteen minutes. That's how arranged marriages get fixed," I said.

Shefali became pensive and said, "Yeah, I know. You tell me your opinion."

"My parents liked your profile a lot. And as far as I'm concerned, your yes is my yes," I spoke casually.

Shefali smiled but said nothing. The discussion stopped when I saw Dad walking towards us. I'm sure Shefali's parents were worried.

At home Dad asked for my answer. "Rishu, we liked Shefali and her parents a lot. What do you think? Should we confirm?"

"I've to marry someone or the other. So, why waste time looking for any more? If you find her good, I'm okay with it," I replied, popping my anti-depressant.

Dad looked happy – finally after so many years. He came forward and embraced me. Mom too smiled, but did not interrupt us. The next day Shefali's father called to find out our answer. And this one phone call confirmed my life partner.

I informed Aarti about Shefali. She sounded excited and asked me to send her Shefali's photograph. I obeyed subserviently. Aarti was happy with my choice and encouraged me to go ahead with the wedding. This time, Dad fixed an early date; the wedding was to be held in three weeks' time with only close relatives invited. Roshini didi came from UK, but Jiju gave it a skip. I didn't invite any of my friends, not even Sam, Phani or Joy. My boss happily extended my medical leave hearing about my wedding. He was the only person who'd admired me in the past few years, at least professionally.

Dad booked a banquet hall in Mahanagar while Shefali's Dad took care of the catering. Though we had only a handful of invitees, every possible effort was being made to keep the guests contented. Both our dads were spending a great deal of money on this wedding. It was just me who wasn't so excited about it.

Aarti called me on the D-day, "Rishu. Promise me you won't do anything silly."

"Just relax. Have faith in me," I gave her an assurance.

"No. Promise me you won't do anything stupid this time, before or after the marriage. Promise me that you'll make it work. Or else…"

"Haan haan, god promise."

Aarti hung up promising to call the next day.

I was far more stable this time, maybe because somewhere in my heart, I had accepted that Aarti couldn't be mine. But love, it hadn't yet given up on her. It was still standing tall.

After a full night's chanting of sacred Sanskrit texts and pouring in ladles full of ghee into the fire, I was married to Shefali.

My parents, especially my Dad, looked very happy. He'd finally taken the monkey off his back, just in time before his retirement. He was now a man free from all responsibilities.

Shefali, the newlywed girl had worn a light smile all night. Sometimes for the camera and sometimes for the relatives. But whenever our eyes met, her smile broadened and turned radiant.

I remember our first night together, the two odd-hours before the sun rose like it always has.

When I entered the room, Shefali was sitting on her side of the bed, dressed in a stunning magenta-coloured traditional Indian bridal dress. She drew her knees to her chest as I bolted the door. I could see the goosebumps building up on her forearms. She was waiting for me to come and sit next to her, raise her ghunghat, look her in the eye, make her blush, gently hold her hand, place it on my throbbing heart, tell her what she meant to me and then, go spelunking for the rest of the night. I did nothing close to that. I just went off to sleep. I broke my wife's heart.

Aarti kept her promise and called the next day. She asked me to share a marriage photograph. She wanted to be sure that I wasn't lying. So, I sent her the photo.

Aarti called back minutes later. "Rishu, I'm so happy for you, happier than I'd ever been for a long time. I wish you and Shefali a successful married life. You'll always be my bestie, my prince, and my hero…" the call got disconnected before I could say anything. I called back, but the number was unreachable. I sent out a WhatsApp message asking Aarti to call, but somehow, it went undelivered. So, I left her a note on Facebook messenger instead.

Two days later, Shefali and I left for Munsiyari, a comely hill station, for our honeymoon. The trip was restricted to sightseeing only. Nothing happened between us because I didn't take the initiative and Shefali was too shy to expect an initiative from.

I called Aarti almost every day, but kept getting a message saying that the number was unreachable. At times, even the calls weren't possible as the signal bars on the phone hardly showed any activity. Unfortunately, I was unable to access the internet because of infrastructure limitations.

I checked my Facebook and WhatsApp messages as soon as we were back. There weren't any from Aarti. Strangely my last WhatsApp message to her was still undelivered. So, I tried to message her a fresh one on Facebook. But she'd disappeared from my friend list! I searched for her, but she was untraceable. I created a fake profile and searched again. No sign of her anywhere. I tried all the other popular social networks, microblogging sites and chat messengers, but she didn't appear anywhere. Even her LinkedIn profile had disappeared. I e-mailed her, but didn't get a reply.

I got restless. Each second became a torture. I kept sending e-mails and then waited, waited and waited for Aarti to reply. But she didn't. Dad got concerned. I had started to show absolutely no interest either in Shefali or in any of the household affairs.

"Rishu, I totally understand what you're going through. But beta, you're married now. Stop waiting for her. She loved you enough to let you go. If not for us, then just do it for her. Make your marriage work. Show some care for your wife," Dad asked curling his arm around my shoulder.

I kept silent and returned to my room. Maybe Dad was right. Now when Aarti was sure that I'd gotten married, she had distanced herself from me so that I could be free. My love for her grew even more.

Days later, I came back to Gurgaon and resumed work after a gap of almost six months. In our earlier days together, Shefali and I talked only when it was unavoidable, but slowly, got accustomed to bearing each other's presence. Shefali was a reserved type of a woman who hardly made friends. Had there not been any newspaper, magazines, TV, phone or the internet, she'd have gone insane for sure. But when it came to me, she did try to strike a friendship... with her new recipes and frequent surprise gifts.

▼

It was our first wedding anniversary. The last one year had been uneventful and kind of mundane. From the perspective of my married life, it was more like two people sharing an apartment with only one of them paying the bills. Though there were no fights, but there was also no fun. Shefali and I were more good friends than husband and wife. We were one for the world, but there was a sea between us.

I made an effort to make the day memorable and took leave from office. At breakfast, Shefali came and sat next to me. She looked into my eyes and then placed a small gift-wrapped box on the table.

"What is it?" I asked slurping the milk from my bowl of cornflakes.

"I hope you like it," she said pushing the box forward.

I picked it up and tore open the gift wrapping. It was an Archies calendar with 365 Love Quotes. "Oh Shefali! This was unnecessary," I said softly.

Shefali smiled and started playing with her hair. "Sorry Shefali, I don't have a gift for you… I'm really sorry," I apologized. She didn't respond and kept playing with her hair. I felt ashamed for not bringing her a gift and tried to lighten the mood, "Hey! Shefali. Look at me. Come on… tell me. What gift do you want? A sari? A necklace? Or maybe an iPhone?"

She slowly shifted her gaze to me, mulled over something and then said, "I don't want all these things. I want something else."

"Ah, I know what you're looking for. Let me see if I can get you some good referrals," I said showing some excitement. Shefali had been a full-time housewife all this time, but now wanted to start working in a school.

"No, it's something else. Would you mind if I ask for it?"

"Uh-huh, go on," I said nibbling on my toast.

"Rishabh, I want a child."

I froze as Shefali placed her hand on my knee. "We've been married for a year now. And we're not yet husband and wife. I often think you don't love me. You just married me because your parents wanted you to," Shefali said with tears brimming in her eyes.

I swallowed the half-chewed toast and spoke in a consoling tone, "Shefali, it's not like that. It's just that I'm not yet ready to become a parent."

"What about sex? We've not had any intimate moments even once."

I wouldn't have believed Shefali knew that word had I not heard it from her mouth. I just looked down at my plate even as Shefali asked, "Rishabh? Do you have a medical issue?"

I was embarrassed, "No, not at all."

"Then what? Have you taken an oath of celibacy?"

"Why is physical intimacy important to you?" I asked.

"I can do without getting physical, but who'll explain it to your Mom? She often taunts me about having a child. What should I tell her? Her son is impotent or he is interested in men? Tell me. You have no idea how I feel when your Mom suspects me to be barren," Shefali grumbled.

"How dare she talk to you like that?" I groaned and took out my cell.

Shefali snatched the phone from my hand. "No Rishabh, no! Don't do that or she'll think I'm poisoning your ears."

"My ears are already poisoned," I said without realising Shefali didn't know about my past.

"What?"

"Nothing. Just give my phone back."

"No. First tell me. What made you say what you did?"

"None of your business," I replied rudely.

"It is my business. I'm your wife."

"Okay, then listen, dear wife. I don't love you. You hear that? I don't love you. I've just chosen you. Because I love somebody else.

Someone your bloody mother-in-law didn't approve of," I blurted out my secret.

Shefali instantly broke into tears. "Then why did you marry me?" she said crying.

"I had no other option," I said.

Shefali kept crying. I felt bad for her, but didn't console.

"Listen Shefali, listen! I have absolutely nothing against you. And I also want our marriage to work. But I'm sorry, I just can't love you."

Shefali looked at me. Her eyes were red. I felt guilty. She kept looking at me.

"It's gonna hurt me, but we need to end this now. And I know that it's for the best," Shefali said and then all of a sudden she pulled out the kitchen knife from the chest of the butter bar.

"Are you mad Shefali? Drop it. Come on Shefali… what do you think you're doing?" I shouted as Shefali changed her grip on the knife to stab it into her own chest.

"Your choice is making its own choice," Shefali said standing up and raised her hand above her shoulder to get that killer momentum.

In that split-second, I acted like never before. I leapt forward and caught hold of her wrist. She tried to break free, but I was too strong for her. I forcibly opened her grip and threw the knife down. I don't know why but I hugged her tightly. She immediately pulled away. She was inconsolable. I tried again, a lot more gently. Shefali relented and let me embrace her. She then buried her face into my chest. I wrapped my arms around her. Shefali kept crying with deep long sighs, her tears trying hard to wash off my love for Aarti.

Shefali wept for a long time. I waited until her shower of pain had eased off. She drew back and looked at me absently, her face smudged with dried tears. I pulled her close. Close enough to kiss her on the lips.

She resisted a little, but as my hands wandered over her waist and up to her blouse, she gave up the fight. I picked her up in my arms and walked towards the bedroom. I set her down on to the bed and then went on to draw the curtains. I turned on the AC and then walked up to the bed. Shefali was sitting curled up with her head resting on her knees. I gently pressed her arm. She raised her head and looked at me with her lovely little eyes. They were still red. I placed my hand on her face. A tear-pearl trickled down her eye. I let loose her beautiful long hair and then made her lie down on the bed. She looked at me endearingly. I couldn't control myself and leaned forward to put my lips over hers. Shefali responded by pressing hers against mine. She put her arms around my head as we kissed ardently. I slowly drew my hand inside her sari. My fingers reached her thighs and then sailed north. Her whole body began to shudder. I helped her out of her clothes and then quickly got rid of mine. Shefali was beautiful. And unexplored! She closed her eyes and moaned in ecstasy as I licked her nipples and then gradually slid down to taste the rest of her being. Moments later, I moved inside her. She was in immense pain. She clutched me hard between her legs. I couldn't move. We remained interlocked for a while. And then, she loosened her grip. I took the control back. The strokes began lightly and then started to gain momentum. By the time I exploded, we both were on cloud nine – screaming hard with unbearable pleasure. It was hard to say whether we'd consummated our marriage out of need or was this the beginning of an actual relationship. But we had, for sure, made the day memorable.

▼

It took Shefali a while to come to terms with what I had said, but gradually, she got over it. As for me, sex had always been a powerful motivator. It was something that had gone on a hiatus for a really long time. And now when it was back, I didn't want it to end so soon. So, I slept with Shefali every other day. I even made her feel special and desirable. But somehow, I found myself incapable of loving her. Aarti was the one I yearned for.

▼

"Sirji, I just got to know that you're going to be promoted," Shefali said over the phone. I was extremely busy, so I grumbled, "Shefu yaar. Don't disturb," and disconnected. She called again. "What do you want? Be quick," I said.

Shefali teased again, "Sir, your hard work is soon gonna pay the dividends."

"What nonsense? What hard work are you talking about?"

"Tsk. *Bhondu Basant*, I'm expecting."

"Fuck!" I said it so loudly that my boss shot up in his cubicle like the release of a coiled spring.

"Yes, my dear. We're soon gonna be parents. Thanks to the 'f' thing," Shefali giggled.

"You naughty girl!" I said grinning.

"I love you Rishabh. I love you more than anything else in this world," Shefali made a kissing sound.

"Yeh, I know," I said in a muted tone as my boss stared at me like a red traffic light.

I hung up saying we'd talk more at home. I don't know why, but I wasn't excited about the news. Rather I found the idea of being a Dad quite atrocious. And I can't lie now and say that I didn't think about abortion.

Though Shefali had given me what I'd always wanted to have from Aarti, but even then, I was still confused between these two women. Maybe I was trying too hard to keep the promise I made to myself that I'd never love another woman, ever. Maybe I was just being obtuse.

▼

"Rishabh, our child," Shefali cried as I picked her up in my arms.

"No, don't even think about it. Everything will be all right," I said as I made her lie down on the backseat of my car.

"Rishu, drive fast. We are losing her." Mom screamed from the backseat even as we rushed to Fortis at an alarming pace. Dad called up the doctor.

"Akritiji, I'm Shefali's father-in-law. She spoke to you this morning. We were coming to the hospital, but something unfortunate happened with us. Shefali is unconscious right now. We are bringing her to the hospital. Please arrange for a stretcher. I think you need to carry out an urgent delivery," Dad spoke in one breath. Akriti was Shefali's gynaecologist. She confirmed her availability and disconnected the call. We reached Fortis in another fifteen minutes or so. Akriti was in the emergency ward.

"What the hell happened?" she said shocked as I entered the ward with Shefali in my arms. Blood was dripping all around.

"Later, doctor later. She needs you right now," I said and carefully set Shefali down on to the stretcher.

"Is this an accident or something else?" Akriti questioned staring me in the eye, standing akimbo.

"O god! She fell from the stairs. Do you hear that? Now don't waste time. She has already lost a lot of blood. And if you want, you can even call the police. I'm not going to run anywhere. *Now please, go!*" I literally shouted back at her.

Akriti discussed the case in haste with the EMO, the emergency medical officer and then asked me to complete the registration process while she prepared for an emergency procedure.

There were five counters at the registration desk, all lined up with customers. I barged in, got abused and was shouldered out. I begged people to let me get the billing first. I told them about Shefali, showed them my bloodstained clothes, and the tinge of crimson over my hands. Just one old person relented. He swapped his place with me. I thanked him for his kindness and asked the lady behind the counter to make it quick. What followed thereafter was an altercation as she irritated me with questions related to medical insurance, cashless hospitalization, payment options, and so on. She even pushed forward a leaflet advertising massive discounts on full-body checkup. She seemed to be in no haste.

By the time I reached the second floor, the place where the OT was, Shefali was already being operated on. I handed over the papers, gasping, drenched in sweat, to a junior doctor and then blindly signed a bunch of consent forms.

While Mom went to the prayer room, Dad and I waited outside in the corridor, a small waiting area where attendants either chose to stand or struggled for the lone three-seater visitor reception chair that was set along the wall. A few eyes turned to me. They checked out my clothes and then got back to what they were doing prior to that. Someone prayed, someone paced up and down the corridor, someone toyed with the hospital leaflet, someone whiled away time checking Facebook feed or playing Candy Crush. As the clocked ticked away, Dad and I got restless. I don't know why, but I called Sam. He was in office. "Hey Pappu! How are you? Long time since we talked," he said enthusiastically.

"Sam, Shefali is in the OT. I'm really scared. My heart is sinking," I cried over the phone.

Sam became serious. "What happened? Is everything alright?" he asked.

"Sam, Shefali is expecting. She is in her thirty-fourth week. Last night she was watching TV when all of a sudden, her water broke. So, we took an urgent appointment with the gynaecologist this morning. We had even planned to take admission at the hospital, if needed. But everything went bad because of a motherfucking sales executive. Shefali picked up his call while I was out to bring the car from the parking. She didn't even wait for either Dad or Mom to help her down the stairs. One wrong step and she tripped. We just couldn't understand what happened in those few seconds. There was blood all over the floor. Sam, I can't explain to you how horrifying it was. It's been two hours and the doctor hasn't come out yet. Why Sam, why... Why the fuck does this shit happen only to me?"

"Rishabh. Hey... don't lose heart. Have faith in god. Everything will be alright," Sam consoled me.

"Sam. I'll... I'll call you later," I hung up as I noticed Akriti coming out of the OT in green surgical scrubs. She looked extremely grim. She came up to Dad. "I'm... I'm sorry sir. I tried my best but... but couldn't revive her. There was too much of internal bleeding," she said looking at the floor.

My heart stopped beating. My mind went numb. And face expressionless! The news had left me in a stupor. I just couldn't believe my ears. Shefali, my wife, was no more.

My world was wrecked. Tears showed up in my eyes. I moaned in despair and sank to my knees. I cried out a river. The pain of my misfortune hurt me in places that I never knew of. My howls echoed down the corridor.

Shefali wasn't just my wife; she was the woman who'd loved me despite all odds. She'd accepted me the way I was. And now she was gone.

"Rishabhji, you're now a father. She's a little angel," Akriti informed me as she put her hand on my shoulder to console. I raised my head and looked at her with tears trickling down my eyes.

"The baby is critical. Next seventy-two hours are quite crucial. Pray for her," Akriti continued.

I never wanted this child. Even thought about getting rid of it. But she seemed to mean everything to me now. Shefali's soul was hidden somewhere inside her.

Dad, who was in tears too, wished to see the child. Akriti asked us to wait. An hour later, the pediatrician allowed only one of us to access the neonatal intensive care unit. While Dad stayed outside, I entered the room wearing shoe caps, mask and a cap. The first sight of my child was heartbreaking. She was held captive in an incubator with a feeding tube running through her nose. An intravenous catheter was inserted in her umbilical cord. She also had chest leads, pulse ox and a temperature probe taped around to display her vital stats on a connected monitor. Her eyes were closed and her tiny feet convulsed every now and then. Her fists were shut tight. She was trying hard to hold on to her life.

I requested Akriti to let me see Shefali. She turned me down saying that it wasn't allowed until the hospital formalities were completed. Rather I should be grateful that she didn't register an MLC, Medico-Legal Case, though the EMO was pressing for it. I begged Akriti to give me just five minutes with my dead wife. But she said her hands were tied. Dad stepped forward and bent down to touch her feet. She felt mortified and eventually relented. She took us into a corner and agreed to allow me in only if we gave her an assurance that we'd not mention it to anyone from the hospital.

Ten minutes later, I was sitting next to Shefali. She looked at peace. And why not? She'd got rid of me, a selfish bastard who'd failed to understand her value. I took Shefali's hand in mine.

It felt soft. But was pale and lifeless. Her ring finger was barren. Our wedding ring had been taken off by the nursing staff, leaving behind an impression on her skin. I remembered taking an oath before the holy fire that I'd always protect and be there for my wife. But I had failed to do so. I had failed to be a good husband. I had failed to leave behind an impression, much like the ring.

I drew Shefali's hand close to my chest and broke into a monologue.

"Shefu, if you loved me, why did you leave me? Take me along or please, please come back. All I need is you and nothing more. You're the woman I love. You're the one I care about. If not for me, then for our daughter, please open your eyes. I'll never be able to give her the love, the care and the upbringing that a wonderful mother like you would do. Please Shefu, please don't abandon me just like everybody else did. I'd never be able to come out of it."

And I started to cry. Shefali was no longer a choice for me. She was the woman that I had eventually fallen for, the woman I couldn't imagine my life without, the woman who'd turned into a sweet memory now. I love you Shefu. I love you.

▼

A swarm of mourners, all dressed in white, walked in to the house, leaving their shoes at the entrance.

My relatives were already there, sitting cross-legged on the rugs spread on either side of Shefali's open casket. It was the wake service. A pandit presided over the proceedings. He chanted mantras which we repeated after him whenever he asked us to.

I was sitting next to Shefali with my palms folded. Her body was washed earlier in the day and was now dressed in the same bridal dress that she wore on our wedding day. She had turmeric applied on her forehead, vermilion in the parting of her hair and the mangalsutra together with a marigold and basil garland around her neck. Her big toes were tied together and her hands were folded in a position of prayer. A one wick sesame oil lamp and a single incense stick were lit and kept close to her head. A Shiva photograph was also placed at her head side.

Shefali's parents were in deep grief. She was their only child. Her mother rocked back and forth as she wailed with deafening cries. Her father, though sober in the way he grieved, was being comforted by my Dad. Mom was at the hospital as my daughter was still struggling for her life.

Mourners offered flowers, exchanged a word with my father and then condoled me on their way out. A few curled an arm around while others restricted themselves to a simple namaste.

Later at the crematorium, as I walked around Shefali's funeral pyre carrying a clay pot of holy water on my left shoulder, I realised that I'd never be able to see her again. I had lost her for ever. It was a heartbreaking moment. Life felt meaningless and empty.

It was then that I made a promise to Shefali for every completed circle around her body. A promise to care for her parents. A promise to provide our daughter with the best in the world. A promise to be good again.

I stayed with her until the embers turned cold.

Three days later, we all went to Haridwar for the *asthi visarjan* ritual. As I alighted the steps of the Asthi Parvath ghat, into the strong and freezing current of the river, a strange feeling swelled up. I wanted to keep Shefali, whatever was left of her, with me. I looked up at the blood-red morning sky, heard the pandit recite a mantra, briefly closed my eyes and then opened the urn to immerse Shefali's ashes in the holy waters of the Ganges. I wanted to walk deep into the river, take a dip and never to rise again.

On the thirteenth day, we had the last prayer of the mourning period. Meals were distributed to the poor as a symbolic gesture. By now, Roshini didi, Jijaji and Adit had also arrived. Though they'd called several times, but this time, Phani, Joy and Sam came by along with their wives. And that is when the tears came back.

▼

My daughter was a warrior. She fought courageously and triumphed over death. I used to visit her daily, but never dared to touch her or pick her up in my arms. I was scared to lose her as well. We brought her home after a month-long care at the hospital. My parents and in-laws stayed back as everyone else went back to their routine lives. During this time, I also went to Kanpur for the bereavement ceremony. The number of children who visited Shefali's house and the wreaths that followed made me realise how many hearts she had broken with her untimely demise.

▼

It was a little less than a year since my life had taken a downturn. I had named my daughter Smriti as she made me remember Shefali. She was her memory for me. A little part of her mother lived inside her.

Mom and Dad had shifted in with me after Shefali left us. All our waking days were spent on giving Smriti a good life.

"Rishu, don't take it otherwise, but I think you should get married again. You look languished. Smriti also needs a mother," said Mom one day at the dinner table.

A dormant volcano woke up. I pushed the plate off the table and wailed like a werewolf, "Disgusting! How can you even think like that? If it was me instead of Shefali, and had she remarried within a year... then? How would you have felt – happy or languished?"

Mom turned her eyes to the carpet. But I continued, "Just for a minute, think about Shefali's parents. She was their only child. And now when she's gone, it's only me who's left in their life. They are my responsibility and I cannot show my back to them. They are as important to me as you both are. So, let me make it clear – if you bring up this remarriage topic again, then I don't have a place for you, either in my house or in my life."

Dad walked up to me. "Rishu, I'm really proud to be your father," he said and embraced me with tears of admiration in his eyes.

After a few days, I convinced Shefali's parents to come and stay with me. They were reluctant to stay with my parents, so I rented a house for them a few houses away from ours.

▼

Four years later

It was a torrid Monday morning. I had gone to the New Delhi railway station to receive one of Shefali's younger cousins, Swati. I came to know that the train would arrive around an hour late than its actual schedule. I was thinking about how to kill time when suddenly a kid emerged on the opposite platform and jumped on the tracks. A train was fast approaching. Like everybody else, I too stopped to watch if he was destined to live. He was quick in his reflexes and within no time climbed up the platform on my side. Then out of nowhere, he came and caught my arm.

"*Saabji, saabji. Bacha lo. Meri ma ko bacha lo*," he begged me to save his mother, as I tried to push him away.

"*Ae, dur hato*," I scolded him, asking him to get away.

But he was unmoved. He fell at my feet and touched his forehead to my shoes. I felt ashamed and sat on my haunches. "Look son. If you need money, take this. But please let me go. I'm getting late," I said offering him ten bucks.

He took the money, tore it into two and put it back on my palm. I was miffed.

"Bloody bastard," I abused him and gave him a tight slap. He started to cry, but kept touching his forehead onto my shoes. My heart melted. "What do you want son?

"My mother. They'll take her away," he said.

"Who'll take her away?"

"Rajan and his men."

"Who's Rajan?" I asked.

The boy pointed to a group of men misbehaving with a woman who looked like a ragpicker. I understood the scene. Must be some local gang, I thought. I didn't want to get into it, so I said, "Son, I cannot help you in this. Ask the police to help you."

"They'll do nothing. Rajan pays them money," snivelled the boy.

I looked across the platform. The woman seemed to be in real trouble. I don't know why and what made me do so, but I jumped off the platform along with the boy. We carefully crossed over and came face-to-face with the gang. One of them was holding the woman by the scruff of her neck while the other was yelling at her. Her messy hair hid her face.

"Hey you! What's the problem? Why are you troubling this woman?" I asked one of the men, who was in all probability Rajan.

"*Oy tu kaun hai be? Chal nikal yahan se,*" he yelled back rudely, telling me to get lost.

"Listen. Let that woman go. I'll pay you the price," I said.

"*Aisa kya? Chal nikal paanch lakh,*" he demanded five lakhs to let her go.

One of his men stepped forward and grabbed my collar. I immediately caught him by his throat. A fight became imminent. And I was sure to lose a lot of blood in the time to come.

But just then a group of armed men dressed in army greens showed up from somewhere and quickly came marching towards us. The goons looked at each other and hurried out of the platform. I was still standing with the boy. The woman stood still for a while and then sank to the floor. She started to cry. One of the army men asked me if everything was okay. I narrated the incident to his team. His entire group encircled us within seconds. One of them bent down and patted the woman on her shoulder. "Hello. *Ae suno. Upar dekho.Woh chale gaye,"* he said to her, assuring her that she was safe as the goons had run off.

She kept crying. Her son sat down on the platform and started to console her. She remained motionless, but then lifted her face to look at us. She was dusky and had scars all over her smudged face. But somehow, she looked familiar. And then suddenly I realised... Oh my god! It was Rajjo, Aarti's housemaid. I was speechless.

"Rajjo. Is it you?" I said, my voice shaking.

The woman looked at me confused. Then out of nowhere, she too started to do what her son had done a while earlier. *"Bacha lo bhaiyaji, bacha lo,"* she begged me to save her.

An army officer asked me if I knew the woman. I confirmed, but expressed my concern in taking her to a safe location. I was obviously scared about my own well being now. The army officer understood my apprehension and devised a plan. He got his colleagues to take Rajjo and her son out of the station and smartly snuck them out. The officer gave me a number and asked me to contact from a PCO sharp at seven in the evening. He didn't provide any other details. I had no other option but to trust. Two of his men helped me out of the station to the Metro train. The officer had instructed me to go and blend with the crowd at Rajiv Chowk, which was the busiest interchange station and then change trains at Mandi House, Central Secretariat and Hauz Khas before finally getting off at a station which wasn't my destination. He had also asked me to have my car picked up from the station parking later on. Though I was terrified about the repercussions of my sudden act of bravery, I was proud to have been able to help, more so because it was Rajjo, a girl I had seen since she was ten. I sent out a WhatsApp message to Swati asking her to hire an Uber or something and not wait for me as I had some urgent work to attend to. I just wanted to ensure her safety as well.

Later, at seven in the evening, I called the given number as was directed. A lady picked it up. She enquired about the physical description of her two refugees and then asked me to come to a specific point at Azadpur Mandi, Asia's largest wholesale market for fruits and vegetables. She gave me a specific dress code and asked me to use public transport. Such meticulous planning is done only for covert operations. Though panicky, I reached the location holding on to my nerves.

Azadpur Mandi was an assault on the senses. It was a place where commotion ruled. After a bit of haggling with a jackfruit vendor, I noticed a lady in her late forties throw a glance at me at repeated intervals. She was probably the one I had a word with on the phone. Her eyes gestured that I'd follow her lead. I complied without a second thought. Fifteen minutes later, I was standing in front of what looked like some sort of a servant quarter. The lady didn't provide nor seek any personal details. She just frisked me head to toe and then knocked at the door five times. Somebody unlatched the door from inside. The lady used a key to unlock it from outside. We entered the dwelling. It was dark and dingy inside. There was no electricity. Only a fluttering flame from an overworked kerosene lamp. There weren't any windows either. Just a ventilator through which the moonbeams fused with streetlights streamed through. The room also had a tattered charpoy along with a slimy table and a three-legged stool wedged in one of its corners. There wasn't any kitchen. Just a doorless stinking bathroom.

As I stepped towards Rajjo, her son ran to her. He clung to his mother wrapping his arms around her hips. He mistook me as Rajan, I guess.

I tried to strike up a conversation with Rajjo, but somehow, she didn't talk much. She seemed to be scared. So was her son. I tried for a while, but then gave up. I think they needed some alone time. While I left, the lady asked me to pay up two thousand bucks per day for the upkeep of my guests. I didn't mind.

I hid Rajjo and her son Shyam under the lady's able security for over a week and then cautiously brought them home. It was a big risk that I had taken. I hoped Rajan and his men never find out. I even instructed both mother and son not to step out of the house for the fear of being recognised in the market. I told everyone at home that Rajjo was a full-time babysitter that I had hired via a maid agency to take care of Smriti. Mom had her reservations, but didn't dare raise an objection. I asked Rajjo to maintain her silence. Shyam was smart enough to understand too.

At Azadpur, Rajjo was initially quiet, but she opened up on our third meeting. Her story moved me to tears. Her father (Aarti's gardener) had got her married to an artisan in Odisha. The 2017 flash floods took away their home and forced them to come to Delhi in search of work. But as time passed, instead of getting better, their miseries kept piling up. Rajjo's husband lost an arm in a factory accident. He took to drinking. Matters became worse thereafter. A year later, Rajjo's husband broke her trust and sold her to a brothel for fifty thousand bucks and disappeared. From there on, the pimps took over her life. She was held captive inside a stinky room for weeks and tortured. Later, she was forced to bed an army of lechers. It took her almost two years to escape from that dungeon. But somehow, Rajan got a tip off from one of the guards posted at the railway station. And it was then that I bailed her out. As Rajjo ended her story, both she and her son touched my feet with their heads. Though at that time I kept my emotions in check, when I came home I lay in tears in bed all night. I felt the pain Rajjo had gone through, the pain that I had given to Priyanka, Ruhana and my very own Shefali. I looked in the mirror to see what I truly was. All I could see was a loser who had failed to understand the value of a woman.

Remorse is like quicksand. The harder you try to redeem yourself, the greater you get pulled into the trench of psychological warfare. I visited temples, joined satsangs and even went on to give anonymous donations to charitable trusts. But the emptiness I felt within didn't appear to cease. I did everything that felt right to make my conscience get away from the guilt of my past actions. But nothing seemed to work. This, in fact, was my salted wound.

▼

One day I went to Bangla Sahib, a prominent gurdwara, with one of my colleagues. To my surprise, I saw a young Sardarji, dressed in a white safari suit with a couple of gold rings on his fingers, tirelessly polish shoes of total strangers. I couldn't understand the need to do such a menial job and approached him out of curiosity. He turned out to be a jeweller from West Delhi. I'd never met such a humble person in my entire life. His words of wisdom changed the way I perceived life as well as the *one* who is believed to be the creator of everything that exists.

The great man said, "No one has seen Him. Not even those who preach about Him. Yet we believe in Him." He went on to say, "When we can so strongly believe in the one that no one has ever seen, then why can't we believe in the ones that each one of us can see. Your wealth and your incantations don't have the power to please Him. You cannot reach out to Him. But He can. Sincerely atone for your sins and rise above your flaws. And He shall seek you. Be good to those who are in distress. Be their hero. And god, the supreme Hero who lives above us all, shall Himself come to you."

Our brief conversation ended on a remarkably noble thought, "He is the happiness that you feel burbling inside your blood when you feed a hungry stomach. He is the peace that quietens the chaos inside your head when you clothe a naked child. And He is the beat that keeps your heart alive when you save a dying man."

Sometimes in life, the biggest lessons come from total strangers. My serendipitous meeting with Sardarji had opened up a new school of thought inside me. He'd taken out my soul and wiped it clean, just like those shoes he attended to. After six months of soul-searching and discussions with numerous people, I finally started an NGO for the girl child. I named it Shefali Smriti. Both Shefali's parents and mine got actively involved with the program. Shefali had always loved children and this was my gift to her. I had never respected women and had always seen them as objects of lust. But Shefali's demise and Rajjo's heart-wrenching tale had brought out the best in me – a part of me I'd never seen before. This NGO was a way to repent what I'd done in my life. A way of keeping the last promise that I made to Shefali at her funeral pyre. A way to be good again.

Imperfectly Perfect

"Congratulations Dad. I'm so proud of you," Smriti screamed over the phone. She was thrilled to bits.

"Thank you bachche," I said in an endearing tone.

"When is the ceremony?" she enquired.

"I haven't received the date yet. But it's usually around March and April."

"Let me know as soon as you get to know it. I want to be there. I want to see it with my own eyes," she said bubbling with excitement.

It's been twenty years since I had started Shefali Smriti. Our untiring and fearless work on female foeticide, child abuse, rape, human trafficking and most importantly, women empowerment has been recognized by the state and central governments. We even got a five crore grant from the Ministry of Women and Child Development and had been covered by the print media and television. Today, on the eve of the Republic Day, we got an even bigger boost. I've been nominated as one of the recipients of the coveted Padma Shri for this year. When I sometimes think about how far I've come from what I was, I'm amazed at my own transformation. Maybe the good born out of a devil transcends the holiness of a saint. Maybe I didn't choose this path. Maybe I was the chosen one.

My daughter Smriti is now a beautiful young woman of almost twenty-six. She works and lives in Boston. Yes, my daughter too is in IT – a field I don't understand even after being in it for four decades.

From the seniors, only Mom has survived. She's mostly bedridden as she suffers from Alzheimer's and has an incontinence problem. We still don't get along and I haven't forgiven her for what she did to me, but I make sure that she has the best of care. Forgiveness is something I still need to work on.

Roshini didi, Jijaji and Adit still stay in the UK. Jiju took an early retirement due to poor health and now stays mostly at home. My nephew Adit is married; has a kid and is working as an AVP at RBS.

My friends Sam, Phani and Joy are doing well and have been in constant touch with me through all these years. Sam made it to the cover page of a business magazine eight years ago, as one of the top ten advocates of India. I use his free services from time to time. Phani made it big in the corporate world. He had moved to France for some time, but returned to start his own company called GREEN (**G**lobal **Re**newable **En**ergy) – an organization rated amongst the top in its category. Joy too spent eight years in the US and made enough money to fulfil his dream of buying his parents a house. He now lives in Kolkata. But unlike Sam and Phani, Joy did something that left me awestruck – he donated fifteen lakhs from his hard-earned wealth to my NGO. As a mark of appreciation for his philanthropic contribution, I started an extension centre of Shefali Smriti at Kolkata and asked Joy to take charge of it.

Rajjo, the woman who inspired me to become what I am, is now an integral part of my life. She assists me at Shefali Smriti. One of her jobs is to motivate women who have become victims at the hands of this cruel society. She tells them about her own struggle, her willingness to come out of it and her determination to live with her head held high. She often tells the women she interacts with that they needn't be ashamed of what happened to them. Those who did it need to feel the guilt. Rajjo's spirit of courage and personal achievement was recognized in the form of Rani Lakshmi Bai Award for the year 2035. I salute this great woman for her bravery and resoluteness in the face of adversity.

And finally, Shyam, the kid who once begged me for help, is now a well-known martial arts instructor! That child impressed me the day he tore the money I gave him on the railway platform. He had great dignity as well as the guts to confront men like Rajan. I educated him and let him get trained in martial arts. Today he runs his own academy where he teaches people self-defence. I've made it mandatory for each woman at Shefali Smriti to be trained in self-defence at his academy.

▼

One night, my phone beeped at around 1 a.m. I was still awake. It was an e-mail on my Shefali Smriti mail account. I was wondering who it could be so late at night. I opened the inbox. It was from some R. Zaidi.

The minute I opened the message, my pupils dilated and my heart shuddered. It was impossible. It was my past. It was Ruhana.

Hello Rishabh
It's been a long time since we last interacted. Although I thought of never communicating with you again, I couldn't hold back after I heard about your nomination in the news. At first I couldn't believe that you had started an organization like this, but then I realised it was you. Your true concern and altruistic efforts for the society have

made the world bow in reverence. The admiration you've earned for
your good work, especially from women, is commendable. Your life
is an inspiration for today's generation. It's a lesson, a direction, a
motivation to turn your life around. By respecting and by bringing
respect to women, you've truly become a complete man.

I regret what I once said to you. I think you're the best man a
woman can ever come across. I wish you the best in life and more
success to your NGO.
Ruhana

Every word of that e-mail unearthed pangs of regret from the confines of my heart. I had outraged a woman's modesty and survived all these years without being incarcerated. And now, the same person was praising me, calling me the best man, and absolving me of all the wrong-doing. How could she do that? How could she be so exonerative? I would've understood her anger, but not this. This was worse than being punished. I couldn't hold back the strange feeling, the remorse, the uneasiness that Ruhana had left me with. I wept, and I wept copiously.

It was four in the morning and I was still awake. Melatonin had failed to lullaby me to sleep. I went up to my laptop and tried composing a response to Ruhana. But couldn't find the right words. All I could manage in the end was a lame sorry. I'm very sorry Ruhana… for what I did to you.

Ruhana didn't reply. I sent out another e-mail the next day, but she didn't respond to that either. I got restless. I had to get it out of my system, so I called Sam.

Though I never thought I'd do it, but I confessed everything to him. Sam listened silently, but said nothing.

"Hello! Sam? Are you there?" I asked, thinking that the call had got disconnected. Only the background noises responded. And then

I heard his voice, "I always thought god had been unfair to you. But now I know – he did it for a reason. He gave you the same pain you gave to others. What you did cannot be undone, but yes, it can be atoned for. And I think you chose the right path. Take that e-mail as a mail from god. He has finally forgiven you. Keep doing the good work and start living a guilt-free life. You're now a complete man."

And the phone got disconnected. I understood Sam's anger over my past misconduct, but also remembered what he had once said. Ruhana's mail embodied something that Sam had warned me about when we were younger. It was only me who never understood it. I spent that night tossing and turning in my bed, praying for an end to my pain.

▼

I'd been a lifer at XLSL and am now its global IT head. Though automation has wiped out most of the jobs, but even then, XLSL has grown to a company employing over 200,000 people and is one of the fastest growing IT service firms of India.

Just before hanging up my boots on the 28th of February 2042, I attended the wedding of the son of one of my colleagues. I was sitting in a corner with some subordinates from my company and discussing my post-retirement plans. Suddenly, I felt a tap on my shoulder. I turned to see who it was. It was a beautiful graceful woman smiling and looking straight into my eyes. I stood up, "Yes ma'am. How can I help you?"

"Idiot! Since when did you start helping older women like me?" she retorted loudly.

Jesus Christ! It was Aarti. She had aged, but as gracefully as ever! The wrinkles made her look a little old, but overall, she was looking fabulous – far better than I looked.

"Is it really you Aarti?" I was stunned.

"Yes, my dear. It *is* me!" Aarti replied jovially. My juniors had become silent and were looking at both of us expectantly. "Excuse me gentlemen. Your boss needs to attend to his beautiful friend. Please don't mind," Aarti told them snappily and tugged me out of the crowd.

Although we were both close to sixty, Aarti had the same old peppiness that I was accustomed to.

"How have you been, my dear dear friend?" Aarti asked, taking both my hands in hers. Thank god she didn't hug me.

"You tell me first. What are you doing in India? That too here, in this party," I asked.

"Gulabo, I mean your friend Amit Gulabani is Rajat's childhood friend. He told me that you were here too."

"He knows that I know you?" I asked a little worried about Amit knowing about my past.

"No, he just happened to mention your name to someone when I heard. You know me – I squeezed out each and every detail of yours from him. He says you're a famous man," Aarti said.

"No, it's just the love of people," I said with a grin. Thankfully, unlike my hair, all my teeth were still intact.

"Oh my! Look at that. What a politically correct statement, Mr Awardee," Aarti teased me in her usual style.

"Please now… let go of my hands. I have a reputation to protect here!" I said freeing my hands from hers.

"Oh yes! I forgot. After all, you're a celebrity. Can I please get your autograph, Agrawal sir?" Aarti teased me again, putting her palm in my hand.

I kind of blushed and changed the topic, "Where's Rajat?"

"Rajat is somewhere around… must be busy ogling some crones," Aarti replied.

"Tsk, same old habits. God help Rajat. What about junior? Where's he?" I asked.

"Junior? Oh! You mean Ayush. He still lives in the US. But he'll be back in two-three years," Aarti said.

"Back to where? Have you guys moved here permanently?" I asked.

"Yup. It's been a month now. Rajat and I decided to spend our last days here in India, the place we grew up in. We've spent our lives working hard to mint money and now want to sit back and enjoy life."

Finally, they understood that money isn't everything, I thought to myself, and asked once again, "So, you guys are here to spend a retired life, right?"

"Kind of. Rajat has joined a small start-up and I'm still thinking what to do," Aarti clarified.

"Why don't you join my NGO?"

"Me and NGO? What will I do there?"

"We'll work it out. I suggest you visit it sometime," I said offering my visiting card.

Aarti scanned it in a rush. "Impressive sir, impressive," she said rolling her eyes.

"As always, ma'am. As always," I replied with a smile.

Aarti laughed out just the way I remembered her doing. "How's your daughter Rishu? What's her name?"

"How do you know I have a daughter?" I was surprised. Aarti always knew everything about my life.

"Arrey yaar. Gulabo Aunty told me. Who else? Now tell me. What's her name? Where is she?"

"Her name is Smriti. She's working now and she stays in your adopted nation. She's very much like you in certain habits."

"So, you didn't miss me that much. Or do you?" Aarti smiled.

I shook my head in frustration. She was talking as if we were still twenty-something.

Aarti smiled again and carried on, "By the way, where does she live? I'll ask Ayush to get in touch with her."

"In Boston. She'll be coming home for the award ceremony. You can meet her then. She knows about you," I replied.

"Really? Don't tell me you told her everything?"

I nodded. Aarti slapped her forehead. "Kids should be kept out of all this," she said.

I explained why I had told Smriti everything. "Listen, I can explain. After Shefali left, Smriti was the only one I had to share my feelings and thoughts with. As she grew up, we became friends more than father and daughter. I told her about us only after she turned twenty-three."

Aarti became serious, "I'm sorry to hear about Shefali. When? How?"

I became silent, so she diverted the talk to Smriti again. "I'm sure Smriti is a lovely girl who shares an everlasting bond with her wonderful daddy."

"Yeah, you're right. Anyway, do you have any other children or is it just Ayush?" I asked.

Aarti giggled and said in a muted tone, "Ayush also happened by accident. After he was born, I told Rajat straight on his face – I can't make any more children. After all, it's a matter of my figure. See how fat I've become," and she twirled around displaying her not so-fat self.

I shook my head in embarrassment. "You're too much Aarti. Age hasn't changed you at all," I said.

"Dude, you're old! I'm not! You're so…"

"Ugly?"

"Serious. You've actually become very serious. Where's that fun-loving guy I knew? "

I just smiled as Aarti carried on, "Now that I'm here, I'll turn you back into the same old Rishu within a month. Just wait and watch. And… oy Mr Oldie! Give me your number."

"It's on my card," I replied.

"Oh, come on! Don't act smart with me. I can still slap you," Aarti threatened.

I knew her very well. She was not joking. So, I called out my number like a scared deer. Aarti told me that they'd bought a flat at Dwarka and we chatted on about everything that had happened in our lives. I was happy to learn that Ayush wasn't nicknamed Rishu or Rishabh, but Aarti said that her three-year-old grandson's pet name was Rishu. And that she really enjoyed changing his diapers!

Rajat joined us a few minutes later. He had a charming personality and quite unfortunately, knew everything about me. I did feel a little embarrassed about being his wife's one-time 'one-sided lover', but he brushed it off by saying that it was all okay unless I started it off again!

▼

It's been a year since I met Aarti at that party. She has joined Shefali Smriti and is helping me take it to newer heights. Rajat is extremely supportive and we've now become good friends. We catch up with each other almost twice a week.

Aarti met Rajjo the day she paid her first visit to Shefali Smriti. I cannot explain the surprise I saw on her face. At first, she didn't believe that it was Rajjo, but when Rajjo started to unfurl her hidden secrets (which I was still unaware of), she quickly accepted it. Aarti wept when Rajjo narrated what had happened to her. She then embraced her tightly, and for the first time in her life, touched my feet as a mark of appreciation. Tears of satisfaction rolled down my eyes.

Aarti finally got to meet Smriti during the new year and had no qualms in declaring her prettier than herself. Smriti is happy for me and often says that I'm lucky to have a friend like Aarti. She sees her mother in Aarti and I was surprised to see them bonding so well. I met Ayush too at the same time. He's a fine young man who has a lovely Indian wife and an extremely naughty kid.

Aarti also met Mom, although I didn't want her to. I was amazed to see that Mom remembered Aarti. She had no recollection about even Dad. I couldn't hold back my tears as Mom cried and apologized to Aarti with folded hands for whatever she had done to both of us. Aarti too got very emotional. She wiped the tears from Mom's shrivelled face and embraced her as if nothing had happened. At that instant, I understood the big-hearted act of forgiveness. The forgiveness that Ruhana had granted me. The forgiveness that I finally bestowed on Mom.

I wish these days never end. I feel alive again. My life has never been so peaceful. Sometimes I think it was Ruhana who brought me all this happiness. I wish I'd never done all that to her. I feel sorry for Priyanka and hope that she too has forgiven me for whatever I did to her.

I still miss Shefali, but the exuberance that Aarti has brought back to my life has made me want to live again. And I want to live life to the fullest. God has finally sought me. He has actually come to me. My life is imperfectly perfect again.

▼

No matter how distinguished and exceptional my contribution is, but, after all, I've commited a crime in the eyes of the law. Accepting an honour such as Padma Shri not only would have been disrespect to the award, but also an insult to the greats who'd been bestowed with it. So, after much deliberation, I gave up the fourth highest civilian award of India. Family, friends as well as the media made a lot of hullabaloo on this matter. The same state government that had recommended my name for the award turned around and called me a narcissist. They even had our accounts scrutinized. But I know, my decision was purely personal and absolutely fair.

A snippet from my guest lecture at IIT Kanpur (I finally made it to their campus)

Director sir introduced me to you as a real-life hero. No, I'm not. I'm just a man who lives among you... a man who has learnt the lesson of life quite well.

But yes, I certainly am somebody's hope. And hope is a good thing. Maybe the best of things. And that is what keeps us alive.

My dear friends, you can also be somebody's hope, a hero in your own way. Go out and write your own story, a story with a perfect ending.

•••

Note from the Author

They say it all starts with a dream. So was this book. Initially it was just a vague idea, but with time, the storyline matured and eventually took the shape that it currently is in.

To be honest, I don't have any prior experience in writing. This is, in fact, the first time that I've written anything longer than two pages. I can't lie and say that storytelling was cakewalk. It took six long years for this book to find your hands! But it did make me learn a lot. I not only got acquainted with the nuances of the publishing industry, but was also able to discover a lot about myself. The journey was tough, but then, the road to success is never a straight line. All we need is perseverance and hope. And this, I believe, is just the beginning – which is always the hardest.

I'd like to thank my publisher for taking a chance on this book. I'd also like to express my heartfelt indebtedness to my editors, designers and typesetters who worked tirelessly and went on to treat this as their own personal project. And finally, I'd like to thank the select few individuals who stood by me all these years, despite all odds.

To learn more about the latest developments around the book, please visit: Facebook: /authorprasoon, Twitter: @authorprasoon or write directly to me at authorprasoon@gmail.com.

Thank you with all of my heart.